Ashes

Visible & Invisible

By Catholic Teen Books authors:

Leslea Wahl
Cynthia T. Toney
Marie C. Keiser
Carolyn Astfalk
Amanda Lauer
Ellen Gable
Corinna Turner
Antony B. Kolenc
T. M. Gaouette
Theresa Linden

This book is a work of fiction. Characters and incidents are products of the authors' imaginations. Real events and characters are used fictitiously.

First Edition

Cover design by Corinna Turner
Edited by Cynthia T. Toney and Theresa Linden

The following short stories are the work of the individual authors. Their inclusion here does not imply endorsement either by Catholic Teen Books or its individual authors.

Visit CatholicTeenBooks.com for more
title and author information.

Manufactured in the United States of America

Library of Congress Control Number: 2022918004

ISBN-13: 979-8985348514
ISBN-10: 8985348514

Praise for *Ashes*

"It would not be easy to write for a teen audience about confronting our own mortality or facing up to the impact of death on our lives. Death brushes up against each of these main characters in different ways. In several stories, characters need to adjust to a different and financially challenging life following the death of a parent. In others, characters are struggling with the unfairness of life and death. Then there are stories where death is frighteningly close and requires an immediate response.

What binds these stories is that each young person must make a leap of Faith, take a step into a fuller, more mature understanding of their Catholic Faith. Characters are called to forgive, to resist temptation, to be courageous, to be steadfast and responsible. All of them come to understand on a deeper level the sacrificial nature of Love.

(Full review on CatholicChildrensStories.com)

Melinda Harrington, CatholicChildrensStories.com

The Catholic Teen Book authors have done it again! We loved this book from page one; it's a great way to dig deeper into Lent with your teens. The book has a story for everyone, and they all share the faith in different but wonderful ways. Highly recommend!

(Full video review on Catholic Mom and Daughter YouTube Channel)

Catholic Mom and Daughter Channel (YouTube)

This is the fourth anthology from the authors at the Catholic Teen Books collective. Each has been a great read. This Lenten volume is also, to be honest, my favourite of the four now . . . Many of the contributors to this collection, in their own way, imitate Christ and are master storytellers in our own generation.

I have a great deal of respect for the ten authors who contributed to this series. And a couple of them are among my all-time favourite authors. And I read a couple hundred books a year. This is a collection of 10 faith-filled stories by 10 great authors.

(Full review on BookReviewsAndMore.ca)

Steven R. McEvoy, BookReviewsAndMore.ca

DEDICATION

For Saint John Bosco, patron of youth, who reminds us all: "Carry your cross on your back and take it as it comes, small or large, whether from friends or enemies and of whatever wood it be made." Thank you for working tirelessly to help, give hope, and share the Gospel with poverty-stricken youth.

CONTENTS

Then I turned my face to the Lord God, seeking Him by prayer and supplications with fasting and sackcloth and ashes.

(Daniel 9:3 RSV-CE)

1

Contemporary

FINISHING THE JOURNEY

by Leslea Wahl

"Oh."

Something about the way Mom says that one word makes me nearly forget the search for my sleeping bag. I close the basement door behind me and focus my attention on her.

Mom's sitting in the kitchen, a stack of mail on the table before her, her gaze locked on a white envelope. I'm unable to decipher the elegant cursive from my vantage point. It doesn't look like a bill, her usual cause for consternation.

"What's that?" I step closer.

She holds the envelope out toward me. "Liz, it's from your grandmother."

I stop and stare, my stomach sinking a bit. This can't be good. I have only one living grandparent, my dad's mother. She is not the warm and fuzzy stereotype of a grandma. She is hard, cold, and has always scared me. And since my parents' divorce years ago, I've barely had any contact with the woman. I only hear from her on

Christmas and my birthday—when she sends me a card and a check. Being mid-March, neither of those occasions are on the horizon, so this unexpected correspondence makes me uneasy.

As I gingerly take the lightweight envelope, my phone buzzes.

Grateful for the distraction, I glance at my best-friend Josie's reply to my sleeping bag query.

Yep, it's here with our camping gear. I'll bring it over now.

"Josie's on her way to drop off my sleeping bag."

Mom's forehead crinkles. "I sure wish she was going with you this weekend. It would make me feel better."

I unsuccessfully fight the eye roll. "Mom, it's a church retreat. I don't think you have anything to worry about."

She bites her lip—her go-to habit when trying to formulate her thoughts. I patiently wait. "It's just that I don't know these people. And you'll be several hours away."

I offer an encouraging smile. Since I'm an only child and Dad's not around much, I often need to reassure her about things like I'm the adult in the relationship. "Mom, we talked about this. Even though Josie won't be with me, there will probably be some other kids from school." Not sure that's true, but it could be.

"You'll call if you feel the least bit nervous—about anything? And you'll stick with the group?"

"Yep."

"And you'll drive safely?" Her crinkled brow turns to look out the window as rivers of rain slide down the glass.

"Those curvy roads through the woods can be dangerous."

"I've driven them before." I give her a quick hug. "It will all be fine." Truth be told, I don't exactly want to spend my entire weekend at this diocesan-wide Confirmation retreat. In fact, I'm not at all sure I should even be going, but there's no way I'm telling her that.

With envelope in hand, I head up to my room to finish packing. If I'm going to make it to the retreat center before dinner, I need to hit the road soon. All this rain will slow down the drive. I shove the envelope into my bag along with my clothes, not eager to discover what my grandmother has to say. I toss in my Bible and rosary as well.

"Are you excited?"

Josie stands at my door, sleeping bag in hand.

I sigh. "Excited? Not exactly the word I'd use." More like afraid I've made a colossal mistake.

She steps forward. "Retreats are always fun."

"I'll take your word for it." Considering I've never been on one, I relied on her counsel when I agreed to go. I look from my bag to her, doubts weaseling into my mind. "What am I doing? Should I even be going?"

She takes my hand and pulls me down to sit on the bed with her. "Are you having second thoughts about joining the Church?"

I shake my head no, even though that's precisely what's on my mind. Last year when I informed Josie that I wanted to join the Catholic Church, I was excited about becoming a member of the church that I'd been attending with her and her family for years. But, at the time, I had no idea what that decision would entail. Now, with only a few weeks left until the Easter Vigil, where I'll be baptized into the faith, I'm suddenly questioning the whole thing. Having to attend this retreat without my sponsor and best friend, Josie, is not helping my unease.

She gives me a hug. "I wish I could go with you, but it's only for the teens receiving sacraments of initiation. I'm sure you'll enjoy all the group discussions. You have such a different perspective than all those cradle-Catholics. They could learn something from you."

"Yeah, right." I appreciate her pep talk, even though I don't believe anyone can learn anything from me.

All the other teens this weekend will be there because they somehow missed their Confirmation retreat or didn't receive the sacrament when everyone else in their grade did. I recently found out that I'm the only teen in the entire diocese going through RCIA—Rite of Christian Initiation for Adults. The misfit kid—the story of my life.

Father Dominic thought it would be good for me to go. Earlier in the week, when I confided my sudden reluctance with him, he didn't seem overly concerned. He patted my hand and replied, "Ah, then, even more reason to go. Liz, you need time to pray and discern. And remember, there is no pressure." He went on to assure me that if I returned from the weekend and still didn't feel comfortable going through with the enormous, life-changing decision, I could continue my studies and join the Church next year.

Josie nudges me. "I'm serious. I'll be praying that you'll

experience exactly what you need this weekend."

"Thanks." I know she'll always support me—that's what best friends do. But if I tell her I've changed my mind, she'll be disappointed and feel like she failed as my sponsor. So, instead of saying anything, I plaster on a smile. "Time to get this show on the road."

Between having to drive slowly in the rain and taking a wrong turn down one of many secluded roads through the woods, I end up at the retreat center a half-hour late. The nearly empty parking lot causes me to re-read the information letter. Did I mix up the day or time? No. This is right.

If I had arrived on time, I'd have had a chance to take my things to my room and settle in before the opening service. Instead, I find myself sliding into one of the back pews in the little chapel while the woman who is retreat coordinator introduces herself. A glance around at my fellow retreat participants, and I realize why the parking lot is so empty. Besides the speaker, I'm the only person present who is old enough to drive.

I slump back and squeeze my eyes shut. Just perfect. I should have anticipated this—Josie had been Confirmed several years ago. But since this particular retreat is for teens that missed their Confirmation requirements for some reason, I assumed there would be at least a few older teens present. Riddle me this, Father Dominic—how is being surrounded by a bunch of middle-schoolers all weekend going to help me discern anything besides the fact that I'm thankful I'm about to graduate high school and will be leaving the drama of teen angst behind?

The middle-aged woman shares a long list of rules and then welcomes everyone with a huge smile. "You'll find plenty of reflection opportunities during this retreat. So often in our daily lives, we are unable to spend time in prayer and quiet solitude so we can hear God and His guidance. This weekend, we'll also listen to a few talks by Father Nate, attend Mass, Adoration, and enjoy time in fellowship through music and games. Oh, and I hope you all brought your rosaries. Besides praying the Rosary together, Father Nate will also lead us in the Divine Mercy Chaplet."

Panic surges through me. What's the Divine Mercy Chaplet? I spent a year figuring out the Rosary. Josie might have mentioned there were other important prayers to know. I glance around. Even though I'm mostly looking at people's backs, no one else seems particularly confused. Why am I the only one who never knows what's going on?

The woman shares a few logistics, then announces that since it's a Friday during Lent, we will start with Stations of the Cross. I breathe a sigh of relief—at least that's something I'm familiar with.

I pick up one of the ready-made plates of fried fish, coleslaw, and French fries, then scan the tables. Where to sit? With the chatty group of girls who seem to all know each other? Perhaps at the mixed table of guys and girls who are slyly sneaking glances at one another? Should I find a table where I can be alone? Or, how about running as fast as I can to my car and leaving this place in a spray of rainwater? Instead, I choose option number five and sit at a half-empty table with three girls.

"Hi, mind if I join you?" They stare at me with wide eyes like I'm a teacher who just caught them passing notes.

I take their silence as an invitation and settle in. Two boys join our table as well. The awkward silence threatens to smother me.

I spread my napkin across my lap. "Shall we introduce ourselves? My name is Liz."

"Are you a counselor or something?" the petite girl to my right asks.

"No. I'm here for the retreat, just like all of you."

"Really?" Across the table, a boy's jaw drops in astonishment, revealing a mouthful of braces.

"Why?" asks another of my young tablemates.

"I'm going through the RCIA program, and my priest thought it would be a good idea to attend a retreat."

From the various glances around the table, I can tell they don't quite understand. But my wish to end the uncomfortable silence is granted, suddenly broken by a barrage of questions.

"RCIA? My aunt went through that. Isn't that just for old people?"

"Um, well, it's for people who haven't grown up in the Catholic Church who want to join."

"So, are you doing it with your family?"

"Nope. Just me."

"Is someone, like, forcing you?"

"No." I suppress a smile.

"How long is the program?"

"I started it about a year ago and will get baptized at the Easter Vigil."

"Like, in front of everyone, at that crazy long service?"

"Yep."

"Why would you do all that if no one's making you?"

At the moment, I'm not really sure, but I answer anyway. "Because I want to."

"Huh. Weird."

After the questions, they seem comfortable enough to begin introducing themselves, sharing where they go to school and church, and how they ended up at this particular retreat. The reasons are similar—they missed their parish retreats due to being sick, traveling, or extracurricular activities. Now in order to get Confirmed in the spring, they need to fulfill the retreat requirement of the program. Not one of them mentions that they want to learn more about Confirmation or are discerning if they should even be joining the Church. Once again, I'm on my own.

After an evening spent playing goofy get-to-know-you games, followed by several praise songs, we scatter to our rooms. The solitude that I've longed for all evening fails to comfort me. Instead, I'm suddenly without distraction and alone with my inner turmoil.

When I unzip my bag to pull out my pajamas, the white

envelope greets me, daring me to open it. How had I forgotten about that? With trepidation, I unseal the envelope and smooth out the folded hand-written note.

Liz,

Your father told me about your misguided judgment. I blame him for not being the role model you needed. However, you must know that we are not a Catholic family. I believe you are aware that I most graciously help pay for my grandchildren's college education. This is a gift, not an obligation. As I do not feel it appropriate to support your decision, I regret to inform you that if you continue on this errant pathway in your faith, I will have no choice but to hold back my portion of your college education. I expect a phone call or letter from you to discuss this further.

Grandmother

My hands shake and my stomach clenches as I stare at the letter. There are strings attached to her gift? She's serious? Of course she is. She always is. Did Dad know about this? A little heads-up from him would've been nice. While I've never had much of a relationship with her, I have been counting on her generous assistance for college. My promising future suddenly looks bleak. I've received a few college acceptances with some offers of scholarship assistance, but tuition remains ridiculously high.

My mind reels. Dad will help, but the additional financial strain on Mom would still be difficult. She's already constantly stressed about money. Loans are an option, but I'm thinking of becoming a teacher or counselor, and from what I hear, on those salaries, paying back loans will take forever. Do I need to kiss my dream of going to school out of state goodbye and settle on living at home while attending community college?

I flop back on my bed and stare at the plain white ceiling. Why is life so hard? Why am I constantly feeling alone? The white tiles above me blur as tears fill my eyes. Time to stop daydreaming about living a fantasy life and finally face reality—the stark, cold truth. As much as I wish I belonged to Josie's family—or any normal family—I don't. I have a single mom who struggles. While things are better lately with my dad, for most of my life, he's not been there for me. My one living grandparent is as warm as an iceberg.

Did I somehow think joining the Church would change things for me? That I'd suddenly feel like I belonged somewhere? What a joke. Instead, this decision will actually alienate me further from my family and make life infinitely harder.

Time to be honest with myself. I've been working toward my goal of joining the Church for a year now, and in some ways, I feel even more distant—like an outsider trying to join a secret club. I'm so pathetic I can't even remember when to stand and kneel at Mass. A year ago, I thought I figured out what I needed. It all seemed so clear to me. So, what happened? Had I fooled myself into believing a lie—achieving something that I could never attain?

Sleep eludes me for most of the night as I try to make sense of my thoughts. All my concerns seem to boil down to one question—as my baptism day inches closer, shouldn't I be excited and full of peace about finally joining the Church? Doubts and sadness can't be a good sign. I should quietly bow out and wait a few years until I'm older and then decide, when life is easier. My college would be paid for. I wouldn't have a mountain of debt. And I wouldn't need to constantly seek my family's support or permission.

As painful as the message is, Grandmother's letter might be the needed proof that I'm making the wrong decision. In a few years, when my life is in order, if I still want to join the Church, there will be nothing holding me back. Yep. Putting the kibosh on this decision makes sense. It will be hard to break the news to Josie, but it will be for the best. And I need to do what is right for me.

Father Dominic was wise. He knew I needed this weekend to discern and realize I'd rushed into something that I'm not ready for. I throw back the covers. Better to leave now and not waste any more time.

To avoid any confrontation, I write a note explaining why I've decided to leave. Then, in the wee hours of the morning, I gather my items, place my note on the registration desk, and quietly exit.

The incessant rain matches my gloomy mood as I trudge to the car. My sleeping bag and duffle get tossed into the back seat, then I slide in behind the wheel and start the car. I should leave before someone comes running out to stop me. But as I stare at the retreat center, something holds me back. Not indecision. More like frustration that I wasted so much time and resources chasing my misguided dream. I push away the sadness by reminding myself that joining the Church can still be in my future. Right now, I need to focus on what's best for me and for Mom—college being paid for and peace in the family. With one last look at the large crucifix on the building, I finally pull out of the parking lot.

The limited visibility keeps me focused on the road, but I do manage a quick glance at the clock on the dashboard. If all goes smoothly, I'll make it home around lunchtime. Mom will be happy to see me, probably relieved by my decision. Explaining to Josie will be much more difficult—but since she's not expecting me to be home this weekend, I can probably avoid that conversation until Sunday evening or even Monday. No need to worry about that now. I turn up my music to silence the thoughts circulating in my brain.

As the overcast sky lightens to a slightly less depressing shade of gray, I slowly make my way down the winding road—the only car journeying at this hour through the remote woods. After about an hour, I finally spot another vehicle. Up ahead, an old pickup truck pulls out from a narrow side road and onto the road in front of me. *Please don't be some pokey driver.* Now that I've decided, I'm anxious to get home to a hot shower—simultaneously ridding myself of this chill and the disastrous weekend.

The road curves, and around a bend, rocky cliffs come

into view. I've always liked these cliffs. On sunny days, light reflects off the pyrite, causing them to shimmer and making me daydream of medieval castles. Today though, they appear dark and foreboding, more like an evil fortress. I sing a little louder to one of my favorite tunes, the windshield wipers moving in syncopation to the beat, when I hear a weird rumble. The pickup truck in front of me suddenly swerves across the yellow line. I tap on my brake, searching the road for what he's trying to avoid—a fallen branch, an animal? Out of the corner of my eye, movement draws my attention. A gasp escapes as I watch part of the rocky cliff break away and crumble onto the road. I slam on the brakes, hoping I'll stop before being pummeled by rocks.

Debris pelts my motionless car with sickening pings, then quiet descends. My worry about any damage vanishes as my gaze focuses on the giant boulder resting on the road in front of me. The entire road is now impassible, covered in mud, rocks, and even a small tree. *Whoa.* I tear my gaze from what's left of the road in search of the pickup—but it's nowhere in sight. While the truck swerved in the nick of time, avoiding the massive boulder, it couldn't have completely avoided the rockslide. Moving like a lava flow, the loosened dirt probably pushed the pickup off the far edge of the road, rolling it down the embankment.

I sit there frozen. *Oh, my gosh.* What do I do? *Think*. The driver may need help. With shaking hands, I grab my phone. My call to 911 doesn't go through. Did I push the wrong buttons? I try again before realizing there's no service. *Seriously?* Now what?

I should check on the driver. But, what if there's another rockslide? Do I turn around and drive back to the retreat center? I squeeze my eyes shut, forcing the panic away. *Dear Lord. What should I do?*

It takes me three tries to unfasten my seatbelt with my useless, trembling hands. I pull up the hood of my rain jacket, ready to face the weather, but am still surprised by the cold, wet raindrops that pummel me as I exit the car. I squint at the cliff, surveying the area as if I'd be able to tell if another slide was imminent. Then I remember the odd rumble—there had been a warning. If I'm observant, I should be able to tell if another slide is about to happen. That should give me time to get out of the way. Hopefully.

Inching toward the edge of the road, I send up another quick prayer.

God, please help the driver to be okay. Please, help me know what to do.

I peer over the edge of the road. The vehicle, looking like a wounded animal, rests about twenty feet below me. Though it's facing the wrong way, it landed upright—the front end crumpled like a smashed soda can. The driver's door is wedged against the embankment, the front windshield a web of shattered glass. From its position and the amount of damage, I presume the truck not only spun but rolled. After another glance at the offending cliff, I make my way toward the vehicle, mud oozing up the sides of my sneakers. On my third step, my feet slip out from under me and, just like the giant boulder, I tumble down the rest of the little hill, coming to rest against a decaying log.

Landing with a jolt, I brush myself off, but my feeble attempt only smears mud everywhere. Continuing my cautious trek toward the truck, I focus on the passenger side door in front of me. The window is partially rolled down, and the bottom of the door panel looks like the Hulk used it as a punching bag—making opening the door impossible.

What if the driver is seriously injured, or worse? How am I going to help him? I take a deep breath, then lean close and peer into the vehicle.

There's only one passenger—a man slumped over the steering wheel, his face angled toward me. Blood trails down his cheek from his mostly brown hair to the white whiskers that color his beard. Is he conscious?

As I watch, his eyes peel open. *Thank goodness he's alive.*

He glances around at his predicament then pushes himself back—his face contorting in pain. Eventually, his gaze lands on me.

"Are you alright?" I manage to squeak out of my dry throat.

His eyes narrow in a squint. He's got the tanned, weathered face of an outdoorsy man, while the lines of wisdom—as my mom likes to call her wrinkles—hint at a long-lived life.

"Are you alright?" I ask again.

He shakes his head. "My legs are pinned."

My gaze travels to his legs, but I can't see anything—they disappear into a dark, compacted mass. That can't be good.

"We need to get you some help." My words, while true, sound ridiculous. No kidding.

He nods, then gives me a little grimace. "Seeing as I'm a little out of service at the moment, maybe you could help with that?"

"I tried to call 911, but there's no service." I pull my phone from my pocket and hold it up as if to prove my failed attempt.

He lets out a strained sigh. "Was afraid of that. The cell coverage is spotty around here."

"I came from a retreat center. I could drive back there and call for help." I study his face. His coloring seems a little off. Is it just the dim lighting, or could he be going into shock? "It's about an hour away, though."

He gives a slight shake of his head. "No. That will take too long."

"Do you live nearby? I could drive to your home and use your phone."

He rubs his face. A gold wedding band adorns his leathery hand. "My hunting cabin is about a half-mile away—that's where I was headed. It's pretty rustic, but my wife insisted it needed a phone. You'll have to walk though, as the road is on the other side of the slide—it'll be the first one you'll come to." He pulls his keys from the ignition. They jangle as he hands them to me. "Use the dark gray one."

I reach in and clasp the keys. "Don't worry. I've got this." Hopefully. I give him my most reassuring smile. "By the way, I'm Liz. What's your name?"

"Glenn."

Despite the slipping and sliding that thwarts my upward momentum, I finally make it back up the small ravine. The road that Glenn mentioned is easy enough to find, and soon I'm jogging down the isolated dirt lane, failing at my attempts to avoid puddles. While it's technically spring, nothing has started to bloom or bud. The dreary day, desolate forest, and barren trees with their gnarled branches brings to mind every creepy movie I've ever watched. I pick up the pace.

Eventually, I spot a little wooden shack. He wasn't kidding when he described it as rustic. The logs are weathered after years of intense winter weather, and the porch sags. I fumble with the key but finally slide it into place. The door sticks, but an extra push with my hip jars it open with a groan—from both the door and myself.

The small space reminds me of one of those tiny homes, only instead of being simplistically chic, mismatched, worn pieces furnish the space. It's no warmer than outside, but at least it's dry. I spot the phone in the tiny kitchenette—an old-fashioned rotary dial. Even though I've never used one, it's not hard to figure out. But thank goodness 911 has only three numbers since the old dialing system takes forever. I quickly tell the operator about the accident and that they need to send help immediately.

The telephone cord is so long that I'm able to walk around the entire cabin as she types in the information. While I describe the location as best I can, I check out the photos hanging on the wall. Each framed picture features Glenn with different kids enjoying some kind of outdoorsy activity—fishing, hiking, boating, and roasting marshmallows. Must be his grandchildren. My favorite photo features him and a girl side by side on separate alpine slides—like they are racing. Hard to tell who's winning. He appears to be the kind of grandpa I always longed for. But it wasn't meant to be—both of mine passed away when I was young.

When I'm done with the call, I leave the dry sanctuary of the cabin and hurry back to my car. Soon the accident scene comes into view. Seeing that massive rock lying in the middle of the road sends a shiver coursing down my spine—and not just from the wet, damp cold. If Glenn hadn't reacted so quickly and swerved out of the way, that rock would've landed on his truck.

I glance both ways down the desolate road. If I hadn't been here, how long until someone would've found him? How horrible to be trapped, injured, and by himself. My moments of feeling alone are nothing compared to that isolation. Well, thank goodness neither of us are alone right now. I grab a few supplies from my car, then repeat the slip and slide routine down the embankment.

Proud of myself for making it down a little more smoothly this time, I once again peer into the truck window—not liking what I see. Glenn's eyes are closed, and he definitely looks paler than before. I rap on the glass. *Please wake up.* His eyes slit open, and a slight grin forms on his face.

I smile—the only warmth I can offer at the moment. "Me again! Mind if I come in and join you while we wait for help?"

"Sure." He gestures with his hand. "Welcome to my humble abode."

I like this guy's spirit.

"'Fraid that's as far down as the window goes, though. Been stuck like that for a while."

"No problem." I shove my sleeping bag and a small grocery bag into the truck, then make the very ungraceful climb and shimmy through the partially lowered passenger window and plop onto the seat next to him.

He eyes the sleeping bag. "You plannin' on staying a while?" An attempted joke seems like a good sign, despite the strain in his voice.

As I unroll the sleeping bag that will hopefully help keep him warm, I share what I learned. "Well, the good news is that help should be on the way."

"And the bad news?"

"The 911 operator informed me that there have been numerous calls about rockslides. So, it might take a while for the emergency vehicles to arrive."

Grim-faced, he nods at the news.

I tuck the sleeping bag around him, careful not to touch his legs. "I've got snacks and some first-aid supplies. But, before we eat, let me look at that head wound of yours."

"You always so well-prepared?"

I laugh. "No. I'm supposed to be at a retreat for the weekend. Snacks and bedding were required. The first-aid kit stays in my car. My mom insisted that you never know when you may need one. So, thanks to you, I'll have to hear her I-told-you-so."

He grins. "What kind of retreat?"

I tuck a wet strand of hair behind my ear, then with supplies in hand, scooch closer to get a better look at his head. "Just a church thing. But I left early." He's not bleeding profusely, so it doesn't appear to be a deep wound.

"Why? Not your thing?"

I pour some water from my water bottle onto the washcloth I packed for the retreat. I hand him the bottle to hold, then dab at the gash. "Something like that."

He winces.

"Sorry. Are you in a lot of pain?"

He grunts. "I've felt worse." He takes a swig of water.

"This isn't the worst accident you've been in?" I gently push his hair away and place a Band-Aid on the cut. Next, I try to wipe the blood from his face.

A mischievous gleam lights his eyes. "Well, I did break my back once."

Ouch!

Satisfied with my work, I settle back and pull the hand sanitizer from my bag. Time to clean myself up. "I think I got the bleeding to stop."

He hands me the water bottle, then leans his head back

against the headrest. "Thanks, but that was just a little scratch. Nothing like the time I cut my hand so badly it wouldn't stop bleeding. Messed up my truck's upholstery."

"Dare I ask how it happened?"

"I was hunting and sliced my hand while field dressing an elk. None of my buddies could drive me from our campsite to town, which was a few hours away."

"Are you saying that you drove yourself?" I shiver at the thought.

He gives me a sheepish little grin. "Yeah, my wife wasn't too happy when I told her about that one." His gaze drops to the grocery bag. "Did you say something about snacks?"

I hold up the bag. "Getting hungry?"

He nods. "I missed breakfast."

"Me too, but all I have are chocolate-chip cookies—not exactly the 'breakfast of champions,' as my dad would say." I offer for him to take the first one. He reaches into the bag, which rattles due to his shaking hand. "So, do you have more such stories?"

He smirks. "Well, there was the time I was skiing and started having chest pains. I was pretty sure it was a heart attack." He sinks his teeth into a cookie.

"Oh, gosh. Did they have to take you down on one of those toboggan things?" I reach into the bag.

He brushes away my suggestion. "Nah. I ended up skiing several more runs because the snow was so good. Then I went to the hospital."

I cover my mouth, stopping myself from spewing my bite of cookie at the poor man as a laugh escapes. "Let me guess. Your wife wasn't too thrilled with that decision either."

"Sounds like you know her." His grin quickly transforms into a grimace.

Hurry up, ambulance. Not only am I worried about him, but if I keep sitting in this cold truck in wet clothes, I may end up with hypothermia and also need medical attention.

Maybe if I keep him talking, it will take his mind off the pain. "I must say, I was quite impressed with how quickly you reacted when that rockslide began. You handled it perfectly—so calm and cool."

He slowly reaches for another cookie. "I've had a few scary driving moments in my life."

"Now you've piqued my curiosity. Do tell—unless you have somewhere else you need to be." I try to match his forced lightheartedness.

"Well, I was a truck driver for many years. Driving over the Rocky Mountains during a white-out blizzard will prepare anyone for what may happen."

"That sounds terrifying. What did you deliver?"

"I hauled lots of things over the years. Groceries, steel, even ducklings."

"Oh, sweet." I rub my arms, attempting to create some warmth.

"The ducks were a long time ago. Back when I was sixteen." His voice catches, from the memory or pain, I'm not sure.

"Wait. You were driving a delivery truck when you were sixteen?" I reach for a second cookie but keep my eye on him to gauge his well-being.

He slowly nods, then grasps the steering wheel, his knuckles white.

"Like around a farm?" Come on, Glenn, keep talking.

"I delivered them from a farm in Pennsylvania to upstate New York."

"When you were younger than I am?" That's crazy. I hate driving to places that I'm not familiar with. I'm about to tell him that, but my chattering teeth prevent me.

Glenn raises an eyebrow, then lifts the edge of my sleeping bag, offering me a bit of the makeshift blanket. I acquiesce and nudge a little closer.

"Tell me more about this church retreat that you were escaping," he says as I gratefully drape part of the warm sleeping bag around myself, making sure not to uncover my elderly patient.

"I wasn't escaping." Well, maybe I was.

"Your parents make you attend?"

"No. It was all my brilliant idea." I watch the rain slide down the side window before trying to explain. "My parents never really attended church much. We only went on holidays and when we visited family. When my parents divorced, my friend Josie and her family started inviting me to go with them to their Catholic church. I never really thought about joining the Church until last year. Things with my dad went from bad to worse, and I found myself in a dark place. Josie gave me this Holy Family Novena to pray, and things miraculously started to improve. The more I thought about it, the more I realized the Church was my rock, so I decided to make it official. I was supposed to be baptized at the upcoming Easter Vigil." Remembering back to that time when I was so sure about things causes my heart to plummet. *Why can't I feel like that again?*

"What did your parents think about you joining the Catholic Church?" His gravelly voice is barely over a whisper.

"Well, they always seemed fine with me going to church with Josie, but they were definitely surprised when I told them I wanted to become Catholic. While they haven't tried to talk me out of the decision, they haven't been overly excited either."

"So, that's why you didn't stay at the retreat?"

I shake my head. "Not entirely." Even though I barely know the man, it's nice to have someone to confide in. "Lately, I feel like such an imposter, trying to fit in someplace where I'll never belong. Everyone else always seems to know all the right prayers. They know about different saints. They know when to stand and kneel during Mass. I can never get the responses memorized. I still stumble over the Rosary. I don't know. I just feel like I rushed into this decision."

"Because you don't know the prayers and responses yet?"

I feel the tears gather in my eyes. "Seeing the other kids at the retreat this weekend just made me sad and extremely jealous. None of them seem to understand how lucky they are. They get to go to church each week with their families. They've grown up with all these wonderful sacraments, yet most seem to take them for granted. They are all so blessed and don't even know it. Sometimes during Mass, I watch the large extended families, and it makes me want to cry because I'll never have what they have." I bite my lip, forcing the threatening tears to stay away.

He pats my hand in amiable silence. What's wrong with me? I've already made my decision to stop the RCIA process. It makes sense. Instead of spending Easter being baptized into the Church, Mom and I will enjoy a brunch somewhere by ourselves. And it'll be nice—a relief. I won't have to worry about how uncomfortable she is during the long Easter Vigil. I won't have to feel guilty, knowing I gave up my college tuition. I won't have to try and explain my decision to Dad once again. It's good—the right decision.

So, why am I still trying to convince myself?

"When you think of Easter, what do you think of?" The question blurts out of my mouth.

"Colored chicks."

"Colored chicks?" I shift to look at him. Is delirium setting in? His eyes droop a little, but otherwise, he seems okay.

He nods. "That farm I drove for as a teenager, dyed chicks for Easter. They'd color the newborn chicks blue, green, and pink—for the kids' Easter baskets."

My eyes narrow. "Live chicks?"

His shoulder raises ever so slightly. "Wouldn't be allowed nowadays."

No kidding. How was it ever allowed? Real-life Peeps? Hmm . . . maybe that's how the colored marshmallow-y treats came about. I find myself smiling, picturing a teenage Glenn with a truckful of pastel-colored chicks. I'd never really understood why Josie enjoyed chatting with military vets. But now I get it. The stories from a different generation are fascinating. His eyes shut, increasing my worry. *Keep him talking.*

"Okay, Mr. Glenn. You've obviously led an interesting life. Tell me five more things about yourself that you haven't already shared."

His eyes remain closed with no indication that he's heard me. Did he lose consciousness?

I throw my head back in frustration. *Lord, You bring people together to help one another. Why not now? Glenn needs someone useful—someone with medical knowledge—not me.*

I have no idea what to do. Let him rest? Try to wake him? Thankfully, before I make a decision, his eyes flutter open.

"Well, let's see." He lifts his hand and, accepting my challenge, raises his fingers one at a time as he rattles off his list. "I owned my own business. I've traveled around the world. I've met a president. I've attended Mass with a pope." He pauses and clears his throat. "And I still think my bride of sixty-three years is the prettiest girl I've ever met."

Aww . . . "That's quite an amazing list."

His right hand strokes his whiskery cheeks. "Mind if I share with you my philosophy of life?"

"Who wouldn't want some advice from the *most interesting man in the world*?"

That smirk of his returns, though not with as much gusto as before. "Life is a journey. The destination being heaven. I've lived my life with three founding principles—my work ethic, my family, and my faith. But the key to it all is faith." His voice catches, and I realize that he's having trouble breathing. "Faith should be the center of your life, guiding all your interactions. You see, working hard enabled me to always give generously. It provided the opportunity to travel to many different countries and meet President Carter through my volunteer work with Habitat for Humanity. I've had a lot of success, but you know what I consider my greatest accomplishment in life? My family. I wisely chose a wife who shared my faith, and together we passed on our values to our children and grandchildren. No matter what trials come along, such as this, I'm assured that God has everything under control."

Wow. How amazing to have such a strong faith, to be at peace even when facing something so scary. I close my eyes and some of the crazy things I learned through RCIA come to mind—like some of the Eucharistic miracles and the unbelievable stories about the saints. Like, seriously, how can there be incorruptible bodies? Dead bodies that don't decompose? That defies all logic. How can those things be explained except that they are miracles? Miracles that have happened in the Catholic Church—God's little proofs that this is His Church. Am I really ready to turn my back on all that I've learned, just to make my life a little easier?

The glorious faint sounds of a siren cut through the silence. Help has arrived!

I squeeze Glenn's hand. "Hey, are you okay? I hear sirens. It shouldn't be much longer."

His head bobs, and his eyes slit open. "Hey, if I'm able, and you change your mind, I would be honored to attend this Easter Vigil thing of yours. I don't mind being a fill-in grandpa if you need one."

I lean against him, breathing in his scent of rugged masculinity, wisdom, and comfort. "Thank you."

After making sure I'm alright, the first responders shoo me away and quickly take charge—finally someone who can help him. At some point, the rain has stopped, leaving a cold, wet dreariness in its wake. I watch them work for a while, then decide there's a better way to help. Pulling the sleeping bag around myself, I perch on a large rock on the side of the road. Too weary to search for my Rosary cheat-sheet, I skip the opening prayer and dive right into the parts I know.

Eventually, my new friend is extracted from the vehicle and brought up to the road. As the stretcher moves toward the ambulance, I scurry over and clasp his hand.

"I'm praying for you," I tell him.

He gently squeezes my hand in reply.

While he's loaded in, I plead for some reassurance that he'll be okay. The paramedics only say that he's in good hands now.

After the emergency vehicle pulls away, the siren now diminishing, I'm left staring at the boulder that smashed into the road. If it hadn't been for Glenn's defensive driving skills, this could have ended quite differently. A jolt of realization hits me—that had almost been me. If I hadn't sat in the parking lot at the retreat center for those few extra moments, I would've been ahead of Glenn on the road and the rock might've landed on my small car. Possibly ending it all. What a sobering thought. Life really is precious. None of us are guaranteed tomorrow.

A new thought comes to me. I pleaded for God to bring someone to Glenn's aid, but maybe our chance meeting was actually for my sake—so I'd realize that putting my faith on the backburner is not the answer. My gaze lifts to the sky. *Thanks, God.*

Suddenly things align into sharp focus. Even though there may be stumbling blocks along the way—minor crosses to bear—faith has to be my main priority. Sure, I wasn't blessed with a family that passed down their religion to me, but a family's faith journey has to start somewhere—why not with me? And maybe my future won't be as easy as I'd always assumed, but paying back college loans or living at home certainly aren't the worst things in the world. Just like Glenn, I'm not afraid of a little hard work.

I offer another prayer of thanks to God for bringing him

into my life and helping me realize that as long as I focus on my faith, I'll never be alone. I turn toward my car. Time to head back to the retreat center and finish the journey I've begun.

###

As an adult convert to Catholicism, I'm impressed with teens who make the decision to go through the RCIA program to join the Church. Their dedication and commitment is inspiring. For this story, I thought it would be fun to explore that idea, and Liz proved to be the perfect character to use. She and her best friend, Josie, can be found in my full-length novel, *Into the Spotlight* (formerly *An Unexpected Role*).

While I was writing this story, my father, Glenn, was very sick—in the last stages of life. He had always been a huge supporter of my writing—eagerly reading my stories as soon as they came out and sharing them with his friends. Making him a character in this story seemed like a wonderful way to honor him. He was not able to see this story in print, but I was able to share it with him. I hope you enjoy this glimpse into the life of a very special man.

ABOUT THE AUTHOR

LESLEA WAHL is the author of the award-winning Catholic teen mysteries *The Perfect Blindside, eXtreme Blindside, Where You Lead,* and *Into the Spotlight*. Leslea's journey to become an author came through a search for value-based fiction for her own children. She now not only writes for teens but also has become a reviewer of Catholic teen fiction to help other families discover faith-based books. Leslea lives in beautiful Colorado with her husband and children. The furry, four-legged members of her family often make cameo appearances in her novels. Leslea has always loved mysteries and hopes to encourage teens to grow in their faith through these fun adventures. For more information about her faith-filled Young Adult mysteries, please visit www.LesleaWahl.com.

2

Historical

FOLLOW ME

by Cynthia T. Toney

Vince Farano

Men in black suits and winter overcoats filed in front of Mama and me, their backs as stiff as the funeral-home chairs in which we sat side by side, me a full head taller than she.

Smiles that slid across teeth in pock-marked faces belied the calculating minds behind their cold, dark eyes. One Chicago goon with a scar across his cheekbone reached out a bronzed hand and touched the shoulder of my suit coat, a new one since my sixteen-year-old back had broadened beyond the size of Papa's.

I jerked my elbow upward to meet his arm and release his touch.

Mama leaned toward my ear and whispered, "Vincent, please. These men are Papa's friends."

More than likely, one of them was his killer. But I had decided to let Mama believe that Papa had been murdered by an enemy, not someone she had served coffee and cookies on Saturday afternoons.

I struggled to convince myself that Papa had repented for his sins before the first bullet struck him. Just in case he'd made it to purgatory, I asked God to have mercy on his soul.

Swallowing my anger over the circumstances of my life, I prayed I would quit thinking that Papa had brought his death upon himself. I had to quit to make my stomach stop hurting.

And if these men believed I would follow in Papa's footsteps, if that's what they hoped—or feared—they were mistaken.

But each tear Mama shed diluted my beautiful watercolor dream of attending seminary later this year of 1929.

The day after the funeral I awoke at dawn, just as I had done the previous days of Lent, to pray in quiet solitude until the aroma of Mama's black coffee from her aluminum pot on the gas stove wafted into my room.

I lingered over breakfast with Mama to provide her with some company, although neither of us felt much like talking. With a check of the wall clock, I wiped my mouth on my cotton napkin. I rose from my chair and carried my dishes to the tile counter next to the sink.

The sound of Mama's shallow breathing filled the room.

I could only guess what filled her mind. I bent over her to kiss her cheek in good-bye.

She grabbed my hand and held tight, her eyes pleading with me to stay.

"Father James is counting on me, Mama. It'll be okay. I'll see you in a little while." I gently peeled away her fingers with my free hand.

Besides, serving a weekday morning Mass with Robert Brown, my best friend in our eleventh and final year of high school, was probably what I needed to feel somewhat normal again.

In spite of my brisk walk in the cold air, Robert had beat me to the church. We both liked to get there early enough to talk before we dressed and prepared the altar, but he was already slipping his white surplice over his head when I stepped into the sacristy.

He spotted me as his brown eyes appeared through the neckline opening. "I'm sorry I couldn't make it to the funeral, Vince. My parents . . ." Robert shrugged, his expression soft, his eyes cloudy.

I removed my black cassock from its hanger. "It's okay, Robert." It was the same with all my friends whose fathers weren't among Papa's business associates. Their families didn't want their sons hanging around those goons, so they avoided my parents and me outside of school activities. Who could blame them?

Robert ran a slim black comb through his hair, almost as dark. "Have you heard from the seminary?"

"Not yet." I worked the buttons down my chest. "And now . . . I don't know what I should do."

The pitch of Robert's voice raised. "What do you mean? I thought you wanted to dedicate your life to Christ."

My cheeks warmed. Why should I have to defend myself? My papa had just died! "I do want to serve Christ, but who would take care of my mama? There's no one else."

Robert's voice dropped to a soothing timbre. "To perform his ministry, Jesus had to leave Mary at home when she couldn't travel with him. Saving souls requires sacrifice."

I dipped my chin and looked up at Robert. I didn't need a Bible lesson. Or one on the merits of sacrifice. Jesus probably wasn't worried about some goon trying to marry his mother and take her house or money. And keep her trapped forever in a criminal husband's life.

From his reflection in the wall mirror, Robert's eyes grew big and round. "Hey, maybe your mama could move to be near you. And get a job like my mama did."

That was exactly what I needed to hear to stop feeling so sorry for myself. Robert and his parents hadn't had an easy time money-wise during the few years I'd known him.

"Maybe." It would be great if Mama and I could both leave this life Papa had created, with all its risk and secrecy. Regardless of what had led Papa into the criminal life, though, at least he'd encouraged me to become a priest from the moment I showed an interest in becoming an altar boy.

Smiling, Robert turned away from the mirror and began to pick lint off his cassock.

Imagine Mama working! What kind of job could she

do? Humph. As smart as she seemed to be, she'd find something. And with that thought, the watercolor image of the seminary reappeared in my mind's eye, this time a little clearer.

Dressed, I faced Robert and drew my eyebrows together. "I thought you were thinking of seminary too. I was sort of hoping you'd decide to at least *try* to go." It would be nice to have a friend on my very first day there.

Robert scratched the back of his neck. "I have prayed about it, but I think God is calling me to do something else. To finish something I didn't finish. I need to go home . . ." Robert's face reddened and he looked away.

My tone became insistent. "And?" Would he finally tell me something about his past?

Robert stared out the window as though intent on studying squirrel activity in the trees.

"Is it a girl?" I could imagine Robert as a good husband and father, same as the kind, soft-spoken Mr. Brown.

He squinted for a second, like he had when Mama dug a splinter out of his finger after we carried in her firewood.

I'd hit my mark.

His voice was a whisper. "I'm thinking of a holy type of life too, if it's done right, just different from the one you'll have."

I nodded. Marriage was a sacrament, after all.

"If I find her again and she feels the same way . . ."

I cracked a weak smile. "Look, I always knew you weren't from around here. You don't even sound like it." *Robert Brown*? Not likely his real name. His olive skin and strong facial features seemed as Italian as my own.

He cut his eyes to the side, toward me.

"Come on. Tell me where you're from." I chuckled low beneath my breath.

He faced me head-on and smiled. "I guess we all have our secrets."

I acknowledged his statement with my steady gaze.

Maybe Robert or his family regretted their choices. Maybe Papa had too.

Lying on my bed with my hands behind my head, I stared at the molded tin ceiling. The alarm clock on my bedside table ticked its familiar rhythm.

I'd talked to Mama, but I should've known she wouldn't easily accept the idea of selling her beautiful house and moving, even to be near me. And I couldn't blame her. The idea of leaving my comfortable surroundings to enter the seminary and a life without the luxuries I'd grown used to was hard for *me* to think about.

A gentle rap sounded at my door, and I sat up. "Yes?"

Mama eased the door open and stepped inside the room.

I snatched clothes off the armchair near the bed. "Wanna sit down, Mama?"

She sat, folded her hands in her lap, and sighed. Dark crescents lay below her eyes.

Her soft voice joined the ticking of the clock. "I need you to understand something."

"Sure, Mama. I'll try." I leaned forward from my seat on

the edge of the bed.

She scrunched her nose. "It's not so easy for someone like me to leave."

"I understand. You've been in this house a long time."

"It's not that." She pressed her lips together and shook her head. "Being married to your father, I sometimes . . ." She took a deep breath. "Well, his associates might think . . . that I know things. And they wouldn't want that information to leave this house."

Heat rose to my cheeks. "Mama, are you afraid? For your life?" Christ had died for our sins, but Mama shouldn't have to die for Papa's sins.

Her gaze met mine. "No. No, I'm not afraid. I'm tired of being afraid. I refuse to live like that any longer. And I don't think anyone would try to physically harm me—or you." Her jaw tightened.

"What, then?" So much had been kept secret from me through the years, but I wasn't a kid any longer.

"They can make it very hard for me to sell this house." She twisted her hands.

"Hard—how?"

"Their influence and connections reach further than you can imagine. Without selling the house, I'd have trouble starting my new life, even if I could find a job."

"So you're trapped?" I chewed my lip. Would I be able to concentrate on my studies, knowing I'd left Mama behind and alone? I shook my head. There had to be a way out. "I'll pray for the house to be sold just the same."

She smiled and stood. "I expected as much from you.

Just try not to worry about it too much right now." She kissed my forehead.

I nodded. I'd pray and give our problem to God, but urgency tied a knot in my belly.

God, please help us.

Alone again, my muscles twitched. I leapt from the bed, unable to pray, and paced around my room. What Mama had said changed everything. What if she couldn't sell the house? What should I do?

Don't be a fool, Vince. You can postpone going to seminary for a year. Let Mama stay in her house and be comfortable for a while. You deserve some time to adjust to your papa's death, too, don't you? Wait and let things settle down. Both of you can act like everything is normal instead of fleeing right away. Why arouse suspicion that she might confide in the authorities? You can attend a small college close to home and get a local part-time job.

I stopped dead in my tracks. Yeah, I could work and save up. Maybe not go to college at all. Really help Mama out. Then later we could escape.

With determination growing, I pounded my fist into my palm.

At school the next day, Robert and I settled at a lunch table, prayed, and opened our paper sacks.

I eyed Robert's meager selections. "Are you fasting?" I'd forgotten about my decision to fast at least three times a week during Lent. That was before Papa was murdered.

Robert spoke without looking up. "When you fast, you're not supposed to announce to everybody that you're fasting. But I will say that it helps me understand a lot of things."

"I know about fasting." Irritation edged my voice.

Robert took a tiny bite of his mama's homemade bread and chewed slowly. "Have you decided what to do about seminary?"

I sighed. He was like a dog with a bone about seminary. Reluctantly, I laid out my plan to him about staying and working for a while, omitting the part about it possibly being forever.

Robert started slicing an apple and placing the slices on his paper sack. "But didn't Jesus say 'Come, follow me'? He didn't say think about it for a year first."

The side of my fist struck the table top, and a few heads turned in my direction. "I know!" I'd heard those very words, clear as day in my head, when I'd first felt called to join the priesthood. Peter and Andrew had left their nets, their house, their kin, to follow Him. Jesus was asking the same of me. Nothing more and nothing less.

Robert raised his eyebrows but focused on his food. "Just wondering if this decision is only about the money."

My face heated, and my back tensed. Did he doubt my sincerity about the priesthood? He'd never made me this angry before. I scowled at Robert, who stole a sideways glance at me as he bit an apple slice.

Okay, it didn't matter what he thought. I had to do what was best for Mama and me. But what was that exactly?

Everything was muddled. The harder I tried to figure things out on my own, the further I got from the outcome I knew in my heart was God's plan.

I inhaled a huge breath and bowed my head. My clasped hands pressed my forehead.

Why couldn't I trust in God? He had called me to His service. Wouldn't He help me get there? Why was I fighting Him by making my own feeble plans? *Lord, tell me what to do!*

With my lunch sack in hand, I shoved against the table's edge, forcing my chair backward.

Leaving Robert chewing like a cow on its cud, I handed my lunch to a skinny boy named Frankie, seated at the next table, who never seemed to have enough to eat.

It didn't take long for God to give me an answer. That evening. Through an unlikely source.

I stood in the front doorway of my house, face to face with one of the goons. I should've looked out the window before answering the bell.

He pushed the brim of his hat backward with one finger, tilting it off his forehead. "How ya doin', Vince?"

What did he care? "Fine." I scowled.

"I was wonderin' if you'd help me with somethin'." Sleazy grin.

Somethin' was surely nothing good. Probably a delivery of drugs or dirty money or who-knows-what. "I'm really pretty busy. You know, with school and all. And preparing to become a *priest*."

The goon blushed through his leathery skin. He must've been one of the few who didn't know about my papa's plan for me.

Without waiting for a reply, I slammed and locked the door. Trembling, I leaned my back against it.

Mama called from upstairs, "Who was at the door?"

"Nobody, Mama. Just somebody trying to sell something."

The pressure for me to enter "the life" was already on. My future, should I remain in my home, unfolded within my mind's eye. Illegal activity, violence. Mama and me stuck in the middle of it all.

God sometimes worked in mysterious ways. But He'd made His intentions clear to me.

I tried to study in my room but laid my books aside, unable to concentrate. If only I could spill my guts to Robert. Not just about the goon visiting me, but everything. All the awful details about the life I'd been a part of. Things I'd suspected Papa had been involved in.

But Robert, so innocent, from such a mild-mannered and ordinary family—how would he understand?

At any rate, I owed Robert an apology for being so grumpy and angry with him at school. He didn't deserve that. And for him to keep after me like he had about the priesthood, he must truly care about me reaching my goal.

Something fluttered in my chest. Could he be worried what would happen to my future without the seminary?

The next morning before the school bell rang, we met up at our usual spot in the schoolyard.

"I'm sorry I got so mad yesterday. I know you were just trying to help." I stuck out my hand.

Robert grinned and shook my hand. "That's okay. I've dished it out to you a few times."

I laughed. "Yeah, like right after you moved here. I couldn't teach you anything about how to get along. You thought you knew everything."

"I still know more than you." He poked me in the chest and chuckled.

I chuckled too and shoved his shoulder.

We both tossed our books on the ground and sank to the grass under a tree.

Robert's eyebrows drew together over his nose. "Hey, did you hear about Frankie?"

"No, what about him?" We'd just seen him at lunch the day before, but we didn't see much of him other than at school. Without a papa, he helped out at home while his mama worked at a factory.

Robert spoke in a quiet voice. "He was shot last night."

My stomach flipped. I sat up straight and faced Robert. "What? How? Is he—" I couldn't speak the word. Frankie never got into trouble like some of the other boys did.

"He'll be all right. He was delivering a package to a speakeasy when police raided the place. Somebody fired at the police and they fired back. Frankie was in the way and got winged."

I took a deep breath and exhaled through my mouth.

He wasn't killed. *Thank you, God.*

Robert cupped my shoulder. "If you want, we can visit him together."

I nodded and swallowed hard. The school bell rang.

As Robert and I trudged toward our school's front entrance, the scenario Robert had described ran through my mind. But in place of Frankie, I pictured myself.

Could the "somethin'" the goon wanted me to do have been the errand that Frankie ran? I shivered.

If I checked on Frankie later, I should have a serious talk with him about what he was getting drawn into. He probably had no idea what the consequences of that kind of life could be. And not just the physical consequences. Sure, he could've easily wound up dead. Just as I could've, in his place.

But more than that, he should consider the consequences for his soul. What about sin? Lots of it. A priest would know how to talk to someone about that. Could convince someone to avoid it. I would someday have that ability if I became a priest.

The compulsion to enter the seminary was back as I approached my first class. I couldn't accept a future other than the one God—and Papa—had chosen for me. *Thank you for that at least, Papa.*

The question remained, though. How? How could I accomplish the move to the seminary while protecting Mama from the life Papa had created for her?

Robert and I put our heads together with Mama's and

came up with a plan for making some money. Money to help Mama get away, with or without selling the house.

Saturday, Robert and I grinned at each other as we plodded down the sidewalk in our overcoats, blending with the other pedestrians dressed the same.

We looked like we'd each gained twenty pounds—and probably had—with the items Mama had strapped onto our bodies and stuffed into our pockets. Silverware, jewelry, rare coins.

Our final destination would be the home of Mama's trusted friend who lived halfway across the city. She would sell the things to friends in her own neighborhood, or to pawn shops, and give the money to us for Mama.

We carried books in our arms so we could use the excuse of going to the public library, should anyone ask us where we were headed.

"Be careful not to rattle." I barely got the words out before Robert and I exploded in laughter. We held our stomachs until we had to wipe tears from our eyes.

The library lay just ahead.

We composed ourselves in time to enter its doors and deposit our books to be returned. Each of us eyed the doors behind us.

"Let's stay a while, just in case we were followed," I whispered.

Robert trailed behind me to where large daily newspapers from around the country hung on wooden poles, waiting to be read. He began looking through them as I used them for cover and watched library visitors mill about. No one seemed interested in us.

"You look serious," I said over his shoulder.

Robert jerked his head around, his face flushed. "I may as well make good use of the time."

I eyed the masthead of the newspaper in front of him. "New Orleans? That's in Louisiana, isn't it?"

He shrugged and quickly returned the newspaper to its home.

Maybe I'd received the first clue about the origins of my mysterious friend, Robert.

Mama's plan with her friend succeeded throughout the winter, with Robert's and my help. We'd collected a tidy sum, which Mama hid in small amounts all over the house.

But even if Robert and I had been able to continue after the weather became too warm to wear overcoats, it would've taken too long to make enough money for Mama to move very far and set up a new life before I had to leave for seminary. And we couldn't start selling the furniture without arousing suspicion.

My praying intensified as I begged God for another solution.

Two weeks before Easter, letters began arriving. Addressed to me, typewritten, short, unsigned. Never the same postmark twice in a row, although all from our general area of Illinois.

Within the folded page in each envelope lay crisp paper currency, sometimes a little, sometimes more. Each letter described the good fortune that had come to the sender from an unexpected source and explained the desire to share it. Each included a recommendation that Mama take the Illinois Central railroad south to a tiny town in Louisiana called Freedom, where she would meet kind people of Italian heritage and be able to start a new life.

I tucked the envelopes into the secret compartment hidden below a loose floorboard underneath my bed.

I probably should've told Mama right away about the first letter and the money but was afraid she'd try to find out who the sender was. That would've made even more trouble for her—and me—and would've done nothing but stifle my plans for us. As the money kept coming, I prayed the Holy Spirit would inspire me with the right words to explain to Mama that God had used someone to help us. That He wanted me to attend seminary and her to be safe, and this was the way.

Her mouth hung open for a few seconds when I finally showed her the letters and the money. And told her that I thought God's hand was in this.

Little spurts of breath escaped her lips.

I clenched my teeth, unsure if she was about to laugh or cry.

If she agreed, all I had to do between my high school commencement exercises and departure for the seminary was to buy her a train ticket and help her pack her bags.

Eyes bright, she placed a hand on my cheek and smiled. "How can I tell God that His plan is no good?"

"Then you'll do it, Mama? Leave here?"

"Keep praying, Vince. I'm doing the same."

My shoulders sagged. Why didn't she just agree? She even admitted it was *His plan*.

She reached up with both hands and smoothed the frown from between my eyebrows with her thumbs. I hadn't realized I'd been frowning at her.

I found Mama on her prayer kneeler, rosary in hand. I joined her on the rug next to her. We hadn't prayed the Rosary together in months, not since before Papa died.

When we finished praying, I helped her rise to her feet.

She slipped her rosary into a pocket. "Let's sit together in the formal living room, Vince."

She led me to the room containing her best furniture that had been off-limits when I was growing up. She perched on the edge of the high-backed sofa I'd always thought was the most uncomfortable-looking sofa I'd ever seen, nothing like the broken-in leather one in the family living room.

I stared at the wingback chair that had been used only by Papa when he and Mama had guests.

"Please, sit in Papa's chair." She extended her hand toward it.

I sat and rested my forearms on my thighs.

She smiled. "I'm very proud of you, Vince."

For . . . ? "Thank you, Mama."

"Papa would be proud of you too. It always meant a lot to us that you wanted to become a priest. It also means a lot to me that you haven't given up on entering the seminary in spite of our family's loss."

Warmth rose to my cheeks. Good that she didn't know I'd almost done that very thing.

"Even before . . . You were willing to make the sacrifice of not ever having your own family in order to serve God as a priest. Now, I know you're concerned about me, about leaving me alone, and I appreciate that. But I've always known I'd have to make sacrifices too, because of your vocation. I'd already resolved myself to the fact that you'd be going away. Every mother faces it eventually anyway."

My chest pounded. "What are you trying to tell me, Mama?"

"I want you to go to seminary with all the joy and hope for the future our family planned together for you, focused on following your calling. And I want to stay here for a while."

I sharply pulled some air into my lungs, my mouth open to protest, but she held up her hand.

"I'm not saying I'll never leave. Actually, I'll probably leave a few months after you do. Freedom sounds like a wonderful town with citizens who share our heritage. Thanks to you and Robert and the mysterious benefactor, I feel a lot more confident that I can survive without help from people here I'd rather separate myself from."

It was great to hear her say that she wanted nothing more to do with Papa's circle. So why would she stay? I joined her on the sofa. "Why not leave when I do, Mama?"

She squeezed my hand. "So you can leave like the apostles did when they chose to follow Jesus.

Unencumbered. Not wondering if someone has pursued us because we left at the same time and I didn't return. And I want you to concentrate on your studies after you get there, not be concerned with me settling into a new life in a strange place. I will be fine by myself for now. I'll have time to grieve the way I should for your papa, in the house we shared together."

"But I feel like I'm abandoning you." I wiped my eyes with my fingers.

"No, please don't. I'll miss you, but I was willing to make that sacrifice for the rest of our lives."

She spoke the truth. Neither one of us could predict where I might serve in the decades that lay ahead of me.

The decision made, relief and gratitude for God's grace flooded my heart.

"Robert, look at this."

Robert and I sat on my bedroom floor, studying for final exams, textbooks and composition books scattered around us. I pressed my chest to the floor and reached my arms under the bed. Lifting the loose board, I grabbed the envelope at the top of the stack. I removed the letter but left the money in the envelope.

Robert's face held no expression as he read the letter and handed it back to me.

"What do you think? Pretty incredible, huh?" My eyes wide, I couldn't wait for his reaction. Any reaction.

Robert took a deep breath and focused on my hands, which held the letter. "I think somebody understands how badly you and your mama need to leave."

"Well, he must be a very caring person to do this, maybe at great personal sacrifice." I sought the eyes of the best friend I'd ever had.

Robert pressed his lips together as his gaze met mine.

I spoke in a low voice. "Do you think maybe something happened to him that makes him want to help someone else?"

Pain flashed in Robert's eyes.

There was something he wasn't telling me.

He swallowed hard. "Maybe."

"Yeah, well, I think so."

Robert looked down and flipped through a composition book.

I scooted back to my bed and stored the letter.

Returning, I sat in front of him. "No matter what, I really appreciate what he's done. And I plan to pay him back as soon as I can, after I find out who he is."

The tiniest smile formed on Robert's lips as he stared into his composition book. "You'll find out someday. And I'm sure he knows you'll pay him back."

Robert Brown, a.k.a. Salvatore (Sal) Scaviano

What a gift from God that Uncle Enzo had evaded the mob's wrath all this time and was alive somewhere! Sal had always felt it during the years of hiding with his parents, but now he was sure of it. Who else would've sent him the money? And God's hand had caused it to arrive in time to help Vince and his mother escape the mob. Just as his own family had done, under different circumstances.

###

If you'd like to find out why Robert Brown, a.k.a. Salvatore Scaviano, and his family had to flee from organized crime, leaving behind their friends and loved ones in the town of Freedom, please consider reading *The Other Side of Freedom.* This historical novel set during Prohibition and widespread prejudice in the U.S. demonstrates the determination and strength of character of thirteen-year-old Sal, his friends, and family members as dreams are shattered and attitudes challenged in their Italian immigrant farming community. The book has received a number of literary awards, including third place for Children's Books in the Catholic Press Association 2018 CPA Book Awards.

ABOUT THE AUTHOR

CYNTHIA T. TONEY writes characters that show tweens and teens how wonderful, powerful, and valuable God made them. Her current novel will accompany *The Other Side of Freedom* and will give readers more of Robert Brown (a.k.a. Sal) and Antonina, the girl he left behind.

Cynthia is also the author of the Bird Face series: *8 Notes to a Nobody, 10 Steps to Girlfriend Status, 6 Dates to Disaster,* and *3 Things to Forget,* as well as short stories in the Catholic Teen Books anthologies *Secrets: Visible & Invisible* and *Gifts: Visible & Invisible.* She is a member of Catholic Writers Guild and a volunteer with the Independence Italian Cultural Museum in Louisiana. She has a passion for rescuing dogs from abuse, neglect, and euthanasia and lives with her husband and several canines.

Find Cynthia T. Toney and her books on Amazon and other retail sites, Facebook, and Goodreads. She co-founded the Facebook group Books for Catholic Teens, where families, professionals, and readers can recommend and discuss Catholic books appropriate for Catholic tweens and teens. The public can also connect with her through her website www.CynthiaTToney.com and her blog www.BirdFaceWendy.wordpress.com. Look for her books and other writing at CatholicTeenBooks.com and her publisher's website, www.WriteIntegrity.com.

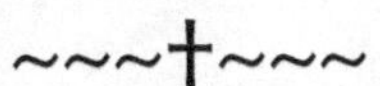

3

Science Fiction

TAKE UP YOUR CROSS

by Marie C. Keiser

My head ached and my stomach growled as I rounded the corner into the trauma recovery ward that Ash Wednesday. Wanting to start Lent right, I'd skipped breakfast, and that never went well, especially with my grueling schedule as a nursing assistant.

I'd just turned eighteen—legally a man now—so this was the first Lent I actually *had* to fast, though I was starting to wonder why I bothered with any of those rules. It had been well over a year since we'd last found a priest willing and able to sneak onto Mirawii and say Mass under the shadow of the Fleet installation.

What was the point anymore? Why cling to an outlawed religion we could scarcely practice? I knew plenty of decent people who weren't Catholics. Doctors, nurses, soldiers, other nursing assistants like me, all working to help other people and make the Galaxy a better place. Why couldn't I just be like them? They were good people, and they didn't have to worry about the government tracking them down and—

"Hey, Justin," the duty nurse greeted me as I walked past the nurse's station. "You've got a new patient in Room 301. They just brought him in an hour ago. He's in pretty bad shape. If he wakes up, make sure to call me in to figure out his pain meds."

I nodded and moved on, groaning to myself. I loved my work. I did. Usually.

Room 301 was first on my route. I stopped outside for a second. The first few days were always the hardest with new patients. They had to get used to whatever had happened to them, and I, well, I had to get used to dealing with them. I wasn't very good at that yet. Delivering bad news . . . seeing strong men at their weakest with pain and drugs lowering inhibitions and leaving them stripped of whatever masks they usually wore . . . being sworn at . . . I wasn't very good at handling any of it.

I glanced through the chart. Major Hector Alvarez, a thirty-one-year-old male. The name sounded familiar, but I couldn't place it. Training accident. I skimmed down to the list of injuries, let out a little whistle. Whoever he was, he was definitely having a worse day than I was. A lot worse.

Bracing myself, I opened the door and stepped in.

He was propped up in the bed, his torso wrapped in bandages. One leg was in a cast from the knee down, while the other, bruised and discolored, had metal pins and bars sticking out of it. Broken femoral shaft, the chart said. Must have been one heck of a training accident. His right arm was immobilized and draped in gauze to allow the burns to heal. An IV drip with antibiotics and painkillers was hooked up to his left hand. His eyes were closed, and his face—pretty much the only part of him that wasn't damaged—was puckered as though he was trying to solve a hard problem.

I checked the monitors for his vitals and made a few notes.

"What happened?"

I looked up to find a pair of golden-brown eyes fixed on me.

"You had an accident," I said. Stupid answer. But I only knew what was on the chart.

"Yes. We crashed. What I want to know is, how bad is it? I can't seem to move."

I hadn't yet gotten used to seeing that kind of fear in men's eyes. The fear that they were broken beyond repair, that they'd never be the same again. But I *had* learned that they wanted the truth and nothing else would satisfy them. Fortunately, in this case, the truth wasn't as bad as it could be. I took a deep breath. "You broke both your legs. Right one above the knee, left below. You've got some pretty deep wounds in your chest and abdomen, so you're bandaged up, and you've got severe burns on your right arm and shoulder. You've been in surgery and intensive care for the last four days. It'll take several weeks, but you'll recover."

He nodded, taking it in.

I couldn't tell if I'd just delivered good news or bad news.

"What about Darrell? Did he make it?"

I started carefully lifting the gauze so I could check the burn site and reapply ointment. "I'm sorry, sir, but I don't know who Darrell is."

"Darrell Lewis. My gunner. He was in the fighter with me when we went down."

The fighter? With a jolt, I realized who he was. This was Hector Alvarez, possibly the best fighter pilot in the Fleet. "I'll find out for you and let you know."

"Thank you," he said, and bit off a curse as the gauze pulled on the raw flesh below.

"Sorry."

He gritted his teeth as I finished the job. I changed the dressings on his other wounds as well. The surgeons had done their best, but he was going to have ugly scars. I could only imagine what he must have looked like before they put him back together. No sign of infection, though. That was good.

I helped him relieve himself, took his vitals, adjusted his pillows and promised to send the nurse in to take care of pain management.

"Anything I can get you before I go?" I had ten other patients I had to look after, and I needed to be going.

He shook his head, and I walked out shutting the door behind me.

Hector Alvarez! He was the best of the best. I'd been obsessed with fighters and ships and things as a kid. Well, to be honest, I wasn't really over it yet. But a year or so ago, I'd finally figured out that my family and other people around me didn't want to hear about it *all* the time. Those space fighters were awesome, and when Hector Alvarez flew them, they were even better. Or so the stories went.

It didn't take too long for me to find the right person to ask about Darrell Lewis, and the next time I went into Major Alvarez's room, I was able to tell him his gunner had survived the crash and was stable, though still being cared for in the burn unit.

He was silent for a long moment. "Thank you for telling me." He glanced at his right arm, covered in burn ointment and gauze, as though imagining how much worse his friend's situation must be if he was still in the burn unit. "I got him into this mess," he said, his expression a mixture of anger, disgust, and pain. He muttered something vicious-sounding under his breath.

"Will there be anything else?" I asked, edging to the door. I had other patients to care for, and I would be just as happy to not be around him when he was in *that* mood.

He looked up at me, evidently just remembering I existed. "No. Thank you."

Impressive, I thought, as I shut the door behind me. So many men in his circumstances would have been cursing at me, but Hector Alvarez had remembered to say thank you. A skilled warrior and courteous besides. Maybe in a few days, when he'd gotten more used to being in the hospital and stopped being angry at himself over the crash, he'd be willing to give me his autograph. I certainly couldn't ask him now. He was probably right-handed, for one thing.

"You know what's funny?" Alvarez asked a couple days later as I was changing his bandages yet again. His left hand—pretty much the only part of him he could move without hurting—clenched and unclenched with nervous energy. Stir crazy. I knew the signs when I saw them. But there wasn't much I could do about it. I'd made sure the entertainment system remote was in reach, and I talked to him when I could. That was about all I could do.

"What?" I asked politely, as he seemed to be waiting for a response.

"I volunteered for that exercise because I was bored." He laughed bitterly. "Bored. Can you imagine?"

"You were bored?" That was hard to believe. I mean, he was a fighter pilot. Pretty much the most amazing job ever, right? Flying high performance spacecraft, defending the Galaxy from pirates—

"Yes. Does that surprise you?"

"Well, sir," I stammered. "Yeah. It does. I mean, you're . . . well . . . you." A remarkably silly speech. But the very idea seemed ridiculous. Hector Alvarez, the best fighter pilot in the Fleet, bored with his job?

"You didn't think fighter pilots could get bored?"

I shook my head.

"Do you find your work interesting?" he asked suddenly.

I blinked. Why was he asking me that? "Most of the time. Yes. I'm hoping to be a doctor someday. The Fleet will pay for my training."

Alvarez nodded. "You're working towards something.

You're learning, you're getting better. So even on the slow days, you can keep going with it."

I shrugged. What was he getting at? "I suppose so."

"I've reached the highest rank I can hold as an active pilot. I'm a wing commander. I've completed pretty much all the available training for my position. I don't have a wife or kids. I've devoted my life to serving the Union and being the best pilot I can be. But even if I volunteer for every mission that presents itself, I won't be flying all the time. Now . . ." He looked down at his bandages and casts. "Once I requalify, I'll just be holding position till I can't do it anymore. Not really making progress."

I'd never thought of it that way, never thought about what pilots did when they weren't actually flying.

"My dad was an officer," Alvarez continued. "And so was his dad, and his dad before him. The Fleet is in my blood. I love what I do. It's what I was born for. But it's not enough. And I'm not going to be able to do it forever. Ten years more, maybe fifteen. And then what? Sit around and look at my medals? I've had enough sitting around in the last few days."

I finished changing the bandage and pushed the rolling table back against the bed, where he could reach his water and the remote. He caught the motion and pushed the remote aside impatiently. "I'm tired of watching. It's all the same. No one has answers." He turned those piercing golden eyes on me. "What do you do when you're bored? If you're sick?"

"Read, maybe? Watch something. I don't know." I

shrugged. I felt bad for him. I did. He wasn't used to sitting around doing nothing. But I needed to go. I had a patient who needed meds five minutes ago, and if I didn't get out there—

"Reading," he said thoughtfully. "It's been a long time since I sat down and read a book. Do you have any I could borrow?"

"Yes, of course," I said hastily. "Anything in particular?"

"Oh, just something *different*."

"I'll try to bring you something tomorrow," I said and made my escape.

My brother Robert and I had gotten an apartment together near the Fleet hospital while he did his training and I did mine. That evening at home, I examined our bookshelves. A lot of the books were, if not exactly illegal, at least suspicious, so those were obviously out. But I found some good mystery stories I remembered enjoying. I had no idea what Hector Alvarez would want to read, but a fast-paced mystery couldn't go too far wrong, could it? Everyone liked those. *A Dangerous Mistake* was lying on the shelf, probably left there by my brother. He'd read it before, though, so I didn't think he'd mind if I borrowed it. I shoved it into my bag, little guessing that I was making my own dangerous mistake.

"Hey, Justin," Robert asked the next evening as he walked into my bedroom. "Have you seen my book anywhere?"

"Which one?" I asked, looking up from the tablet where I was doing some pre-med coursework.

"It was a biography of St. Ignatius, but I put the cover from *A Dangerous Mistake* on it so I could read it between classes without attracting attention."

I dropped my tablet. "You did what!?" Hector Alvarez had been reading that book all day.

"I do it all the time and no one has ever noticed. Relax."

"No, no it's not that," I said, still feeling as though the bottom had dropped out of my world. "I lent it to a patient."

It was Robert's turn to be shocked. "You did *what*?"

"He was bored. Asked for a book or something. I thought he might enjoy a mystery story. So I gave him . . ." I trailed off, unable to bring myself to say it.

"You gave him something that might get us both in trouble."

"It's not *exactly* illegal," I pointed out.

Robert snorted. "No. But pretty much the only reason anyone reads books like that *is* and everyone knows it."

I pounded my head against the back of my chair. "I'm such an idiot. I can't believe I did that. Now what do I do?"

"It was at least as much my fault as yours," Robert said with his usual fairness. "I don't really see what you can do now besides act normal and pray it all works out."

Pray . . . right. Robert's solution to everything. I wished I had half his certainty. It never seemed to occur to him to wonder if it made sense or if it was worth it to plan his entire life around an outlawed religion. He prayed, did spiritual reading, and pursued his studies to be a ground car mechanic, not because he was particularly excited about being a ground car mechanic, but because it was a job where he could support a family and probably not be asked about religion. I wanted to ask him where he got his certainty from, but that would mean admitting my own doubts, which seemed so shameful, somehow. Well, praying couldn't *hurt*, could it?

"Oh, good," Alvarez said as I reluctantly entered his room the next morning. "I've been wanting to talk to you."

Beads of perspiration rose on my face and neck. I swallowed, glancing at the book sitting closed on the table next to him. Alvarez didn't look suspicious or angry though, just curious, alert. Alive. More alive than I'd ever seen him.

"The cover threw me off at first, but I liked the book. That man. Ignatius. He was a real person, right? From the same part of Earth my ancestors came from?"

I took a breath and relaxed. "Yes."

"I liked his story. He was a soldier too. And bored while recovering from his wounds." Alvarez chuckled a little, laughing at himself, then abruptly turned serious. "He found an answer. Something to live for, die for if necessary. I've given my life to the Fleet, but it's not the same thing. I think I'm doing something worthwhile, and

I'm good at it, but it's not—it's just . . . not the same. It doesn't explain enough . . ." He trailed off and looked out the window for a moment.

Not sure what to say, I worked in silence, taking his blood pressure and entering it into his chart.

"Thank you, Justin." He turned back to me with a smile. "I asked for something different, and you definitely gave me that."

Not on purpose! "I'm glad you liked it." I tried to hold a neutral expression.

"It said Ignatius read the Gospels. I think I'd like to read them too." He picked up the book and flipped through it. "It might explain some things I didn't really understand."

My eyes widened. Had Alvarez never even heard of the Bible?

He set the book back on the table. "Would you happen to have a paper copy of the Gospels? I find I like reading physical books."

The biography of a Catholic saint *and the Bible*? I winced. The Bible wasn't precisely illegal either. People had Bibles for all sorts of reasons. But most who had them were part of an outlawed religious group, so possession of a Bible tended to arouse suspicion. I'd be asking for trouble to admit having both.

"What's the matter?" Alvarez frowned.

Be careful. "I could probably find you a copy, but . . ." What should I say? Reading the sacred book of an outlawed religion was hardly a good career move. For either of us.

His voice roughened. "Is there a problem?"

"It's just . . . if you start reading that, someone might think you're a Catholic." There. I'd said it. Now I'd just have to hope he wouldn't make the obvious connection and assume I was one. How he would respond to that idea I could only guess.

"A *Catholic*?" He said the word the way I might say some deadly insult. "Why would they think that?"

I swallowed. "Well, I've heard that Catholics like that book."

"So? I imagine they like eating too. I plan to continue doing that. So why should it stop me from looking for answers?"

"I'll try to get my hands on a copy." I started edging my way back out of the room. "But I really need to go now. Are you done with that book?"

"If you don't mind, I'd like to keep it for another day or so."

Now what? I'd lent him one suspicious book accidentally; now I was supposed to lend him another.

Could I do that? I couldn't. I'd get myself into deep trouble and maybe my brother too.

But what explanation would I give Alvarez? I'd as good as told him I had a copy of the Gospels. If he started wondering why I was reluctant to lend it to him . . .

I'd just have to give him one and hope everything worked out. And pray—as Robert would doubtless tell me.

"Here it is," I told Alvarez the next day, handing him my personal copy of the New Testament. My parents had given it to me on my twelfth birthday.

"Have you read it?"

I hesitated. It wasn't *exactly* illegal. And Robert and I *had* done a Scripture reading resolution a couple Lents ago. "Yes."

Alvarez smiled. "Good. I'll have someone to talk to about it."

I groaned internally and made my escape as quickly as I could. Discussing the Gospels with a Fleet officer. Never thought I'd end up doing that. God's idea of a joke maybe. Or maybe just my Lent.

I came in on my rounds later that day and found him reading.

"This is the weirdest thing I've ever read," he commented as I walked in.

I was a little startled. The inspired Word of God weird? "Oh?"

"So this Jesus guy wanders around and magically heals people and cures blindness and raises people from the dead. That part's weird enough. This is supposed to be a true story too, right? I mean the story about that Ignatius guy was a true story and *he* certainly thought these Gospels were, so . . ." He looked at me suddenly. "How does that work? What was he doing?"

"Who? Doing what?"

"This Jesus guy. How was he doing all those things?

Most of that stuff we *still* can't do—not like that anyway—and he was living in pre-space ancient times. Does it explain later?"

"Umm . . . well, He was God, you know."

"God?"

"You know, creator of everything, supreme being?"

"Right. I've heard people talk about God . . . usually talking about whether or not he exists. So this Jesus. He's supposed to be God?"

"Yes."

"Huh. I'll have to think about that some more. Anyway, so in this book, Jesus is going around doing all these amazing things and curing people and stuff. And then there's this group of people who are always trying to get him in trouble. Why are they doing that? I mean, he's healing people. Why are people so mad at him?"

My wristband buzzed. An urgent assist in room 308. "I'm sorry, I've got to go. I'll be back in a few minutes to finish up."

He nodded and picked the book up again.

The assist took longer than I expected, and it was nearly the end of my shift before I came back.

"They killed him," Alvarez said as I walked in. "Why did they kill him?"

I shrugged uncomfortably. "I think they thought He was threatening their position." Though I should probably know more than that.

"But to kill him?" he said more to himself than to me.

"Well, he does rise from the dead," I pointed out.

"He does?"

"Didn't you read that part? He said He would and then He did. It wouldn't make much sense to worship Him thousands of years later if He hadn't."

"People worship him?"

"Well, He *is* God."

Alvarez gave me a look. "So this Jesus guy is supposed to be God. And he lets himself get killed, and then rises from the dead. Why?"

"Because He wanted to save people from their sins."

"By dying. Like that." He pointed at the book he'd just been reading.

"Yes."

"God's supposed to be in charge, isn't he? Why would he need to do that?"

"He didn't," I said. "I mean, He didn't have to die like that. I mean . . . the Church says that He decided to redeem us that way to show us His love . . . and . . . sort of to show us that He was with us. That He had done it all first. If that makes sense."

Alvarez looked thoughtful. "Yes," he said softly. "That does make sense." His lips twitched into a smile. "He's a good officer. You don't order your men to do anything you wouldn't do yourself."

I smiled. St. Ignatius would have liked that idea.

"You said 'the Church.' What church is that?"

I looked up from the chart I was filling out, feeling the blood draining from my face. I met his eyes, saw confusion, then suspicion, then anger.

"You're Catholic." He spat the word like a curse.

I swallowed. Was I? Was I sure enough about it to admit it? To destroy my chance of a career? To get deported, or worse? The courts might interpret what I'd been doing as proselytizing. And that carried a prison sentence.

"You are, aren't you? *That's* why you didn't want to give me this book when I asked for it." Alvarez's hand hovered over the call button.

I didn't want to go to prison. But right after explaining how God loved us enough to die for us, I couldn't bring myself to deny Him. I squeezed my eyes shut and nodded. *Jesus did it first.* There was a long, long silence while I waited for him to push the button, to call in the authorities and have me arrested.

Nothing happened.

I opened my eyes. He'd moved his hand away from the call button and was eyeing me curiously.

"Why did you give me the first book?"

"It was an accident." The words came out almost as a whisper, my mouth was so dry.

He flicked a glance to where it sat on his table. "I see. That explains the cover."

He didn't seem angry anymore, but I couldn't read his expression. Was he still considering turning me in?

My wristband buzzed again, louder this time. It had gone off a couple minutes earlier, but I'd ignored it. This time Alvarez heard it too.

"You should go deal with that," he said.

I went out in a daze, helped the nurse who'd called for assistance, and apologized for taking so long. And then, finally, my shift was over and I went home.

I locked the door behind me and leaned against the wall. Now that I was home, I could afford to panic properly. What was Alvarez going to *do*? He obviously hated Catholics—no surprise there. *Everyone* hated them these days, ever since the last war got blamed on them. Not that it was really their fault, but since when had anyone cared about the truth?

But he hadn't called anyone in to arrest me. Was he waiting? For what?

"Justin? I thought I heard you come—" Robert's voice trailed off as he came into the kitchen and saw me. "What's wrong?"

"He figured it out," I told him. "Alvarez figured it out."

"What are you talking about?"

"He knows I'm Catholic."

Robert paled slightly. "Just from that St. Ignatius book? I had no idea—"

"No. I lent him my *New Testament* too," I admitted in a very small voice.

"Why?"

"He asked me to."

"He *asked* you to?"

I nodded miserably.

Robert ran one hand through his hair. "So now what? He's figured out you're Catholic, you say. What is he going to do about it?"

"I don't know."

"He didn't denounce you?"

"For a second I was sure he was going to, but then he didn't. I have no idea what he means to do. What d'you think *I* should do?"

Robert leaned against the counter and let out a huff. "I don't know. If you *knew* he was going to denounce you, it might be worth trying to run, but if you don't know . . ." He chewed on his lip. "I'd say you'd better just go to work as usual. You've got your Fleet Reserve contract to consider. Running out on that would get you in trouble all by itself."

I sighed. He was probably right. Our parents hadn't been too excited about me joining the Fleet Reserve as a medical trainee. But since they couldn't pay for regular medical school, and I really wanted to be a doctor, I'd gone ahead and done it anyway.

"What about you?" I asked. "You don't have a contract. You could . . . go on vacation or something."

He shook his head. "My name's on the apartment lease. If they start looking at you, they'll be looking at me too. It won't matter where I am. And if I start ordering last minute tickets right now, that probably won't look good. Worst case scenario we get deported to some awful desert planet where they dump trash, right? Not my first choice, but there's worse things."

Like going to prison. I shivered. Probably better not to tell Robert that I was afraid I'd be charged with proselytizing.

He was worried enough as it was.

"When you came in, I was going to ask you if you wanted to say a Rosary with me," Robert said into my thoughts.

I smiled weakly. Count on Robert to suggest praying. "Let's do it," I said. "I know just what to pray for."

After a restless night, I woke up, still unarrested, and got ready for work. I considered doing my rounds backwards so I'd see Alvarez last—but then I'd be dreading it longer.

Eventually, I just went in.

Alvarez was dozing but as I started marking down his vital signs, he woke up and noticed me. His face hardened.

"I should denounce you," he said. "I almost did, several times last night. It's just . . ." He looked up at me suddenly. "Why did you come back?"

"I have a Fleet Reserve contract. I'm not allowed to leave."

"You're not allowed to be Catholic either."

"That's true, sir."

"So tell me, then, what does all of this"—he gestured at the two books that still sat on his table—"have to do with destabilizing the government, disrupting galactic unity, and murdering innocent civilians?"

I winced. "You're talking about the war."

"Damn right I'm talking about the war."

Of course. No one knew—or cared—what Catholics

actually *believed* anymore. Not since Javier O'Mara had crashed a small moon into the planet Delphi's surface during the war, just two weeks after the Pope had publicly commended him for heroism. Never mind that it had been the work of one man—and likely accidental besides. Ever since then, when people heard Catholic they thought of billions of people dying a fiery death.

"Those books, those ideas don't have anything to do with the war, sir."

"Then what do they have to do with being Catholic?"

"Everything, sir."

Alvarez clenched his fist impatiently. "That's not—"

"Sir," I cut him off. "I know you want answers. But I have patients I need to take care of right now. I promise I'll come back on my break or after my shift to answer that and whatever else you want to ask me."

"Do that," he said after a moment, his voice grim. "But understand one thing."

"Yes, sir?"

"If I'm not satisfied with your answers, I *will* turn you in."

"I understand, sir." But did I? What would satisfy him?

All day, I debated with myself. Should I run? No. I'd promised. And anyway, if I didn't show up at the end of the day, he'd simply denounce me then. Could I get far enough away by then?

Or I could just deny it. Say it was all a mistake and I didn't really mean it and of course I'm not Catholic and I'll swear the oath of allegiance as many times as you like. No.

I couldn't do that either. The worst that would happen to me was I might go to prison for a while. Others had died. Christ himself had died rather than deny His divinity. It was like I had told Alvarez. Jesus did it first. All I had to do was follow.

When my shift was over and I couldn't put off facing Alvarez any longer, I went to his room again. For my trial.

I answered all his questions. I told him the whole story of the war as I'd learned it—a very different story from what most people had heard. How it had originally started as a protest over a human rights violation, then turned into a dispute over the boundaries of corporate and government power and how, finally, after the Delphi incident, it had turned into a crusade against Christians and any other group that had been so unwise as to align itself against the corporation that committed the initial human rights violation that started the whole thing.

I also told him everything I knew about my religion. He asked probing questions, and it didn't take him long to show me just how meager my understanding of my faith was. But at least I had answers. Not the best, not the deepest, but something. My parents had insisted I learn those things, and for the first time I genuinely appreciated their insistence.

Finally, Alvarez leaned back with a thoughtful expression. "And—"

The door opened and the duty nurse walked in.

"What are you doing here?" she asked me, glancing at

the clock. "Your shift ended almost two hours ago."

"I . . . uh . . ." How exactly was I supposed to explain?

Alvarez came to my rescue. "He's here because I asked him to . . . explain something to me. He's almost done." He smiled at her. "I won't do it again."

She gave me another look, shrugged, and proceeded to ignore me. For my part, I sat silently and did my best to be invisible as she finished her work.

"So that's what you believe?" Alvarez continued once the nurse was gone.

I hesitated. Usually I believed it. Some days it was harder. I always *wanted* to believe, at least. And I certainly didn't have anything to replace it with.

"Yes, sir."

"You hesitated. Why?"

"On good days, that's what I believe. On bad days, I doubt everything." It was hard to admit, even to him.

"Yesterday was a good day, then?"

I blinked, confused. "Not particularly. Why?"

"Because you admitted your religion even when you thought you'd suffer for it. That doesn't seem like a reasonable choice if you're not sure."

"I know." That was exactly why it was so hard. Sometimes it *didn't* seem reasonable. Sometimes it didn't make any sense to me to keep living this way. Sometimes, God seemed so far away it was as if He didn't exist, or at least didn't care. Like He'd abandoned me. Yes, that was the word. Abandoned . . . like Jesus on the cross, calling out, "God, why have you abandoned me?"

Jesus had done that first, too; he'd felt the same way. Maybe He didn't doubt, exactly—He was God, after all—but He must have let Himself feel the emptiness, the horrible alone darkness of it. It wasn't a sin. It wasn't something I was doing wrong. It was a cross, and a cross Jesus had carried before me.

"That must be very hard," Alvarez broke in on my thoughts. "If it helps, I *am* satisfied with your answers. You should probably go home and rest. I'm sure you're tired."

I looked up. He'd said *satisfied*. "Does that mean—"

Alvarez smiled, the first full smile he'd given me since I'd admitted being Catholic. "Your secret is safe with me."

I took a deep breath and let it out, allowing all the tension of the last day to drain away.

"Thank you, sir."

"Thank *you*. You've given me a lot to think about. And I *will* be thinking about it. All of it."

When I got home, Robert was pacing and talking to someone on the phone. "Oh, he just came in." I could hear the relief in his voice. "Yes, I'll tell him," Robert continued. "He'll be glad to hear. Yes. I'll tell him that too. Thanks. Bye."

He hung up and turned to me, half pulling me into a hug. "Justin, where the heck *were* you? I called you four times!"

I gave him a tired smile. "Sorry. I tried to call before I left work, but you didn't pick up."

"I was probably already on the phone with Mom," Robert conceded, "She says hi, by the way. But why are you so late? After what you told me yesterday, I was convinced you must have gotten arrested."

"I had to stay and answer all his questions. He threatened to turn me in if I didn't."

"He threatened—what kind of questions?"

"He must have asked me the whole catechism, one way or the other, but in the end he said he was satisfied and wouldn't turn me in."

"This whole time? You must be exhausted." Robert almost looked impressed. "I made spaghetti for supper. There's leftovers in the fridge. Oh! I almost forgot. Mom had good news; we're supposed to get a priest this Easter."

Alvarez was quiet and preoccupied for the next week, reading on his Fleet-issue tablet, or just thinking. He didn't talk to me much. They removed the stitches and he had to do two sessions of physical therapy every day, though it would be a long time before he'd be able to walk normally again. At least the bruising and swelling was gone, and he said the pain was better.

"I checked your story," Alvarez said one day, turning troubled eyes on me as I took his blood pressure. "I was hoping you were wrong. But it's all there in the records—the classified Fleet records you're not allowed to see unless you have clearance. We've been hounding innocent people for decades." He shook his head sadly. "I've helped."

I didn't say anything. What was there to say?

"I don't want it to be true," he said quietly, staring in front of him. "I don't want any of it to be true." He looked at me again with a haunted expression. "Do you understand?" he asked.

I shook my head. I had no idea what he was trying to say.

Abruptly, he grabbed my New Testament and slammed it down on his table. "If this is true, then my entire life, everything I've done, everything I've worked for, everything I *am*, is wrong. If this is true—and I don't know why, but somehow I am sure that it is—if this is true, then I—" His voice broke and it was a moment before he spoke again. "If I follow this, I will lose absolutely everything I have. You see that, don't you? Eventually, there will be a mission I can't accept. I'll be stripped of my rank and my uniform and thrown out in disgrace. The Fleet is my life, my family, my friends, everything I know. In my family, military pride is everything. What do you think they would say to me if I was dishonorably discharged?" His hand clenched on the bed sheets.

"If I accept this, there will be nothing left of me. And I'm supposed to think this God is good? "

I stared at him. Was he seriously considering . . . *converting*?

He was silent for a while. "Why?" he suddenly asked me. "Why can't there be another way? If I choose this, I lose everything I have. If I say no, I lose . . . God?"

Hearing it like that—from him—was like being punched in the gut. That was the question, wasn't it? Could *anything* be worth losing God?

Alvarez already had all the things I'd imagined replacing my faith with, and they weren't enough for him. They wouldn't have been enough for me, either. Nothing could fill the place of God, even when God seemed to leave sometimes. My career, maybe even my life, might have to take second place.

"Jesus did it first," I said, the words coming out without my really thinking about it.

"What?"

"Jesus gave up everything, even His life. It's like you said, God doesn't ask us to do anything He didn't already do Himself."

"'Not my will but Yours be done?'" Alvarez shook his head. "Is it humanly possible to say that and mean it?"

I don't know if it is humanly possible. All I know is that Alvarez did it.

Because I stood beside him that Easter as he laid aside his old life and was given a new one.

###

If you want to read more about Hector Alvarez, the underground Catholics, and the Galaxy they live in, Alvarez is also a character in *Heaven's Hunter*, another story about finding faith in spite of danger.

ABOUT THE AUTHOR

MARIE C. KEISER is the author of *Heaven's Hunter*. A former teacher, she now lives in Minnesota with her husband and young children. She is passionate about writing inspiring stories about people who struggle with Faith. When she's not doing dishes, chasing toddlers, or changing diapers, she occasionally blogs about books, life, or ideas at www.EnjoyingWomanhood.com.

4

Contemporary

A BIG ASK

by Carolyn Astfalk

Paul Porter shouldered his way through the throng at the front of the classroom toward the door, squeezing between Sassy and Brassy, his unspoken nicknames for the two girls who argued every point with their not-so-chill Christian Morality teacher. He had someplace to be, namely Room 103B for study hall with Rachel.

With his lunch period early and hers late, they met daily outside the cafeteria. He blocked out the hallway chatter as he mentally scrolled through what he needed to accomplish during his free period. Leaning against the tiled wall, he bided his time until Rachel's bright eyes and perky brown ponytail caught his attention.

Rachel shifted a stack of textbooks from one arm to the other and smiled as she stopped in front of him, her toes nearly touching his. "Hey," she said, her eyes dancing. "How's your day going?"

"Okay." He rubbed a hand along her back, having learned the hard way that any more effusive public display of affection would be reported by some passing snitch. With a nudge to her shoulder, he turned her toward the hallway opposite them, which would take them to study hall.

The noise from students leaving the cafeteria had barely diminished enough for conversation when Rachel stopped short outside the gym doors, nearly tripping him. At least three classrooms stood between them and study hall.

"I guess we'll catch up after school." She inclined her head to the posters hanging on the gym door.

He skimmed the words and pictures, trying to uncover her meaning. Christian Service Club announcement, baseball conditioning . . . blood drive.

She shifted her books again, leaning to tug up her navy knee socks. "You want to donate blood this time? Last one of the school year. For Lent."

Paul had seen the signs around school and had heard the announcements, but he hadn't given them a second thought. "I don't do well with blood." *Anymore.* Since Rachel had fractured her leg in a fall last summer, he'd become uncharacteristically squeamish.

Rachel twisted her lips. "Really? I didn't think it bothered you."

He shrugged. Case in point. Last fall, when he'd gotten scraped up badly while working at the orchard, he'd nearly fainted tending to his own wounds. He should've worn long sleeves, but an unseasonably warm day meant short sleeves. An old cherry limb he'd pruned came down the wrong way, leaving a gash on his arm, wrist to elbow. He'd trekked to the first aid kit at the barn to clean and wrap the cut. By all accounts, he'd turned ghostly pale and swayed on his feet. Nope, no blood donation for him.

"Well, I'm sorry we can't hang out." As the gym door opened and shut, they glanced inside at the tables and chairs set up. "Maybe I can snag you a muffin and juice when it's done."

"Sure." He pulled her into a side hug. "See you after school."

As Paul drove them home from school, Rachel chattered endlessly about some drama in her Government class. He listened as best he could, but not knowing most of the kids she mentioned, the conversation drifted past him.

Stopped at a traffic light, his gaze roamed the intersection, landing on a red-and-white poster affixed to a utility pole. *Kidney Donor Needed for Seth Kennedy.* A website was listed for more information.

He'd seen it before. At least a dozen times here, at other intersections, and affixed to the side of the underpass that ran beneath the railroad tracks. He'd read it once or twice before it became part of the passing scenery. Lately he'd seen the colors and letters and not the words.

A tingling sensation shot through Paul's belly and up his chest, gripping his heart for a millisecond. He committed the website to memory, feeling the urge to look it up. Rachel's words broke into his thoughts.

"It's green," she said, poking him gently on the shoulder. By the honk of a car horn behind him, he guessed it wasn't the first time she'd said it.

Once he'd completed his Lit essay and studied for his Latin exam, Paul dragged his laptop onto the bed and visited the website he'd seen on the poster. Again, an uncomfortable tingling shot through him.

Seth Kennedy was a local man who'd suddenly become ill. Organ donation offered the only cure. Seth had a wife and seven kids. *Seven. Wow.* His ability to work, which he'd lost, was imperative for him to care for his family.

Paul enlarged the picture. Seth wore short, neat dreadlocks and a single small gold hoop earring. His wife had a brilliant smile, glowing skin, and hair piled high on her head in some kind of updo. The kids ranged in age from late teens to a toddler held against his wife's hip. One of the middle kids, a girl, wore a baseball uniform and clutched a trophy.

His heart rate increased slightly as he clicked on more information about living organ donation.

Being eighteen and in good health, Paul might be a candidate. Race wouldn't be a factor. He had no living parents he had to convince to get on board with his decision. He had health insurance and he'd have help during his recovery process. His brother would help. So would Rachel and her family. He'd fall into the Altruistic Donor category—no connection to the recipient.

He blinked and slammed the laptop shut. What was he thinking? You didn't just give some stranger one of your kidneys.

Much to his irritation, a little voice inside his head challenged him. "Why not?"

The knife's blade glinted in the sunlight, a brilliant shimmer blinding Paul momentarily as the hand—his hand?—holding the knife shook. A swell of emotion gripped his chest. He wanted to cry out, but his mouth refused to open. Hot tears trickled down his cheeks while his stifled cries continued. Against his will, his arm lowered, the knife's sharp tip pointing at a boy lying on a stone slab before him.

The obnoxious blare of his alarm clock broke through Paul's dream. He smacked his phone on the nightstand, trying to make it stop. Morning came too quickly. He lay with his eyes closed, his thoughts jumbled by his disturbing dream and Seth Kennedy and his family still on his mind.

Seven kids. They needed a dad. Paul, who'd lost his widowed dad only a couple of years ago, knew the importance of having a dad better than most.

He yanked the covers, twisted onto his side, and flung a hand across his closed eyes in a futile attempt to keep out the morning light.

Minutes passed as he attempted to shake off his unsettled feelings—the helplessness he'd felt at not being able to cry out in his dream and the confusion as to why he'd held a knife over a boy in a scenario that seemed oddly familiar.

He shoved the covers from his body, giving up on catching a few more minutes of sleep. His thoughts turned back to Seth Kennedy. Donating an organ—when he couldn't even muster the courage to hand over a pint of his blood—seemed extreme. Ridiculous, even.

Sometimes God asks us to do ridiculous things. He dismissed the notion. God also asked us to be prudent. He gave everyone two kidneys for a reason. Paul should probably hang onto the ones God gave him. He'd have a family to raise someday too, God willing.

No one has greater love than this, than to lay down one's life for one's friends. Again, Paul dismissed the thought. God wasn't playing fair. He knew what that verse meant to Paul, whose family had been whittled down to only him and his older brother, Sean, precisely because their parents had lived that verse, his mom dying due to pregnancy complications and his dad in service to his country.

Paul fully expected to live that verse too but in a regular fashion. Something more akin to how Sean was living it, running on fumes going from a job he'd grown tired of to home and helping his wife tend to their newborn all hours of the night. Not to mention keeping tabs on Paul as much as he could.

Christian Morality was swapped for a mini-Lenten retreat this morning, leaving Paul slumped in a back pew in the high school chapel. He worked to keep his mind from drifting, as it often did, to Rachel . . . to assignments due . . . to Rachel . . . to his adorable baby niece . . . to Rachel. And now, to Seth Kennedy.

Relentless. He'd been dismissing all those crazy notions of donating his kidney, but like a game of whack-a-mole, they kept cropping up in unexpected spots. And his mental mallet had proven ineffective.

He slid to his knees and dropped his head onto his folded hands. *Is this really what you want of me, God? To give a stranger my kidney?*

Deafening silence.

Paul had been quiet at dinner with Rachel's family, and he'd skirted around answering their questions as to why. Best case scenario if he told them about Seth Kennedy, they'd think he was nuts. Worst case, they'd actually encourage him. Still, since the idea had taken hold and hadn't let go, he needed to talk to someone.

He paced the length of his small living area, cracking his knuckles one by one. First the left hand. Then the right. Then he grabbed his phone from the end table to text Sean.

Been thinking about organ donation. You have an opinion?

After a half-hour, Sean's reply came. A thumbs-up emoji.

Paul rolled his eyes. Probably busy with the baby.

Thinking about the living kind, not the dead kind.

This time, Sean's reply only took ten minutes.

It's a good thing.

This was painful. Paul would have to spell it out.

I'm thinking of donating an organ to a local man on dialysis. He needs a kidney.

Within seconds, Paul's ringtone sounded, and he tapped to answer Sean's call.

"You're what?" Sean's question sounded above an infant's cry and the shushing sounds of his sister-in-law,

Amanda.

"You read it right," Paul said, taking the phone and walking toward the window where he could gaze at the grass, thick and bright from all the spring rain. "I saw a poster, and it's been nagging at me. To help this guy and his family." He stared as a robin yanked a worm from the ground and flew off. "I mean, this is what our family does, right? This'd be nothing compared to Mom and Dad's sacrifices."

The baby noise diminished, and he could imagine Sean stepping into another room, running a hand through his hair like he did when stressed.

"Okay. That sounds generous and all that, but it also sounds crazy. And forgive me for being selfish, but you're the only brother I have, and I'm opposed to you taking unnecessary risks."

Fair enough. Paul had probably given Sean enough scares over the past year to last a lifetime, what with his attempt to help Rachel when she'd broken her leg and then when that guy had tried to rob them of the gold they'd discovered while digging near Rachel's flower garden. But he wasn't Sean's only family anymore; Sean had Amanda and the baby. Plus, from what he'd read, donating a kidney wasn't terribly risky.

"You worry too much." Paul sighed, grateful that his brother worried about him at all. "Listen, it's not like I actually *like* the idea. I just . . . I can't let go of it. I mean, God doesn't talk to me. Like never in my life. At least not that I've heard. Everyone else is like, 'Oh, and God said blah, blah, blah.' Whatever. Not my experience. But this . . . It's like the thought keeps popping into my head, and I keep thinking of this guy. I think God wants me to pursue this. And you know better than anyone I'm not the saintliest guy around. I'm, like, just scraping by, and Rachel's always dragging us off to confession, but even I know it's not a good idea to ignore something God wants you to do."

His monologue was met with silence. And background baby noise, but mostly silence.

Then, "What do you want me to say, Paul? You're not gonna pin refusing God onto me." He laughed then, an exasperated chuckle. "I guess just think about it and pray about it and take the next step. At least look into it, and we can talk about it some more."

Paul did as Sean suggested. He spent a week reading about kidney donation, thinking about it, praying about it. Nothing had changed. It still sounded crazy. It also nagged him.

Saturday night, he and Rachel sat side by side on her family's couch, watching a sci-fi movie. Her mom and little brother had gone to bed, but her dad sat at the desk he'd positioned in the recessed area of the room. Ostensibly, he was doing their taxes, evidenced by his frequent grumbling, paper shuffling, and occasional slamming of the calculator, along with a few salty words. Still, Paul couldn't help but think the location had been chosen so he could act as chaperone for the evening—out of earshot but not out of sight.

Paul's mind drifted from the movie, his brain finally connecting the dots, making sense of the weird dream he'd had last week. He hit pause on the movie and angled toward Rachel.

She grabbed a few Skittles from the bowl on the coffee table in front of them and popped them into her mouth. "What's up?"

"Abraham and Isaac in the Bible. I've always been hung up on that story."

She squinted at him, obviously not understanding his train of thought. "Well, that's out of nowhere, but okay."

"Sorry. Just something I've been thinking about. What must've Abraham thought? God asks him to kill his beloved son. I mean, who would listen to that? How would you even know it was God telling you to do that, 'cause, I mean, why would He? It seems contrary to everything. And I know that's what God did later with Jesus, but Abraham didn't know that. He just obeyed. Even though it sounded crazy. He was ready to do it."

Rachel folded her legs beneath her, as though settling in for a conversation. "Yeah. I always got the shivers from that story. I was afraid God would ask my dad to do that to me."

"Would you do it? Sacrifice your child if God asked you to?"

Rachel bit her lower lip and paused for a few beats. "I don't know. I wouldn't be able to imagine He'd want me to do that. Of course, I know how the story ends. But taking that into account isn't fair, I guess." She unfolded her legs and propped her feet on the coffee table. "It'd be easier to give up my own life, I think."

He nodded. It would. Easier still if it wasn't your life. Just, maybe, a kidney.

"I think maybe God wants a grand gesture from me." He still got that zingy feeling when he thought about Seth Kennedy.

Rachel furrowed her brow. "Meaning?"

He spilled all of it. From the utility pole poster to his internet searches to his prayers and his conversations with Sean.

She stared at him. "Wow."

"Wow?"

"Yeah, wow."

Her dad's chair squeaked as he pushed away from the desk. "Wrap it up, guys. I'm gonna get ready for bed."

Paul glanced at the wall clock. Later than he realized. "So," he said, his gaze returning to Rachel. "Do you think I should do it?"

"I don't think it's for me to decide." Rachel clicked the movie off. They'd have to pick it up another night. "I just know whenever I've gone to Mom about stuff, decisions, she says if I want to have peace, I need to do what God wants me to do, not just what I prefer." She shrugged. "Not like a mistake is irreversible, but, well, I at least want to try to do what He wants. Sometimes I don't know what that is, and I have to guess. Usually. I mean, I'm not great at hearing Him. But if I think I know what He wants, I figure I'd better do it."

He nodded. She'd affirmed what he knew in his heart.

She grinned at him, her eyes alight.

"What?" Nothing about organ donation struck him as remotely funny.

"Just thinking what an epic response you'd have when someone asks, 'What did you give up for Lent?'" She faked admiring her fingernails then rubbed them against her shirt. "'Oh, y'know. Same old stuff. Chocolate. Swearing. Oh, and a kidney.'" She laughed and bumped his shoulder with her own.

He chuckled. Yeah, it would be hard to one-up *that* sacrifice.

By midweek, Paul had repeated the conversation with Rachel's parents, whom he considered almost surrogate parents. Especially her dad. Then he'd rehashed it with Sean. And Sean and Amanda—while he held his baby niece, which made the whole rehashing worth it because she was the most precious thing in the world, and he wanted one or two or more of those with Rachel someday. And then he'd talked to Rachel once more before she sat beside him as he'd filled out the online application.

And then he waited.

A week later, his phone buzzed as he walked to the orchard after school for work. His hand stung as he held the phone, staring at the incoming call from an unknown number. "Hello?"

"Paul Porter? This is Angie. I'm calling regarding your application." The nurse reviewed his questionnaire with him while he followed the path between Rachel's family's property and the orchard. He'd crossed two rows of peach trees and had almost reached the barn when the nurse concluded the medical screening and set him up for a blood draw at a local lab.

He'd done the right thing, moving forward. He knew it. He felt it in his bones. And yet his heart pounded, and anxiety swirled in his belly.

He'd have been anxious the morning of the blood draw no matter what, given his new squeamishness about blood, but the implications of that blood draw propelled his nervousness to a new level. He felt like a preschooler begging for his mommy when he'd asked the nurse if Rachel could accompany him and hold his hand, but the kind middle-aged woman didn't bat an eye, just smiled knowingly.

He lived with a constant tension in his chest for a few days longer while he waited for the results. Rachel excelled at distracting him with conversation, video games, chatter about school, homework, and simply being herself.

After a painfully honest assessment, Paul realized that he'd fight God tooth and nail if He ever asked him to give her up. It made him wonder if he was fooling himself, thinking that he could go through with this kidney donation, should he be a match for Seth Kennedy.

His attachment to Rachel ran deep. He supposed it was understandable given the loss of his parents, but he also knew now that he'd have to address that at some point. He intended to love her 'til his dying breath, sacrificing anything for her. But he also knew that if his love for her superseded his obedience to God, his priorities were messed up. He could take a lesson from Abraham there.

He and Rachel had gone down to her wildflower garden the afternoon the call finally came. He'd been helping her cut back last year's dead blooms and stalks and turn over a new patch for expansion. When the phone rang, he yanked off his work gloves, tossed them on the ground, and pulled Rachel to a seat on a log bench.

"Paul Porter?"

"This is me. Uh, him. He. I'm Paul Porter."

Rachel squeezed his free hand. Hers was warm and strong; his suddenly felt clammy.

He pulled the phone from his ear and held it in front of them, tapping the speakerphone symbol. In doing so, he missed the first part of the nurse's sentence.

" . . . share the results with you?"

She must've been asking if he was ready for the blood draw results. Was he a match for Seth Kennedy? Could the donation of Paul's kidney give Seth a new lease on life? Could Seth stop dialysis and go back to work, continuing to be a father to his seven children?

A zing shot through his chest again, and Rachel dropped his hand and rubbed gentle circles across his back.

"Yes, ma'am," he croaked, then cleared his throat.

"Your blood type is not a match for the donor's." She

paused, giving him a moment to take that in, it seemed.

His chest deflated, and Rachel leaned her head against his shoulder, still rubbing his back. Relief coursed through him. An embarrassing amount of it. He hadn't realized how much he still feared the organ donation despite his resolve and commitment to the process.

The nurse continued speaking, finally asking if he wished to remain on the donor list. He hadn't thought beyond Seth Kennedy, but thinking about organ donation in terms of anyone else left him feeling flat. No zing in the chest. No swirling in his belly.

"Can I think about that?"

She assured him that he could, and they ended the call.

"What are you thinking?" Rachel asked, her head still against his shoulder.

He wrapped an arm around her. "I don't know. I feel like I dodged a bullet. But it's an odd mixture of relief and . . . maybe disappointment. But . . . peace."

She raised her head and turned to him. "I'm so proud of you."

He cringed inwardly, conscious of the utter and immediate relief he'd felt on hearing the results. But he'd said as much to her, and she hadn't been fazed.

"You're brave. And honest. And good." She patted his chest, over his heart. "You're a good man, Paul. Your dad would be so proud."

Well, that did it. Tears stung his eyes, and a familiar lump grew in his throat. "You know what that means to me," he said, staring through watery eyes. "But I'm not—"

She stopped him with two fingers pressed against his lips. "Don't. Just accept the compliments. It's okay to be relieved. I'm pretty sure Abraham was. Besides, I'm pretty sure God's not done asking things of you. Or us."

She lowered her fingers and gave him a sweet smile.

"You're right. I'm sure."

After all, sacrifice was in his blood. Sean had sacrificed much for him. Being a carefree teen and young adult, most of all. Mom had sacrificed her life. Dad, his. But it went back farther. Back even to Abraham, who'd been willing to sacrifice his only, beloved son. It went back to his Father and Abraham's—their Father in heaven—Who hadn't stilled His own hand when it came to *His* only, beloved Son.

Paul could only pray that if God asked something of him again—not if, but when—he'd be ready, no matter how small and ordinary or large and exceptional. And that someone else would be up for the task God obviously hadn't equipped Paul for, and that Seth Kennedy would find his match.

###

"A Big Ask," features the main characters in my coming-of-age novel, *Rightfully Ours,* Paul and Rachel. The story is set mere months after the novel's conclusion. To find out how Paul and Rachel met, forged a friendship, fell in love, and even stumbled upon what may have been buried treasure, you'll need to read *Rightfully Ours*. I

recommend it for mature teens or students of St. John Paul II's Theology of the Body due to the realistic (but non-explicit) way it addresses love, temptation, and chastity.

ABOUT THE AUTHOR

CAROLYN ASTFALK writes from the sweetest place on earth, Hershey, Pennsylvania, where she lives with her husband and four children. In addition to her contemporary Catholic romances, including the young adult coming-of-age story *Rightfully Ours*, she is a CatholicMom.com contributor. She is a member of the Catholic Writers Guild and Pennwriters. When she is not washing dishes, doing laundry, or reading, you can find her blogging about books, faith, and family life at www.CarolynAstfalk.com.

5

Historical

LENT ROYAL & ANCIENT

by Amanda Lauer

Glencoe, The Highlands, Scotland
February 23, 1692

For the past ten months, I, Bronwyn Campbell, a typical American high schooler, had been living the life of a Middle-Ages Scottish lass. Or at least what I thought was the Middle Ages. I never could remember the exact years that the various historical ages started and ended.

I'd come to love this ancient land, the beautiful people inhabiting it, the old Church and its sacraments, and a certain young man named Iain. I truly believed that God had sent me to the seventeenth-century Highlands for a reason.

That being said, I'd experienced my share of heartache too, especially in the last ten days. Tragedy had struck the MacDonald clan. I shuddered just thinking about it. A lump formed in my throat and I blinked back the tears that threatened to spring up again.

While I'd once prayed to go back to my old life, I now

prayed that God would allow me to continue building a life with Iain. Especially after he'd been thrust into the role of clan chieftain and would be depending on the support of the people around him that he knew and trusted.

Watching him stride toward the stables, his ebony shoulder-length hair tied back with a leather string, a range of emotions flooded over me. There was empathy for the grief that he was experiencing, admiration for how he'd embraced his position of leadership, gratitude that he'd survived that God-awful day, and a sense of connectedness like I'd never felt before.

Despite everything that his family had been through, Iain's faith was unwavering. It was the first Sunday of Lent, and this morning we'd gone to Mass in the safe room on the second floor of the manor house. Father Ferguson had been conducting services there since his arrival last year. It would be dangerous to use the chapel on the property.

Hard as it was to believe, practicing Catholicism in Scotland during this time was illegal. It was high treason for a priest to even enter the country. That being the case, having narrowly escaped execution in the Lowlands, Father had taken refuge at the home of his old friend, Gregor MacDonald, Iain's father.

To lessen the chance of being discovered, the priest was consistently garbed in a fashion similar to the other men on the property from his kilt with the matching vest in the MacDonald plaid to the cotton peasant shirt, knee-high socks, and leather ankle boots. It seemed odd to see a priest with a cravat wrapped around his neck rather than the white clerical collar.

As had been the case since I'd arrived in Scotland, Mass was abbreviated and subdued. No singing, no extended sermons, and no adornments in the room other than a candelabra on the makeshift wooden altar.

Mass was said in Latin. After all these months, I wasn't proficient in that ancient language by any means. Not only that, but he faced the altar, just as the family did, and he spoke in hushed tones, so I could barely make out what he said.

The homily was in English and, as per usual, Father got directly to the point. He outlined the three pillars of Lent—prayer, almsgiving, and fasting.

With everything that had gone on in the past week, I'd given no thought to my Lenten sacrifice. Something to think about when I got back to the manor house.

Stepping into my bedchamber, as the Scots call it, I crossed the floor to the vanity and grabbed my leather-bound journal from the bottom drawer. Quill and ink at hand, I started writing.

Prayer, I jotted next to the first bullet point. Since finding myself in old-time Scotland, prayer had become a major focus of my day. The MacDonald family was very devout—even Iain's little brothers, Alastair, Lenox, and Graeme, ages seven, six, and five, respectively. Prayer was woven into the family's daily life.

Morag, Iain's sister, four months my senior, was not at

Mass today. She had just given birth to her first child a few days ago and was expected to convalesce for several more weeks. From what I was told, after the "lying in" period, she would be brought before Father Ferguson and blessed and then welcomed back to Mass. "Churching the mother," as it was called.

Douglas, Morag's husband, had been more than willing to let me hold sweet baby Oda during the service. Morag and I hadn't always seen eye-to-eye, but she too seemed comfortable with me watching the baby. Actually, seemingly more comfortable with me than with herself. Which was somewhat surprising. Mom had abandoned me and Dad shortly after I was born. With no siblings, I had even less experience with children than she did.

Morag did her motherly duty by nursing the baby but was eager to pass her along to one of the chambermaids or her own mother, Isobel, as soon as the task was complete. The once overly confident girl seemed unsure of herself. I figured that soon enough Morag would be back to her normal self. Her *Mean Girls* self, knowing my luck.

For now, I didn't mind helping with the baby's care. I was taking the night shift to rock Oda back to sleep after her middle-of-the-night feeding. I actually looked forward to our time together in the wee hours of the morning. That baby was a cutie pie.

Returning to my journal, I dipped the quill in the ink and made a second bullet point. *Almsgiving*. Hmm . . . that might be a tough one because I literally didn't have one shilling—as they say in this day and age—to my name.

Yet wasn't almsgiving defined as time, talent, and treasure? I had no treasure and my talent—compared to these living-off-the-grid Scottish girls—was definitely lacking, but I did have time.

I could up my game of helping Morag with the baby. Maybe take two shifts?

Last bullet point. *Fasting*. That was built into the system here. The MacDonalds were so fanatical about it that they even fasted during Advent. *Who does that?* As if the pickings weren't slim enough in these times, now that it was Lent, they were restricted from eating meat, eggs, and dairy products, which other times of the year were their major sources of protein.

And no food at all could be consumed on the weekdays until after three o'clock, the hour of Our Lord's death. Nothing but water before then. Ash Wednesday had been a black fast day, which meant no food *or* drink. The Triduum should be fun. *Not.* Fasting would begin at sundown on Maunday Thursday, go through Good Friday, and not conclude until noon on Holy Saturday.

It's no wonder there weren't any obese people. The plague wasn't going around, so I wondered what actually killed people. *They certainly weren't digging their graves with their forks like people in my day and age were, I can tell you that.*

"Have ye come up with a plan fer Lent, Bronwyn?" Iain inquired as we went for our evening walk on the grounds—always within sight of the manor house, mind you.

"I have two of the three pillars of Lent covered—prayer and fasting."

Iain nodded in agreement. "Me mam be adept at making sure the entire household adheres te high standards," he admitted.

"That leaves me with almsgiving. Obviously, I don't have any coins to share, but I can share my time."

"Sounds reasonable enough. By chance, I've a list of at least a dozen projects I plan te implement in the village over the next couple of months."

I'm sure you do, Iain . . .

"Perhaps ye'd like to assist with one of them?"

"That's so kind of you to offer, but I've come up with an idea already. I thought I'd help Morag more with the baby. Your mom has her hands full keeping an eye on your brothers and helping you with the administration of the house and lands. I doubt she has much time to spare."

"True that."

"And Morag doesn't quite seem herself." *As in bossy . . . snooty . . . arrogant . . .* Not that I appreciated those attributes, but it was worrisome to see her so lethargic.

Iain waved his hand as if dismissing that observation. "A number of the villagers be in more dire straits than me sister."

"That could be. But, as they say, charity begins at home."

"I hadn't heard such an idiom. The thought, however, does have merit."

It may have been lukewarm, but it was still an

endorsement, from my point of view. If Iain hadn't been amenable to that, Plan B was giving something up. Seeing that since my arrival in Scotland, I'd given up coffee drinks, chocolate, all electronics—including my cell phone, paper products, and flush toilets, there wasn't much left to forsake.

Laying his right arm across my shoulders, Iain gave me a quick squeeze. "That's very kind of ye. I'm sure she'll appreciate it."

I wasn't so sure, but I treasured his sign of affection. Getting to spend part of each day with such a kind, thoughtful, humorous, dutiful, intelligent, and moral guy as Iain certainly made me grateful that God sent me here, even if the timing was less than ideal.

"One more thing fer ye te consider, Bronwyn."

Tilting my chin to look up at him, I was instantly mesmerized by his greyish-blue eyes. I nodded. He could ask just about anything, and I'd say yes.

"We've talked of this before, and ye've yet te take action on it."

I froze mid-nod. I knew where this conversation was going.

"I'm not lookin' te judge, mind ye, but ye haven't partaken in confession since ye've arrived. Ye're missing out on the grace of that sacrament."

Missing may be a strong term. More like avoiding. I hadn't been to confession since before my First Communion. Not that I was a terrible human being or anything. Just wasn't a fan of sharing my less-than-stellar behavior with a stranger.

"It's important te have yer soul cleansed before Easter. We'll have the opportunity to receive Holy Communion that day."

Considering the fact that Iain had studied in a monastery for several years on "the continent," as they said, I took his word on that.

"Will ye consider it?"

Whatever you do, do not give me the puppy dog eyes.

Even though I wanted to, I couldn't turn away.

Ack, he's doing it. Resistance is futile.

I gave a sigh reminiscent of Jesus' *from the depth of His spirit* and nodded.

"Excellent," replied Iain, planting a kiss on the back of my hand.

"I didn't say I'd do it," I grumbled. "I said I'd consider it."

Was guilt an inborn Catholic thing, or was it just me? I literally couldn't walk by the chapel without thinking about confession and being struck with a jab of remorse. I knew that I should do it, especially with Easter Sunday just four weeks away, but the whole process made me anxious.

It'd been ten years since I'd last been in a confessional. I could only remember the first two lines of the Act of Contrition.

Then there was the fact that I'd have to tell Father Ferguson that I'd been traveling through time. I'd been less-than-truthful about my background to the MacDonald clan. The last thing that I wanted was the local villagers coming after me, pitchforks and torches in hand.

Iain was the only person who knew my backstory. What if the priest heard my tale and thought I'd gone mad, as the Scottish said, or that I was possessed? Was exorcism a thing in the 17th century? I didn't think I could handle that, especially the part where a person's head spun around three-hundred-and-sixty degrees. I'd seen the movie.

Time was on my side, though, so I chose to focus on my other Lenten promise, to assist Morag more with the baby. A couple times a day after Oda's feeding, I stopped by to either rock her to sleep or entertain her so Morag could rest.

I couldn't get enough snuggles from that sweet little babe, so it actually wasn't a hardship at all. That's why Morag's behavior was so peculiar. She seemed to have no interest in rocking the baby or interacting with her on just about any level.

Maybe today would be different. I tapped on the door of Morag and Douglas' bedchamber. "Morag?"

"Come in," came a faint voice.

Stepping inside the room, I saw Morag pushing herself up from the rocking chair by the window and Oda alone on the master bed, gazing up at the ceiling. *Wasn't Morag supposed to be in bed with the baby?* I was under the impression that the lying-in process was quite a bit longer.

I strode over to the infant. "You're awake, little one." I scooped her up and nuzzled her sweet-smelling neck.

With the baby out of the way, Morag settled herself back into bed.

"When did she wake up?"

Morag shrugged, continuing to stare out the window.

"Should we go see Mama?" I asked Oda.

As she couldn't talk, I took her staring at me for a yes.

"Morag, I'll bet Oda would love to be rocked."

"Perhaps. The rocking chair is free."

"I meant rocked by you, Morag."

Turning her head slightly my way, she whispered. "I'm just not up to it, Bronwyn."

"Up to what?"

"The demands of being a mother."

"It's only been a few weeks. You just need time to adjust."

"I don't think so. I'd like you to find a wet nurse for her."

"A wet nurse?"

"Yes. Another woman who has an infant herself and can nurse both the babies. You know most of the villagers. There must be someone who can help."

"I'm sure there is, Morag, but the baby is thriving. There's no need to do that."

"It's a common practice."

My jaw dropped. *It is?* Why would any woman want to miss out on such a significant aspect of motherhood?

As if she were reading my thoughts, Morag continued. "I'm not comfortable with nursing," she stated, replicating her mother's refined British accent. "Babies are so fragile.

And time-consuming, I may add."

I shook my head at her in disbelief.

"If you won't do as I ask, Bronwyn, I'll find someone else."

Not knowing how to reply, I left the room—sleepy little Oda in my arms—with the excuse that I was taking her for a walk.

Pacing is a form of walking, right? I shoved my bedchamber door shut with my foot and proceeded to cross the floor in long strides, fuming at Morag for being so uncaring toward Oda. Treating me like dirt was one thing, but her own child?

Tears burned my eyes as I looked down at that angelic little face and wondered how anyone couldn't treasure her. She was the picture of innocence and all that was good in the world. The thought of finding some village woman to nurse her was dismaying. If I had the capability, I'd take on the job myself.

Despite my turmoil, the brisk pace put Oda to sleep. She snoozed as I ranted to myself, clenching my teeth to keep the volume low.

Since ranting wasn't getting me anywhere, I decided to seek out Iain and get his thoughts on the issue. Unlike me, he made decisions with his head. He'd look at the situation logically and offer sound advice.

With the baby bundled in her blanket, I grabbed my fox shawl and stepped out into the brisk February air. Isobel happened to be approaching the manor house just as I was leaving. She offered to bring Oda back inside so she could have some grand-mum time with her.

The weather was colder than I'd anticipated, so I was happy to pass the baby along to her. I took off in a jog across the yard, doing my best to keep the shawl wrapped tightly around me as I bounced and slid across the frozen ground.

On the pretext of helping Alastair, Lenox, and Graeme work on their horseback riding skills, Iain had taken them to the stables. In actuality, he was helping his mom. Those three little ones running wild in the manor house weren't helping her accomplish her tasks for the day.

Keeping those boys in line was like herding cats, but Iain was doing a good job managing them as they rode their ponies around the stable yard.

"Lenox, if I've told ye once, I've told ye a hundred times, ye're not te stand on the horse's back. I don't care how good yer balance be."

Usually Iain was unflappable, but his jaw clenched as he watched the horse's pace quicken.

"Slow down, Alastair, before ye get unseated. If ye break yer neck, ye shan't come running to me."

As concerning as the scene before me was, I couldn't help but laugh at the admonition. That was a classic. Apparently, it'd been around for eons.

I approached Iain and tapped his upper arm to get his attention. He glanced away from the boys to give me a smile.

"What can I do fer ye, me fine young lady?" he

inquired.

"I'd just like a moment of time to ask you something, if you can spare it."

"Fer ye, always." He gave me a wink and yelled to his brothers. "Trot around the yard six times, and then I'll join ye for a gallop about the property."

Immediately the trio slowed their pace and started the count.

"That ought te give us a few minutes," he noted, rolling his eyes when he heard the youngest two start squabbling.

"Ye make it sound like it's the end of the world fer Morag te request a wet nurse," Iain noted. "It's a common practice, ye know."

"That's what your sister said. But, common or not, I don't think it's best for Oda. Or Morag, for that matter," I insisted.

"As long as the wee one is fed and looked after, what difference does it make who provides the care?"

"What difference? Babies need their moms, Iain. And there's no physical reason why Morag can't feed her own child."

"That may be true, but if she has no desire te do that, who are we te tell her otherwise?"

Arms akimbo, I countered. "Something doesn't feel right about this."

"Morag will still be Oda's mother. In time she'll grow te have affection fer her."

At that moment, the hymn Isaiah 49 popped into my

head. *Does a mother forget her baby or a woman the child within her womb? Yet even if these forget, I will never forget my own.*

I bit my lower lip to keep it from trembling. Noticing my reaction, Iain pulled me into an embrace. "Are ye thinking of ye own mam, Bronwyn?"

Afraid I'd break into tears, I buried my head in his chest and just nodded.

"I know it stings that ye own mother left ye. But this be different."

"I'm not so sure, Iain. I can't understand why Morag's acting like she is. It's not right."

"If ye think this be a spiritual issue, perhaps ye should speak with Father Ferguson."

Stepping back from Iain, I asked, "Would I be able to request a private meeting with him today?"

"Possibly. I saw him near the chapel as I made me way te the stables."

"This isn't just an excuse to get me to go to confession, is it?"

"Would I do that?" Iain asked innocently, eyebrows raised.

"Yes," I muttered.

"Maybe I would, but talking with Father about this situation does have merit."

Putting one hand on each of my shoulders, Iain leaned down, kissed my forehead, and then turned me around in the direction of the chapel.

"Off ye go."

Dragging my feet, I started forward.

"It's not like ye're heading te yer execution, Bronwyn."

"That's what *you* think."

Looking over my shoulder, I ascertained that no one was in the vicinity, so I crept inside the stone building. I slipped a chapel veil on top of my head before genuflecting. There would be no tabernacle on the altar, but I wanted to err on the side of being respectful. The nave was empty, however, I heard whistling coming from the sacristy.

I proceeded forward and bowed toward the altar. With the altar rail blocking my path, I assumed that lay people weren't allowed in the sanctuary. I stopped and called out, "Excuse me?"

"Just a moment," came a voice from the other room.

Moments later, Father Ferguson stepped into the sanctuary dressed casually as per usual. "Good afternoon, lass."

"Good afternoon, Father."

"How may I be of service te ye today?"

"I wonder if you might have a moment to talk?"

"Of course, me dear." He nodded toward the area where the confessional had stood when the building had been a place of holy Catholic worship.

Even if I were thinking of going to confession, the last way I'd want to do that would be face to face with a priest. "This isn't anything formal, Father," I spouted. "I just have a question."

After sharing my concerns about Morag, Father Ferguson noted that it wasn't uncommon for mothers in her societal position to take on a wet nurse. "It's not a sin on her part, Mistress Bronwyn. And, even if it were, it's not yer duty te be relaying it te me."

Ouch. Nothing like getting called out by a priest.

"But, Father, she's uncaring. Just like my mom was when she walked out on me and my dad when I was a baby."

"We're not te judge." Father inclined his head in the direction of the confessional area once again.

The color drained from my face. Dropping my head in resignation, I made my way toward the far wall and dropped to my knees. Within a few seconds, Father Ferguson was on his knees beside me.

I racked my brain trying to remember how to start the session.

"Bless me, Father, for I have sinned . . ." I said uncertainly.

"Yes, me daughter." Score one for my stellar memory. "Ye may begin."

Apparently, that instruction wasn't for me but for the butterflies in my stomach. At once, they went into formation and began circling around my insides.

It felt logical to go back seventeen years to the last time Mom had been in my life. Or ahead three-hundred-and-some years, depending on how you looked at it.

No matter how many times I'd gone through this in my

head or shared it with someone, relating my early-childhood story always made me tear up.

Or weep, as was the case today. Unfortunately, I hadn't thought to bring a handkerchief with me, and Kleenex hadn't been invented yet, so the bottom of my skirt made do.

My confession was broken into two parts. The first concerned Mom and my unrelenting anger toward her. I'm not sure why it took a conversation with an ancient Scottish priest to finally realize that I'd been holding resentment inside me all these years.

The brogue was a bit thick, but I deciphered his every word. Even if I'd never meet Mom again, it was imperative that I forgive her.

"Father, how do you forgive someone who doesn't want to be forgiven?"

"De ye ken with certainty that she doesn't?"

"No . . . But, if she wanted to make amends, she had seventeen years to do that."

"Sometimes, lass, it's as hard te ask fer forgiveness as it is te grant it."

He had a point, but I couldn't help but blurt out, "She doesn't deserve to be forgiven."

"None of us do. Yet Jesus died on the cross in atonement fer all of our sins."

Wow. I was speechless. Thoughts darted through my brain. I'd grown so accustomed to carrying this hurt around inside me, I didn't know if I could let it go.

As if sensing my inner dialogue, Father Ferguson

added, "Lass, this act may benefit ye even more than yer mam."

I could hardly argue that.

"One more thing te consider. What if yer mam felt that her actions were in yer best interest?"

"How could that be?"

"Perhaps she didn't ken how te be a proper mother. Or maybe she was afraid she'd hurt her wee little one."

His words caused my eyes to open wide. That sounded eerily familiar to what Morag had told me earlier in the day.

Could confession be a conversation? It sure felt like it when I was confessing to Father Ferguson. The man was older than the hills, but *with age comes wisdom*. He had a grandpa-type vibe that drew me to him.

Thinking back as far as I could, I enumerated my childhood sins, which I assumed were all venial. He didn't say otherwise.

When it came time to open up about my time traveling, it was hard to determine what he was thinking. His comments ranged from, "Oh, my," to "Ye don't say."

Not that traveling through time was a sin. I sure as heck didn't do it on purpose. The lying about it was where things got a bit sticky. While I'd made amends with Iain and corrected every mistruth—spoken and unspoken—between us, I'd never come clean with the rest of his family.

Those conversations would happen soon. I'd make sure

of it. First, I needed to complete this process.

"Is that all?" asked Father Ferguson when my words died down.

"I think so." I held my breath, waiting for the verdict, praying the word exorcism wouldn't come up.

"Fer yer penance, pray three Our Fathers and two Hail Marys."

That was it? I could easily do that. Why had I waited so long to go to confession? It wasn't nearly as bad as I thought it would be.

"Ye may say the Act of Contrition."

My mind went completely blank.

Realizing my situation, Father stated it one line at a time in English, with me echoing him. He followed that with, "I absolve ye of yer sins."

"Uh, thank you?"

"Amen."

"Amen," I corrected myself.

"God has freed ye from yer sin. Go in peace."

"Okay."

The priest cleared his throat. "Thanks be to God."

"Thanks be to God, I mean."

Kneeling on the stone floor in the chapel, I said the prayers that Father had assigned me. That complete, I turned to face a statue of the Blessed Mother that had somehow been left unscathed when the chapel had been ransacked by the reformers. I looked up at her and she gazed down at me.

"Blessed Mother, what's the deal with Morag? Is she really a crummy mom or am I just overreacting?"

I sat back on my haunches; my eyes locked with Mother Mary's as the staring contest commenced. *She's good, I'll give her that.* Or course, being made out of stone was a definite advantage. Between blinks, I perused her face and tried to read her enigmatic expression.

"Is there something wrong with her?"

I waited for the Blessed Mother's reply, listening with all my might, but nothing was forthcoming. Inspecting her closer, it seemed as though she were wrapped in a cloud of serenity and love. It was almost as if the statue had become animated. Her chest appeared to rise and fall slightly as she inhaled and exhaled. The rosary beads in her hands swung slightly. A chill ran through me.

Mesmerized, my eyes slowly shut. Images flowed through my mind. I watched them as though they were written on a computer screen. Out of nowhere, the word "depression" was highlighted before me.

My eyes sprang open.

"Our Lady, are you trying to tell me that Morag is suffering from depression?"

The lips on the stone face were upturned in a slight smile. Had they been carved that way? Had I missed that before?

I mulled over the possibility for several minutes. Wasn't there some sort of depression that only happened to women who'd recently given birth? Like the baby blues? Or could it be something more serious?

Shoot, what's that called? It took a bit, but the word finally came to me. Postpartum. Postpartum depression.

Could it be that Morag wasn't a bad mother after all, but she was going through some mental health crisis? If that were the case, it couldn't last forever, could it? Somebody should be able to help her through it.

Seeing that I was the only Middle-Ages human who'd ever heard of this concept, it probably would have to be me. I knew next to nothing about mental health, but I did know how to listen. Maybe Morag just needed someone to act as a sounding board.

The next thought caused the breath to catch in my throat. *Had Mom gone through something like this when I was born?*

After bowing in reverence and thanks to the Blessed Mother, I turned to the altar, dropped to my knees, and touched my forehead to the stone floor.

"Thank you, God," I whispered as I brought my head up. "Thank you for giving me a possible answer for Morag's problem. Is this why you brought me here?"

My eyes raised to glance to the outline of where a crucifix had hung on the wall behind the altar. I considered all the pain that Jesus Christ had gone through on His way to Calvary and His crucifixion. Maybe Morag was suffering her own pain and, since it was invisible, nobody recognized it.

"Jesus," I implored, "give me the ability to listen to Morag and convince her that she can do this. Be at my side and let your words flow through me."

Crossing myself, I rose and bowed once more toward the altar.

Before slipping out of the chapel, I removed the chapel veil and stuffed it into the waistband of my skirt. I made my way purposely toward the manor house. Once inside, I noticed Isobel in the great room, lost in thought as she rocked the baby. The scene was so sweet, I couldn't imagine that she had ever had any problem bonding with her babies.

Passing the archway, I crept up the stairs so as not to disturb her or the baby. At the end of the upstairs hall, I knocked on Morag's door.

There was no answer, so I cracked it open to see if anyone was in there. Morag was lying in bed once again. Her nose was red and eyes puffy from crying.

Even though we'd had our issues in the past, I felt empathy for her.

"Morag," I said quietly as I approached the chair, "are you okay?"

She turned her head away from me and dabbed her eyes with a handkerchief. "I'm fine."

"Do you mind if I sit with you for a bit?"

"Do as you please," she replied listlessly.

Pulling up the chair from her vanity, I positioned it several feet away from her.

We sat in silence for a couple of minutes as I prayed for the words to start our conversation.

"It's hard being a new mother, isn't it?" I began.

Staring out the window, Morag nodded.

"You were amazingly strong during Oda's delivery."

She turned and eyed me curiously. "You think so?"

"I know so. You and I are the same age. I couldn't imagine enduring such pain."

"You could do it, Bronwyn. I've been watching you all these months. You've gone through so much yourself, and you've always made it through."

It was my turn to get teary-eyed. Instinctively, I reached out and grabbed Morag's hand. It was limp, and the surface veins were visible. She hadn't been eating nearly enough to sustain both herself and the baby.

Gently pulling back, I waited for more inspiration before continuing. "Morag, if it's God's plan, someday I'll have a child too. What is the experience like?"

"I can't speak for every woman, but I'm exhausted."

"As would be expected."

She rolled her eyes to the left as if looking for more adjectives. "And overwhelmed. The responsibility of raising a child is frightening."

Was that how Mom felt when I was born?

"I would imagine it is."

She was quiet for a while as she considered her next words.

"Even leading up to the baby's birth, I didn't feel like myself. Douglas can attest to that. My emotions shifted from anxiety to irritability. I was having trouble sleeping and was overcome by fits of crying."

"Wow, I had no idea."

Morag shrugged and continued. "I couldn't determine what was happening to me, but I imagined that when the baby arrived, everything would go back to normal."

"And, it didn't?"

"In actuality, it got worse."

Until this conversation, I'd had no idea what Morag was dealing with. She haltingly relayed some of her concerns to me. Again, I thought of Mom. With Dad in the Air Force, she had been living far from her childhood home. Maybe she didn't have anyone on the base to talk to. Maybe she'd felt trapped or helpless.

Relying on the Blessed Mother and my guardian angel, I did my best to validate Morag's feelings and reassure her that there was a light at the end of this tunnel.

She seemed exhausted after our talk but less frazzled than she had been. I excused myself to get the baby from Isobel. When I got back to the bedchamber with Oda in my arms, Morag glanced our way. I took that as a positive sign.

"Morag, Oda was asking for her mama," I noted, seeing the infant rooting toward the blanket that brushed her cheek.

While she didn't seem overly excited about the prospect of feeding the infant, she allowed me to place the baby in her arms.

Would you like some privacy while you nurse?" I inquired.

"That's fine. You may stay."

Once the baby latched on, I leaned over and stroked the smattering of hair on her tiny head.

"She's so pretty, Morag. Just like you."

That statement was no lie.

"Do you think so?"

"She's the spitting image of you. Everyone says so."

That caught Morag's interest. She looked the baby over closer and touched her cheek.

"You're so gentle with her," I added. "She's in capable hands."

Morag tilted her head, checking the baby out from another angle. "I could never be as good a mother to her as mine is to me."

"There's no need to compare yourself to anyone, Morag. You're the best mother for Oda, and that's all that counts."

She considered my words. As she seemed comfortable enough with the baby, I told her that I needed to run to my room and I'd return in a bit when Oda was done eating.

When I came back, I suggested that Morag help me change the baby's cloth diaper. Normally, that task was reserved for the chambermaid, but I wanted her to realize that Oda wasn't as fragile as she may have thought.

With a dry diaper and a full belly, Oda was content and wide awake. Seizing the opportunity, I laid her on the bed for some tummy time with a cloth beneath her to catch any drool and proceeded to do a mini massage on her little arms and legs. She enjoyed that, so I started lightly rubbing her back in a circular motion.

"Give it a try," I encouraged Morag.

Timidly, Morag reached out and set her hand on the baby's lower back and imitated my motions.

Kneeling at the bedside, eye level with the baby, I noticed something. "Morag, look. Oda appears to be smiling. She likes her mother's touch."

Leaning closer herself, Morag observed her daughter. Whether it was a gas bubble or a baby that young could actually smile, I didn't know. But her momma bought it and smiled back.

Not a moment later, a belch came from the little one. *Well, now we know.*

It was relatively loud, considering the source. When a second one came a moment later, I couldn't help myself and burst out laughing. "You'll give your three young uncles a run for their money someday, Oda."

Then I heard it. A giggle. From Morag. I turned and stared at her.

She hid her mirth behind her hand. "We'll need to work on your manners, now won't we, my little one?"

My eyes opened wide in astonishment.

Things didn't turn around overnight. It was more of a two-steps-forward-one-step-back process, but every day I spent some time with Morag and commented on each act she performed that helped strengthen the bond between her and Oda.

"I think she likes hearing you talk, Morag," I mentioned one day. "She listened to your voice continually when she was growing inside of you."

"At least when I was between retching and crying," she replied, a bit of humor returning to her.

"Why don't you try singing to Oda?"

"I don't know any children's songs."

"It doesn't matter, Morag. Your voice is so pleasant, I think she'll enjoy anything you sing."

Hesitantly, she began. I recognized it as a song from church. Even though it was meant to be somber, it brought a smile to the baby's face. Noticing that, Morag's voice caught in her throat.

"It seems as though you're correct, Bronwyn."

That made me smile. Thoughts of Mom came to me again, but I noticed that the hurt feelings were receding, and in their place was a sense of compassion. I said a prayer for her as Morag picked up the song again.

As the days wore on, Morag's requests for a wet nurse trailed off, and I felt that she and the baby were on the right track. Douglas expressed his thanks to me for helping his wife. He'd been at his wits' end trying to figure out how to placate her.

The season of Lent progressed, Oda thrived, and before we knew it, Holy Week was upon us. The Triduum, starting with Maundy Thursday, fell this year on the third of April.

After the Thursday service, which was held in the safe room on the second floor of the manor house, Isobel covered the bare altar with twigs to symbolize the stripping and scourging of Jesus.

There was an interesting custom on that day in ancient

Scotland that Iain referred to as "creeping to the cross." His family entered the chapel barefoot and shuffled on their knees to the crucifix that had been placed on the altar.

St. John's Passion narrative was read by Father Ferguson. The only light came from a candleholder, appropriately enough called a hearse, with the candles extinguished one after another, representing darkness falling on the world, until just the center candle remained, the light of Christ.

Once again, I thanked God for the gift of Iain. I'd have been clueless about what was going on around me if he hadn't kept up a whispered, running narrative during the service. He even knew the Psalm that Father Ferguson quoted, 51:1-2.

The words, in Iain's translation, were so moving. "Have mercy on me, O God, according to your steadfast love; according to your abundant mercy, blot out my transgressions. Wash me thoroughly from my iniquity and cleanse me from my sin."

As the family made their way back to other areas of the manor house, Christ's words as he'd hung dying on the cross echoed through my mind. Father Ferguson had recited them in Latin, but I knew the English translation, "Father, forgive them, they know not what they do."

Mom came to my mind. Did she know what she was doing when she left us that day? She couldn't have realized the implications that action would have on my life, could she? *If Jesus was able to forgive His tormentors, then who am I to hold back my forgiveness?*

I pondered that as the third day in the Triduum dawned. Holy Saturday turned out to be an unforgettable day. I'd never attended an Easter Vigil before—probably because it was the longest Mass of the season—but I was so grateful to have that opportunity this year. Words couldn't adequately describe the sense of reverence and feeling of peace that fell over me as the Mass proceeded.

While the priest incanted the doxology—what I'd always called the "through Him, with Him, in Him" prayer until Iain had set me straight—I recognized from where that peace emanated. My heart. It had been a gradual process, but I was finally ready to completely forgive Mom. I wished nothing but peace in her life as well.

My hand brushing Iain's as the service concluded, everything felt right in my world.

That feeling continued Easter Sunday as we gathered in the safe room, quietly singing hymns of praise and finally being able to proclaim the word *Alleluia*. The sense of joy throughout the small group of congregants was palpable.

As we processed to the front of the room to receive Holy Communion, my heart beat in anticipation, as though this was my First Communion. Cleansed of my sins after receiving the sacrament of Confession again the day before, I felt as if I were a whole new person and eagerly awaited the body and blood of Christ.

Stepping back to my spot after making the Sign of the Cross, I thought over the last six weeks. When I was growing up, I'd dreaded Lent because I hated giving up things I enjoyed. This year I'd faced each day with gratitude. The sacrifices were small in comparison to what I gained, particularly deepening my faith and focusing on the Passion of our Lord.

Seeing that it was a holy day for all the residents of the manor house, Isobel hosted a feast for the entire household. Hearkening back to the day when Jesus washed the feet of His disciples, the family was tasked with serving the staff members, all of whom had been given the day off.

I was introduced to another Easter tradition. As it was on Christmas Day, all the members of the MacDonald household had been fitted with a new outfit. In turn, each of us gave an item of our own clothing to one of the servants. In turn, they would do the same to people in the village who were below them in rank, who then passed an item of their clothing to someone below them until many folks had something new—or new to them—to wear.

Apparently, that same gifting process would happen again on Whitsun, or what I'd always known as Pentecost. It was so heartwarming seeing the delight that the clan members experienced in not only receiving but in giving as well.

All decked out in our new finery, we enjoyed a banquet that rivaled anything that William III would have produced for his English subjects. Watching Iain as we bussed the tables—reliving one of my first jobs at a banquet hall when I was a fifteen—I was convinced that no royal could match his good looks or gentlemanly bearing.

Once we'd finally had the chance to eat our fill, Iain excused the two of us from the table. We stepped away from the crowd to walk the grounds and enjoy the unusually sunny spring day on our own. After two months, the gloom in the atmosphere, both literally and figuratively, was starting to diminish.

"It's beautiful, isn't it, Iain?"

"'Tis enchanting, just like ye."

Color warmed my cheeks. I didn't know if I'd ever get used to his compliments. He saw something in me of which I'd never been aware.

"Thank you," I murmured.

Once we were beyond the noise of the crowd in the manor house, Iain paused and looked down at me. "Bronwyn, I owe ye a debt of gratitude. I've no clue how ye accomplished it, but I believe ye helped Morag overcome her bout of melancholy."

His words brought a smile to my face.

"I may have assisted, but the credit goes to God and Our Blessed Mother for inspiring me to say the words to encourage her. I was just the instrument; God was the conductor."

"Be that as it may, without ye here, she'd still be floundering. Lord knows if she would've ever seen her way out of the darkness that she'd found herself in."

At first thought, I wanted to dismiss that notion and assure Iain that Morag would have been fine without me, but I paused. *Would she have come through this?* Or would this have set up a cycle of mental health issues that filtered down through countless generations?

"Iain, do you think it's possible that my helping Morag will help her descendants? Maybe all the way to the century that I came from?"

Pulling me close to him, Iain said sincerely, "Bronwyn, chances are we'll never know the answer, at least not on this plane. But what I do know is that ye're a good person and ye've made a difference in so many lives. In yer day and mine."

I wrapped my arms tightly around Iain's waist, never wanting to let go of him.

"Ye needn't squeeze me te death, lass. I not be going anywhere."

"You're not, but what if I am? What if this was the mission that I was sent here to accomplish, and now God is transporting me back to my time?"

Iain strengthened his grip on me. "We've an unending bond, Bronwyn. If, somehow, we be torn apart, I'll spend the rest of eternity looking fer ye."

With that comforting thought, I relaxed into his embrace.

"God is great all the time," I whispered. "All the time, God is great. Thank you, Lord."

###

If you enjoyed this Lenten story about Bronwyn Campbell traveling back in time to meet Iain MacDonald

and his family, you'll want to read the full novel *Royal & Ancient*. Discover how Bronwyn came to be in Scotland, learned to negotiate life in ancient times, and survived one of the most harrowing incidents in Scottish history. "Lent Royal & Ancient" takes place where my novel *Royal & Ancient* left off.

ABOUT THE AUTHOR

AMANDA LAUER is an avid reader and history buff since childhood, award-winning author, journalist, and screenwriter. She is the author of the *Heaven Intended* Civil War series. *A World Such as Heaven Intended* won the 2016 CALA Award and *A Freedom Such as Heaven Intended* earned the 2022 Catholic Media Book Awards: First Place Catholic Novels: Inspirational. In addition, Lauer has written two time-travel novels, *Anything But Groovy* and *Royal & Ancient,* and she contributed to the anthology *Treasures: Visible & Invisible* and worked with Archduke Eduard Habsburg to bring his children's tale *Dubbie: The Double-Headed Eagle* to life. In addition, Lauer won the *Red Letter Awards 2020 Best Writer or Screenplay* for her work on the Christian film *The Islands*.

For more information, visit www.AmandaLauer.com.

6

Contemporary

NO GREATER LOVE

by Ellen Gable

There is no greater love than this; to lay down one's life for his friends. John 15:3

Fifteen-year-old Alexis Marie—Lexie—Dugan stared out the window of religion class. Although cold outside, bright sun and blue skies made for a beautiful late winter's New Jersey day. If only she could escape and enjoy it.

Her teacher, Mrs. Eastman, droned on about what treats or activities the students could give up for Lent. "Alexis Dugan, please pay attention."

Lexie sighed and faced the front of the classroom. She had already decided she was giving up chocolate because, quite frankly, she ate enough Kit Kats during the year to keep the company in operation. Besides, while Sundays were considered part of Lent, they weren't days of fasting, so she always enjoyed five or six Fun Size Kit Kats that day. Not that she needed anything special to give up for Lent.

As the oldest of five kids, Lexie dreamed of having a sister but recognized that she likely would remain the only girl in a long line of Dugan boys. Her dad had been one of eight sons, Uncle Frank had five sons, and Uncle Mike had three. Mom was an only child, so there were no cousins on that side of the family. Lexie had no idea what it was like to even have a young female related to her. Her mom and dad weren't even going to bother to find out the sex of the baby beforehand.

Mrs. Eastman broke into Lexie's thoughts. "So, class, what do you think Jesus meant when he said, '*There is no greater love than this; to lay down one's life for his friends*?'"

Lexie raised her hand. "To be willing to die for someone?"

"Yes, that's one of the meanings. Anything else?"

No one raised a hand.

"Well," Mrs. Eastman said, "what do we do when we have to work on a school project or do a chore for our parents, and we'd rather be on social media?"

A hand shot up. "Go on social media," said one of the boys with a laugh.

"Hmm, no. We do the project or the chore. At least that's what we're called to do. Sometimes, laying down one's life means putting others' needs before our own. When we're able to do that, we can love others in the way we're called to."

Lexie never had to worry about social media because she wasn't on social media. Her parents wouldn't allow it. In fact, her parents were so strict that Lexie wasn't allowed to own a cell phone—the only student in her entire St. Michael's sophomore class without one. If she was biking to the movies or to the pizza place, Lexie borrowed her mom's cell phone, but she wasn't allowed to text her friends. It was so unfair. Her parents told her they were "protecting" her, but couldn't they just trust her?

At least her mom and dad allowed her brothers and her to watch two TV stations: TV Land and PBS Kids. TV Land had just started showing old reruns of *Gilligan's Island* at 3:30. If Lexie rushed out at the end of class, she'd be able to watch it from the beginning. The show was corny and unrealistic, but at least the characters acted in fun ways. They all had two goals: to survive on the island and to someday be rescued.

The bell rang. Lexie closed her book, slipped it into her backpack, and headed for the door.

"Alexis?"

She turned to find Mrs. Eastman waving for her. Lexie cringed. Her teacher was nice enough, but she was always asking Lexie to help after school, and Lexie just wanted to get home in time for *Gilligan's Island*. She sighed and dutifully approached the elderly woman.

"Yes, Mrs. Eastman?"

"Would you mind staying after class, dear, to help me with the chalkboards?"

Shoulders slumping, Lexie replied after a moment of hesitation, "Sure, Mrs. Eastman." Of course, Mrs. Eastman, being ancient—at least eighty-five—told her class that she preferred using the old-fashioned board instead of a smartboard. The downside was that someone had to clean off the boards and clap the erasers, something Lexie's grandparents probably did when they were her age.

When Lexie finished erasing the chalkboards and clapping the erasers, the time on the old wall clock was already 3:45. No use rushing to get home to watch the show. Disappointed, she meandered home. The birds chirped as if spring had already arrived, and the sky was a beautifully intense blue. She passed a group of kids staring down at their phones. For one brief second, Lexie was envious. She sighed. If she'd been mesmerized by a phone, she'd have completely missed the beauty of the day. Still, she longed to be like a normal kid, cell phone and all.

As she approached her house, a two-story Cape Cod, her dad's car was parked in the driveway. He rarely came home from work this early. And most weekdays, he was out of town working.

Lexie bounded up the porch and opened the door. Inside, her mom was lounging on the sofa, and her dad was sitting on a chair beside her. Mom had an uncharacteristically serious expression on her face, but she relaxed into happy mode as soon as she saw Lexie. Her dad turned around.

Lexie glanced from her dad back to her mom. "Is everything okay?"

"Everything's okay . . . for now," her dad said.

"What's that mean?"

Her mom's soft voice replied, "Lex, come over here. Your dad and I have something important we want to discuss with you." They both seemed to be forcing smiles.

Uh-oh, Lexie thought. *Important? Why are they smiling if it's so important?*

Lexie sat at the other end of the sofa, near her mom's feet. "What's going on?"

Her mom opened her mouth to respond when two of Lexie's three brothers came racing through the room with model airplanes in their hands. They ran up the stairs.

"Well," her mom said when they were gone, "you know it's two months until this baby is due, right?"

"Um, yeah, I guess."

"Well, I have a medical condition called placenta previa. That means that the placenta is partially covering the cervix. At any moment, part of the placenta can come through the cervix, and the baby's life and my life will be at risk. So I've been put on bed rest until the baby can be delivered by C-section."

"O . . . kay." Lexie nodded. "So the baby's all right?"

"For now, but a C-section means surgery," her dad said.

"And . . . " her mother began.

"And what?"

"Because I need to be on bed rest, your Aunt Kelly will be helping me during the day. But she won't be able to after school. And Dad is out of town most weekdays because of his job."

Lexie was beginning to understand why they were telling her about her mom's condition. "And . . . you want me to help you and the boys while you're on bed rest?"

"Tony, I told you Lexie would want to help."

"Of course, I want to help. But I tutor on Wednesdays

and have choir on Fridays. So I'll help all the other afternoons."

"No, hon, that won't work. You'll have to give up those activities until after the baby is born," her mom murmured.

Lexie had been excited for her new baby brother to be born—she was sure that's what it would be—but why did they ask her to give up the things she loved doing? "I see. All right, whatever you need." The words rolled off her lips, but she had to swallow a lump in her throat. It didn't seem fair that she had to give up the activities she enjoyed.

As she turned to go to her room, her mom called to her. "Lex?"

She stopped.

Her mom held her hand out and on her palm was her cell phone. "Here. I want you to have this."

Lexie's eyes widened. "A cell phone? Really?"

"Yes," her dad responded. "You're taking on more responsibility, so you deserve it. But it comes with rules. You can use it to text but not to surf the internet. This is an old phone anyway, but you can still text. We wanted you to have it as a reward because we know this isn't an easy thing to do, to take care of Mom."

Lexie nodded. Yes, her mom's phone was ancient—at least ten years old—but it *was* a cell phone, so she'd finally be able to text her friends.

"Another thing," her dad said. "Mom or I will ask you from time to time if we can read your texts."

"Of course," Lexie said. She hugged her mom and dad.

"Thanks, you guys. This means a lot to me."

"We know," her mom replied.

Upstairs in her bedroom, Lexie shut the door. Perhaps the biggest advantage of being the only girl in a houseful of boys was that she had her own room. Her brothers all shared another room. At least she had some privacy. She couldn't wait to text her friends. She knew Ashley's, Kennedy's, and Taylor's numbers by heart, so she texted them with the news about her cell phone.

The phone vibrated immediately with three incoming texts.

Super cool!

Wow! So glad!

Great!

In bed that evening, Lexie fell asleep, sure that having a cell phone would make her other classmates at school think that she was more normal.

Lexie responded to texts from her friends all day the next day. Mom and Dad had said not to text during class, but they texted her, and surely she wasn't supposed to be rude? She almost got caught twice, once during math and once during religion with Mrs. Eastman.

When she got home, Lexie greeted her mom, who was resting on the sofa in the living room. "Did Aunt Kelly leave already?"

"Yes, she did." Her mother paused. "Hey, Lex. May I see the cell phone please?"

Lexie stepped backward and frowned. "Why?"

"Because one of the conditions of having a cell phone is not using it during classes."

Shoulders slumped, Lexie gave her mom the cell phone.

Her mom shook her head. "Ninety-six texts today, most of which were sent during classes." Her mom sighed.

"I'm sorry, Mom, but my friends texted me. I didn't want to be rude."

"Nice try." Her mom paused. "You'll have to explain to your friends that you can only text during breaks and lunch, all right?"

"Yeah, all right."

"Can you please start supper for me? There's a chicken casserole in the freezer. It needs to be baked at three hundred and fifty for seventy minutes."

"Sure." Lexie tried to sound upbeat, but right now, she wished that she was like the other kids in school, with cell phones and parents who let them watch anything or read anything and who only had one sibling. Did her parents not trust her? She was fifteen, after all, practically an adult.

While Lexi prepared dinner in the kitchen, the door slammed, and her four younger brothers bounded into the living room, along with their loud voices. Why did boys have to be so LOUD?

Lexie wiped her hands on a dishtowel and went into the living room. Andrew held Micah's hand, but her brothers were hovering around their mom, yelling, "I got an A on my test, Mommy!" and "Look what I did, Mommy!"

"Hey, fellas," Lexie said, "Mom is trying to rest. One at a time, please." She nodded to Andrew, her closest-in-age sibling, to speak to their mom. She waved each of her youngest brothers, eight-year-old twins Peter and Paul and five-year-old Micah, up to their rooms to change out of their uniforms.

Back in the kitchen, Lexie popped the casserole into the preheated oven, then met Peter and Paul at the bottom of the stairs. "Can we talk to Mommy now, Lex?"

"Of course. Please try not to be so loud, though. Mom's supposed to be resting."

Peter nodded and tiptoed over to the sofa. Paul followed.

Bumping noises sounded over Lexie's head. Andrew must already be upstairs changing. And why hasn't Micah come down yet?

She ascended the stairs, and before she got to the boys' room, she heard Micah sobbing. She reached the doorway and stopped. Andrew was crouching down in front of their little brother. Lexie joined them. "Hey, buddy, what's wrong?"

Micah hiccupped but said nothing.

Andrew said, "Some kid is calling him names at school."

"What kind of names?"

Micah spoke up. "Chunky monkey."

"What?" Lexie blurted out.

Andrew patted Micah's head. "That's just stupid talk."

"Am I fat?"

Lexie sighed. Weren't all four- and five-year-old boys chubby? "Of course, you're not fat." Micah just hadn't lost all of his baby chubbiness. "Come on, let me help you get out of your uniform so you can play outside."

Micah hiccupped again and allowed Lexie to assist him.

Andrew said behind her, "A little privacy, please. I need to change."

"Sorry." She finished helping Micah with his pants and shirt, then took him downstairs.

After preparing and serving dinner, Lexie got help from Andrew with the dishes. Then she put TV Land on for her mother and the boys in the living room and headed upstairs to do her homework. This would be so much easier if Dad were home one or two days during the week. While she was working on her religion project on her laptop, Andrew knocked on her door. "Lex?"

"Yeah, Andrew?"

"Mom wants to see you."

Lexie stopped typing and sighed. *It's one thing to help Mom, but can't I even get my homework done without interruption?* She clenched her fists and followed Andrew downstairs.

"Hey, Lex, we're going to watch *The Lion, the Witch and the Wardrobe*. Do you want to join us?"

"No, thanks, Mom. I've got homework to do." Lexie realized that her tone might have come off as sharp, but what did her mom expect? For her to be all sunshine and roses while she gave up her life to take care of her mom and the boys? It wasn't fair.

Mom pursed her lips and nodded.

Lexie stomped back upstairs, annoyance pushing her

shoulders down. When she sat in front of her laptop to work on her project, her cell phone buzzed.

Lex, r u free? It was from Taylor.

Lexie texted back. *Just doing a project.*

Her cell rang. It was Taylor. "Hi, Tay."

"Projects are boring."

Lexie sighed. "I know, but I have to finish it tonight."

Taylor droned on about boys and makeup and things that Lexie wasn't excited about. But Taylor was her friend, so she listened. It was well after 9:00 p.m. when Lexie finally got off the phone. It was hard for her to get a word in edgewise because Taylor talked non-stop for over an hour. She yawned and returned to working on her project.

A timid knock sounded at her door, and she heard her mom's voice. "Lex?" The door opened.

Lexie turned.

"I'm going to bed, honey. Can you listen for Micah? He may need to use the bathroom or want a glass of water during the night."

"Yeah, sure, Mom."

At midnight, project finished, Lexie finally crawled into bed, exhausted, just to be woken by Micah, who was whining. She threw the covers off and tromped over to her brothers' room. Andrew had gotten up and was hugging Micah. Andrew turned when Lexie opened the door. "Bad dream. I've got this, Lex."

"Thanks, Andrew."

She crawled back into bed, exhausted, and finally fell asleep.

The next day was a repeat of the previous one. So was the next. She missed attending choir practice. She missed tutoring after school. She missed her freedom. Yes, she had a cell phone, but once the newness of it faded, it wasn't all that cool.

Soon, only two weeks remained until Easter. Then the baby would be born soon after that, and Lexie could finally have her life back.

That Friday, school couldn't have been worse. One of the jocks, Chris Kramer, had been making fun of her for a few weeks, and she had tried to ignore him. Initially, she thought, *What is this? Kindergarten*? But she soon learned there were just some kids who got a kick out of putting other people down. But that particular day, ignoring him wasn't an option because he got close to her face, then stepped back, saying, "Man, you've got such bad breath. Must be all the *bleep* you're eating."

Offended by his invasion of her personal space as well as his language, Lexie leaned backward and away from him. "Why don't you just leave me alone?"

Chris mimicked her in a high-pitched voice, laughed, and walked away.

When Lexie got to her next class, the teacher handed out a surprise test. Lexie hated surprise tests because she always worked hard to prepare. Without preparation, Lexie was sure afterward that she had failed.

At lunch, when Lexie took out her bagged sandwich, Chris' voice sounded behind her. "Aww, too poor to purchase the school lunch?"

Lexie's fists clenched. Her friend Kennedy said, "Leave her alone." Surprisingly, Chris left. But as she ate her egg salad sandwich, her stomach was in knots.

By the time she got home, she was in no mood for her brothers' whining and fighting. Was there a full moon or something? All of them were acting out, misbehaving, and doing everything to get on her nerves. As she tried to chop carrots for dinner, Micah ran into her legs, and she cut the inside of her finger. Paul was right behind her and rammed her stomach into the countertop.

That was the last straw. She threw the knife into the sink, ran out to her mother on the sofa, and yelled, "That's it. I'm never having kids! Never!"

Mom's eyes widened, and her mouth fell open as if Lexie had just slapped her face. "Oh, Lex, you don't mean that."

"Yes, I do. I've had it." She held the cloth to her throbbing and bleeding finger.

"I know you've given up a lot this Lent, and I'm so appreciative."

"A lot? A lot? Mom, I can't wait until this is OVER."

Mom's eyes watered, but Lexie didn't care. She stormed up to her bedroom and slammed the door. She kept pressing the cloth to her finger, but she couldn't care less if it bled all over her room.

After a few minutes of fuming, Lexie had to finish making dinner. She wasn't happy about it, but she did it.

She plunked the plates of food down for her brothers

and brought her mother one. Back at the table, they said grace loudly enough for their mom to hear and join in.

"When you're finished, scrape your plates, and put them in the dishwasher. Andrew, you can make sure that's done, right?"

"Sure," he mumbled through his full mouth of food.

Lexie took her food upstairs and ate while she studied for a test scheduled for the next day. As the evening went on, she found herself feeling guilty for talking to her mother the way she had. She'd have to say she was sorry, but she wasn't ready yet. These last four-and-a-half weeks had been torture for her, and she hated all of it. If she had been born an only child or with maybe one sibling, her life would be so much better.

Gentle knocking on her door around nine made her turn in her seat. "Yes?"

The door opened, and there stood her mom. "I'm going to bed, honey. I've asked Andrew to take care of Micah in case he needs to use the bathroom."

Her mom said something else, but Lexie didn't catch it. She heard, "Love you, Lex."

"Yeah, love you too, Mom," she said over her shoulder. Lexie knew she should apologize to her mom for the harsh words earlier, but didn't she understand just how much Lexie had given up for her? "Sorry, Mom. I had a bad day."

"It's okay, honey. I know you're doing a lot. And I appreciate it."

The following morning, it was too quiet after her alarm woke her up. Usually, the boys were pounding down the halls, stomping on the steps, and yelling by now. She got up and walked across the hall to their room. She knocked and opened the door. Her brothers were still in bed and hadn't woken up. Lexie shook her head and knocked louder on the door. "Andrew, Peter, Paul, and Micah, time to wake up. Did you guys sleep through your alarm?"

They all groaned. Andrew growled, "It's a PD day, Lex. We're off. Shut the door, would you?"

"Oops," she mumbled, then made her way to her mom's room. She quietly opened the door. Her mom was still asleep, so she closed the door and stepped back out.

She got dressed in her school uniform and slipped her cell into her pocket. She wished her high school teachers also had a professional development day so she could have a day off. But no luck. Downstairs, she poured herself a bowl of cereal, chowed it down, and was just about to go out the door when she heard her mom's distressed voice coming from upstairs. *Something's wrong.*

Lexie raced up the stairs, coat and backpack still on, and stopped at her mom's open door. She was on the floor, and the back of her nightgown was covered in blood. "Mom!"

"Honey, call 911."

She punched in the numbers on the cell phone, gave her address, and explained what was happening to her mother. Then she helped her mother to the bathroom.

Her brothers, now awake, were staring at her with helpless expressions. Before closing the door, Lexie said,

"Andrew, go wait at the front door for help to arrive. Peter, Paul, and Micah, you guys go into your room and read or play quietly."

"Is Mommy okay, Lex?" Micah asked in his high-pitched voice.

"Yes, she's going to be fine." Lexie tried to sound convincing so Micah wouldn't detect her own doubt. She closed the door and attended to her mother.

"Bathtub, Lex. Help me."

"Um, okay." She assisted Mom into the bathtub. It was the first time she got a closer look at the back of her nightgown. It had turned bright crimson. She reached up for a towel and positioned it to soak up more blood.

Mom started to shake. "Lex, listen . . ."

"Yes?"

The door suddenly opened, and the paramedics burst inside their tiny bathroom.

"We've got it, Miss—what's your name?" the tall male EMT asked.

"Lexie. This is my mom. Her name's Susan."

"Okay, Lexie. We're going to take good care of your mom. You go ahead and take care of your brothers."

Lexie squeezed past the three paramedics and the stretcher that took up most of the room in the hallway. All four of her brothers were standing by her parents' bedroom door, staring at the bathroom and the commotion. Lexie stepped in front of them. "Hey, guys, let's go downstairs and get something to eat."

None of them responded, so she took Micah's hand and

urged the other boys to come with her. She instructed the boys to go single file past the stretcher until they made it to the stairs.

She dialed Aunt Kelly's number. Wasn't she supposed to be helping Mom during the day?

Aunt Kelly answered on the first ring. "Um, hullo?" Her aunt's voice sounded muffled.

"Oh, hi, Aunt Kelly. Aren't you supposed to be here helping Mom?"

"I was just about . . ." She coughed long and hard. "To call to let your mother know I have the flu. Sorry, hon."

"I'll just stay home. No problem." She didn't want to stay home from school and babysit her brothers, but she would have to. *Is Mom going to be all right?*

At the dining room table, the boys didn't speak as they slurped cereal into their mouths. Lexie tried calling her father, but it went to voicemail. In the next moment, footfalls sounded on the stairs, voices traveling down with them. So Lexie jumped up and met the paramedics with the gurney at the bottom. Her mom's face was so pale, and her eyes were closed. She had an oxygen mask on her face.

"Is my mom okay?"

"Yes, she may need blood, so we have to take her to the hospital."

Her mom opened her eyes and reached her hand out toward Lexie.

She squeezed her mom's hand, but her mom didn't squeeze back. She looked so pale. *Please let Mom be okay, God. Please let the baby be okay.*

Lexie called her school to let them know she wasn't coming in, and then she called Dad again on his cell phone. He was working in New Hampshire. He answered on the first ring.

"Hello, Lex? Is everything all right?"

"No, Dad. Mom is bleeding, and the EMTs just took her to the hospital."

"I'll be on the next flight home."

Lexie hung up the cordless phone and stared out the kitchen window. Chickadees nibbled at the birdfeeder, and trees were starting to bud. How could such a beautiful day turn into *this*? She fought against the worry weighing her down and the responsibility for her brothers.

Behind her, the boys grew louder, now yelling at one another. She turned to find Andrew shushing the others. He gave her a reassuring glance that said, "I've got this."

After breakfast, she turned on the TV. "What do you guys want to watch?" When her parents were out of the house, only DVDs were allowed. She flipped through a few on the bookshelf. "How about Star Wars?"

"Nah," Andrew said. "As much as I love the series, we've seen that a bazillion times."

Paul picked up a DVD from the wall unit. "How about this one? We never got to watch it at Christmas."

"*It's a Wonderful Life*? But that's a Christmas movie," she said.

"I know, but I like that one," said Peter.

"Even though it's in black and white?" she asked.

"Sure," Peter said.

"Yeah, that's a good movie," said Andrew.

If she put on a black-and-white movie, maybe her younger brothers would doze off, and then she wouldn't have to worry about them getting into mischief. "All right."

She had only seen this movie once before, and that had been a few years ago. She couldn't recall too much about it.

Lexie didn't pay much attention to the movie as it told the story of George Bailey from a child to an adult. When the part came on when George lost the money and was in despair, his family and friends all prayed for him. As he stood at the bridge, wanting to jump off, someone else suddenly fell in, and without thinking, George jumped in to save him. Lexie shivered. *That must be cold*. And yet, George, who at first thought about jumping off and killing himself, jumped in and saved the man in the water. He put the man's life before his own, just like Mrs. Eastman talked about in religion class.

The next scene was in the bridge tender's office, and a goofy-looking guard listened to the conversation between George and the man he saved from the water, Clarence, who revealed he was an angel. George said, "It would've been better if I'd never been born."

Lexie tilted her head and listened closely. Then Clarence showed George what life would've been like had he never been born. In the alternate life, George's wife, friends, and mother treated him like they didn't know him. Finally, Clarence, the angel, said, "Strange, isn't it? Each man's life touches so many other lives. When he isn't around, he leaves an awful hole, doesn't he?"

Lexie's eyes teared. She didn't remember this movie being so sad.

She was so scared for George as the policemen were shooting at him. He finally returned to the bridge and realized that he was back again in his life with his family knowing him.

She was startled when the phone rang.

"Is Alexis Dugan there?"

Lexie gulped. "Um, yes."

"This is Virtua Hospital in Voorhees calling. I'm a nurse, and I'm calling about your mother."

Lexie held her breath. *Please say Mom is okay. Please say Mom is okay.*

"Hon?"

"Yes."

"Your mother wanted me to let you know that she had an emergency C-section and that she and the baby are doing fine."

"Baby?"

"Yes."

She sighed as all the tension she'd built up over the previous several hours was released. "And they're both fine?"

"They're both doing well."

"Thank you for letting me know."

"You're welcome."

When she hung up, her brothers were now all awake

and leaned toward her.

"Mom's going to be fine. And she had the baby."

Andrew said, "Another boy?"

Lexie chuckled. "I didn't ask because I'm sure it's another boy. Now I have to call Dad."

She dialed her father's number, and he answered on the first ring. "Everything okay, Lex?"

"Mom had the baby, and she's doing fine, Dad."

"Thank God. We're just deplaning. I'll call you from the hospital."

She hung up and sank onto the couch. Now all her brothers were chattering.

As Lexie watched the end of the movie, her eyes teared up. What if she had never been born? Or any of her brothers? Or even her mom or dad? Heck, Lexie wouldn't even be alive if either her mother or father had not been born.

The phone rang again. Call display indicated it was her father's cell phone. "Hey, Lex, I'm here at the hospital with Mom and the new baby. Aunt Nora is coming by in about half an hour to pick you guys up to come and visit." Aunt Nora was their dad's aunt and like a grandmother to them.

"Great. I'll get everybody ready."

Andrew said, "I'll get Micah dressed and ready, Lex."

"Thanks, Andrew."

Still in her uniform from this morning, she dashed to her bedroom and changed into jeans and a t-shirt

Aunt Nora picked them up, and on the way to the hospital, she spoke about how blessed they all were with another sibling.

Blessed? Was that how Lexie felt? Her comment about never having kids weighed heavy on her heart. Mom and Dad had welcomed six children, six new human beings for whom they'd be responsible until they were adults. There would never be another Lexie, Andrew, Peter, Paul, or Micah. This new baby would be his own person with unique likes and dislikes. Maybe he would discover the cure for a disease or become a priest.

Lexie shook her head. During the past four weeks, she had been so focused on how much she had given up this Lent that she'd never thought of how much her parents had given up for all their kids. Lexie had experienced a tiny taste of what they experienced as parents, but how did *she* react? She tensed every time she was asked to take on another chore.

She made a mental note to get to confession as soon as possible. Instead of being a happy servant, she turned out to be an angry servant. Instead of seeing this as an opportunity to show how responsible she was, all she could see was what she had to give up.

At the hospital, their dad welcomed them into her mom's hospital room. Lexie was so happy. Her mom's skin tone was much less pale than when she last saw her. One of her mom's hands had an intravenous tube inserted in it—a painkiller since she had received a C-section—and she sat up as she nursed the newest member of their clan. Their dad stood in front of the bassinette as their mom nursed the baby.

"What do you think of the baby, Lexie?"

Lexie inched closer. "He's cute, looks like Micah as a baby."

When the baby finished nursing, Mom wrapped him up and handed the baby to Lexie. "Why don't you change the baby, Lex?"

Her mom glanced at her dad, and he nodded. "Yeah, Lex. You change the baby's diaper."

"Um . . . okay. I never changed any of the boys' diapers when they were this small."

"I know. But you're old enough now. We want you to change the diaper."

"All right."

Their dad said, "The baby was only six pounds at birth, so that's much smaller than you or your brothers."

"Okay." Lexie carefully placed her new baby brother down on the bed. She unwrapped him, and he stretched and yawned. Lexie's heart melted. He was so beautiful. "Mom?"

"Yes?"

"I changed my mind. I want to have kids."

Mom's eyes widened, and a smile stretched across her face. "Really?"

"Yes, really."

She unwrapped the baby as the boys surrounded her, her littlest brothers on their tiptoes to catch a glimpse of Baby Dugan. Her father gave her a diaper and a baby wipe. The baby cooed and stretched when the blanket was completely off. It had been a few years since she changed

Micah's diaper, but he was a toddler. She had never changed a newborn's diaper. She took the baby wipe and pulled off the diaper. A black, tarry poop explosion covered the baby's private parts. Lexie blinked. She wiped, then blinked again. Her mouth fell open, and she glanced at her parents. "Um . . . um . . ."

Mom said, "Yes, it's a girl. And we've named her Leah. What do you think?"

Lexie could hardly speak. "She's . . . um . . . absolutely beautiful."

Baby Leah turned her head and opened her tiny mouth. Lexie's heart just about exploded with joy. She recalled Mrs. Eastman reading the Scripture passage at the beginning of Lent, *There is no greater love than this, to lay down one's life for his friends.* As she gazed down into the sweet face of Leah, Lexie remembered Mrs. Eastman saying that laying down one's life didn't necessarily mean giving up one's physical life but that it could mean giving up things in your life for someone else, like what Lexie did for her mother.

Lexie put a fresh diaper on the baby, wrapped her up, and held her in her arms. "May I hold her a few more minutes, Mom? Dad?"

"Of course," her mom said.

Her youngest brothers whined that they wanted to hold the baby. But Lexie ignored them, lowered herself to the hospital chair, sat back, and gazed into the sweet face of Leah, who squinted and pursed her little lips. Lexie picked up her baby sister's hand, kissed it, and marveled at how tiny it was. She stared in awe at the little peach fuzz on the baby's almost-bald head.

Lexie opened up the blanket. Leah's feet were so little. Micah yelled out, the baby was startled, and her little lip curled up like she might cry. Lexie kissed Leah's forehead. "Shhh. You're going to have to get used to the loudness at the Dugan home, Leah," she whispered.

Her dad said, "This week is Holy Week, then the Triduum, then Easter. Mom and I want you to pick out a dress for the baby to wear for Easter."

Lexie straightened. "Really?"

"Yep," said her father.

"Cool! It will be pink with little flowers!"

"Sounds great," Mom said.

At the beginning of Lent, all Lexie cared about was having a cell phone or getting home after school to watch *Gilligan's Island.*

From now on, however, Lexie planned to race home every day to help her mother with Baby Leah. And that wouldn't change when Lent was over.

###

"No Greater Love" is based on the author's experience many years ago as a pregnant mother on bed rest whose oldest teen had to care for his siblings. Adolescence is a time when teens struggle with self-centeredness, and this struggle is very evident in the story about Lexie. She, like

the author's son, at first resents the extra responsibilities, but like her real-life counterpart, she eventually realizes that self-sacrifice actually brings great joy. This theme of self-sacrifice is also prevalent in Gable's *Great War Great Love* series.

ABOUT THE AUTHOR

ELLEN GABLE is an award-winning author of twelve books (three of which are part of Catholic Teen Books), editor, book coach, publisher, marriage preparation instructor, Theology of the Body instructor, NFP teacher, and ghostwriter. She is also the mother of five adult sons, mother-in-law to three daughters-in-law, grandmother of two, and wife of 40 years to James. When she's not writing, Ellen enjoys playing trivia games, genealogy, watching classic movies, and playing with her grandchildren. For more information visit www.EllenGable.com and her website, www.FullQuiverPublishing.com.

7

Dystopian

A VERY JURASSIC LENT

by Corinna Turner

HARRY

"So I just toss it up into the air?" I eye the contents of the frying pan.

"What? No!" Josh takes the pan from the stovetop and gives it an exploratory shake, making the pancake slide from side to side with a papery sound. "You have to do it just the right way so you can *catch* the pancake again. Watch, I'll do this one."

He steps into the open part of the Habitat Vehicle's living area—such as it is with the table out—then gives the pan a sharp flick. The pancake soars up into the air, turns over—and drops neatly back into the pan, uncooked side now downwards.

Darryl smiles and claps, then raises a hand to stroke Kiko, who had recoiled slightly at Josh's sudden movement, hunching into his four long wing-limbs. The little quadravian—or microraptor as their scientific name is—quickly relaxes, settling more comfortably on her shoulder.

Nope, my big sis doesn't look at all bothered that we're about to try doing what Josh just did. I am definitely going to drop mine.

"Remind me again why we don't just turn them over with a spatula?" I say.

"Tossing pancakes on Shrove Tuesday is traditional," says Josh. "And it's more fun."

"Isn't any Fat Tuesday tradition I've ever heard of." And spending all evening clearing up pancake from the floor or ceiling isn't what I'd call fun, either. We do enough cleaning as it is, cat-like, trying to avoid the notice of any predator large enough to breach the Habitat Vehicle.

"It's a hunter tradition. This guy came over from Britain soon after the Rewilding and married into a big hunter family and brought it with him. Soon everyone were doing it. And . . . there we are." He slides the finished pancake onto a plate and holds out the empty pan, glancing from me to Darryl. "I tossed it, I getta eat it. Who wants the next one?"

I want the next one, I just don't want to toss it, so I let Darryl take the frying pan. Josh only has one—no space for clutter in a HabVi.

Josh ladles out some of the edmontosaur mince that's keeping warm in the OmniProcessor and rolls the pancake up neatly.

Darryl pauses, pushing her long brown braid behind her back, and gives me a meaningful look. Oh, right, it's my turn to say grace. Once I've finished, Josh digs in.

Of course, Darryl tosses her pancake so neatly you'd think she was hunter-born not farmer-born. And then it's my turn.

I catch it! With an undignified lunge, but I catch it. They clap and don't laugh—much.

"So, what do hunters eat on Ash Wednesday?" I ask curiously, in between tasty mouthfuls of my now meat-filled pancake. Something traditional, no doubt . . .

Josh's eyes widen slightly. "Nothing."

"At all?"

He shakes his head, still looking bemused.

Darryl's eyebrows go up. Oh boy. Dad always planned jobs on the farm so we didn't do heavy work on Ash Wednesday if we could avoid it, so we could fast. But we always had one meal and two snacks. Nothing? Seriously?

"You're only fourteen, though," Josh adds, tossing his pancake without missing a beat, "which is real borderline for manhood so you can eat if you wanna. If that's okay with Darryl."

Darryl nods. Josh is the boss, but Darryl's my big sis so some things he defers to her. But *this* . . . My cheeks burn. "I'm not going to eat if you two don't! Though Father Ben said you don't *have* to fast until you're eighteen, right? Darryl's only seventeen, so only Josh *has* to fast 'cos he's nineteen—and even he doesn't have to eat nothing at all!"

"Ain't right to eat on Ash Wednesday," says Josh firmly. "Not if you're young and healthy. But you two are farmers; you can do what farmers do."

"We're hunters at the moment." Darryl sounds stung.

"I'll fast like a hunter—unless it isn't safe." She hesitates. "Are you sure you want to do that T. rex nest tomorrow? Why not leave it until the day after, when you won't be hungry?"

Josh shoots us a sidelong glance, eyes crinkling, as he slides his second pancake onto his plate. "If I do it mid-afternoon, I'll only have missed two meals. What's that gonna matter?"

Ugh, hunters. Tough as rex hide. At home on the farm, large, regular meals were such a fixed part of the day. Whereas Josh thinks nothing of missing one because we're too busy or it isn't safe to stop for it.

If we're doing the nest, then one of us has to be on watch all night and most of tomorrow, until finally—if it's safe—Josh will creep up into those crags and sterilize the she-rex's eggs. All without a bite to eat until the following morning. Oh yeah, the next thirty-six hours are going to be super-fun. Though I guess Ash Wednesday isn't about fun, is it?

DARRYL

I guess it's no surprise hunters do a full fast on Ash Wednesday, since they tend to imitate Saint Desmond, the beloved patron saint of all those who live unSPARKed—outside an electric fence—and that's what he did. I've almost finished rereading *The Memoirs of Saint Desmond the Hermit* so that fact is fresh in my mind as I dig into another pancake.

It'll be tough, but I'm determined to do it. I wish Josh

wasn't planning to tackle such a risky contract tomorrow, though. We all ought to be at our best for that. Maybe Josh will change his mind.

After two or three meaty pancakes, we switch to sweet ones, piling on sugar and honey and the chocolate sauce Josh has saved untouched in the cupboard since New Year. Kiko gets a few morsels that he shouldn't really have since he doesn't brush his teeth, but never mind. It's only once a year.

Sugar granules ping from Harry's plate, making Josh glance around from his pancake-making, frowning.

"Harry, stop spreading sugar everywhere," I say, "or you'll be deep-cleaning the 'Vi before bed!"

"Do you want that she-rex to make sardines of us?" adds Josh sharply.

Harry's winter-pale skin goes bright red, and he puts down the sugar shaker. After almost a year in the 'Vi, he's basically internalized the scent procedures, the same as I have, but I guess in all the pancake-making excitement he forgot that he wasn't at home behind the farm's electric fence, where ants are the worst thing sugar is likely to attract.

At home. It barely feels like home anymore. Home is here in the 'Vi, out in the wilderness, with Josh. Sometimes it feels like we've always known him, like we've always been a family, even though we aren't actually related.

Harry's already fetching a cloth; good. We don't want that nesting she-rex popping down this hill, ripping the roof off and eating us up. After guarding those eggs for maybe a month already with little food, she'll be hungry. The 'Vi is raptor and allosaur proof, but armor heavy enough to protect against a rex just isn't practical.

Josh seems slightly on edge, despite the pancake fun. Maybe he doesn't really like the fasting much . . . no, it isn't that. It's the rex nesting. One of the most dangerous hunter jobs, second only to hunting raptors on foot. His dad *died* rex nesting.

"Oh, and we've got two rex nesting contracts," West told him, last time we met with Josh's "uncles" for re-supply.

"Give us one, then," Josh said, sounding slightly too casual.

And West hesitated, then did it. Had to treat Josh like a man, 'cos he is, even in city-eyes. But not being prepared to avoid something isn't the same as Josh looking forward to it.

When we're stuffed too full of pancake to eat another bite—Kiko sprawls over my shoulder, snoring softly—Harry pays for his sugary lapse by getting stuck with clean-up, while Josh and I settle down on each side of the table with a hot drink.

Josh leans back in his chair, sipping and staring at the photo frame on the wall. His dad's rosary hangs from it, along with a mysterious blue raptor feather that he still won't explain. The familiar family pictures cycle past—his dad, his uncle, and child-Josh at different ages, with the odd photo of West and the others. He doesn't seem to want to talk, returning brief answers to anything Harry says, so I pick up my handPad. I'm hoping to finish Saint

Des's *Memoirs* tonight, because I want to read *The Imitation of Christ* during Lent, the first proper grown-up book of that kind I'll have tackled.

This last chapter deals with the different theories about how Saint Des survived living in that cave of his for twenty years with no electric fence or armored walls to protect him from predators. A miracle, sure, but how did it work?

> Supporters of the Eucharistic miracle theory point to an episode in the life of Saint Clare that tells how, once, a fierce Saracen army invaded San Damiano, entering the very cloister of the virgins. Terrified, the nuns ran to their Mother Superior, Saint Clare, who lay ill in bed.
>
> Fearlessly, she got up and prostrated herself before the Lord. "I pray You, Lord, protect these, Your handmaids, whom I cannot now save by myself."
>
> A voice like that of a little child resounded in her ears from the tabernacle: "I will always protect you!"
>
> So, taking a monstrance of silver and ivory containing the Blessed Sacrament, she confronted the intruders, while her nuns—losing their fear—followed behind. Upon which, quite unaccountably, the Saracens took flight and fled, leaving them all unharmed.

Although the miracle of Saint Clare is categorized as a Eucharistic miracle because of the voice from the tabernacle, it is not clear whether it was the actual presence of Our Lord in the Blessed Sacrament that put the invaders to flight, or the sheer faith of Saint Clare and the nuns, or some other intervention from God. In the same way, we will never know for certain in this life exactly how Saint Desmond lived, preserved from all harm for twenty years amidst fierce predators. But that is all right.

We do not need to know how. Only that he did.

Thanks be to God.

The End.

"I do *like* the Eucharistic theory," I say, putting aside my handPad as Harry finally settles down with his own drink. "You know, Saint Desmond had a little oratory in the cave with the Blessed Sacrament, and that was what kept the predators away?"

Josh nods, glancing at the gun cabinet, inside which our own little home tabernacle nestles in the carefully converted explosives box. We are *so* blessed—a home tabernacle isn't a right, it's an immense privilege. Farms often have one, but HabVis don't usually—long story.

"Yeah, but he didn't carry Our Lord *around* with him," Josh agrees. "So who knows? I asked Father Ben, and he said that if you left the Blessed Sacrament lying outside most often an animal would simply come along and gobble Him up. When an animal does respond to Him, it sure is a miracle, no question."

He glances from me to the gun cabinet again. Right, he wants Adoration. What did I expect, bringing the subject up? It's Josh's 'Vi, but I'm the only one who has permission from Father Ben to expose the Sacrament, even though all I have to do is turn the knob to open the spiral lattice in the front of the pyx.

"Sure," I say. "When Harry's had his hot chocolate."

Josh gets busy folding the table up out of the way and checking the living area is clean and tidy enough to host a divine Guest. By the time Harry's finished, Josh has placed two unlit candles ready on each side of the gun cabinet and is eyeing me hopefully again. Josh is really badly catechized, even now, despite my efforts to pass on what I know—but he's always ready for Adoration. He reminds me of that wonderful, loyal dog Uncle Mau had when I was a child. The way it would just gaze at its master, not *understanding* but loving *so much*. Josh puts me to shame.

When I get up and head for the gun cabinet, Josh and Harry kneel, Harry with only a small, resigned groan.

It is Ash Wednesday tomorrow, after all.

JOSHUA

"Harry, you take the first watch. I'll take the small hours. Darryl, dawn shift."

We've finished Adoration, had another drink, and we're

ready to turn in. Harry's face falls and Darryl gives me an anxious look.

"Josh, are you sure we should do this contract tomorrow? Why not start stake-out on Thursday night and do it on Friday?"

It wouldn't be a bad plan but—I just . . . "We're doing the nest tomorrow." I know I'm coming off as bossier than usual, but I really don't know how to explain why I wanna. Tomorrow is a holy day, and I *need* that . . .

Fortunately, they're well-enough trained now to accept that what the boss says goes. Farmers don't argue back quite like city-folk, but they don't always obey quite like born hunters, neither. That settled, we disperse toward our berths—or rather, me toward mine, Darryl toward hers and Harry up the ladder to the observation turret.

By the time I take over from a bleary-eyed Harry the moon is out, illuminating the nightscape in a wash of clear light. Not that it matters, with the heat-sensors. But it does make the watch more enjoyable.

I scan the landscape by eye, then check the thermal images on the console screens. I send the drone out as frequently as the battery will allow, monitoring the whole of the surrounding area, going a lot farther out than I usually would.

The maze of boulders ahead blocks us from getting the 'Vi closer than a half-mile to the nest, so we need to be very, very sure there ain't any predators nowhere nearby before I set off. Trouble is, raptors can move real fast and we can check as carefully as we like, it still ain't impossible a pack could show up before I could get back to the 'Vi, especially if there were the slightest delay. And that ain't speculation—I *know*. Sure wish I didn't . . .

But the nest has to be done. The Dinosaur Activity and Population department want the eggs sterilized, with one left untouched. Time to let a baby rex hatch in this region. The goal is always to have enough rex to keep the herbi'saur population stable, with as few extra juveniles around to blunder through farm—and even city—fences as possible. It sure ain't worth going out there tomorrow for the money—I'll be going out for the farmers, for Darryl and Harry's neighbors and all the others. Even the crazy city-folk.

Usually I like doing a nest where you get to leave an egg. Nice to imagine the she-rex as a proud mother.

I stare up at the dark line of the crags against the night sky. Anger . . . *hate* . . . bubbles inside. *This* rex . . . I'd rather lug my rex gun up there and shoot the creature.

No. *No.* I struggle to let the horrible feelings go, breathing slowly, remembering sitting quietly in the presence of the Lord earlier. I do love having that tabernacle onboard.

The hate—thank God—fades away again, like water flowing downstream. Unfortunately, that leaves nothing to mask the fear, the fear that's had me on edge all evening. Every time I think about going up to that nest tomorrow it coils through my belly, freeze-drying me from the inside out.

It ain't so much fear of dying—first time I truly thought I were about to die I were eleven years old—that's just life, I can deal with *that*. No, it's the fear that when it's actually time to get out of the 'Vi and head up that hillside, I simply won't be able to do it. That the past will overwhelm me and I'll freeze. That the fear will win.

Saint Des, please help me.

Lord, give me courage.

'Cos that . . . that would be worse than dying. To lose myself like that. To lose *to* myself.

No, the nest has to be done. And I'm gonna do it.

DARRYL

The dawn light bounces off the mist, touching the rocky slopes with gold. It's harder to appreciate the beauty with my eyelids this heavy—usually I'm just getting up about now. Tired or not, I should enjoy the greenery while I can. We'll be heading back to the high snowy mountains as soon as we've completed this contract.

Josh and Harry are sleeping in, no surprise. I scan the landscape, then check the thermal imaging carefully. No sign of any carni'saurs. Time to launch the drone again.

Kiko lands in my lap, seeking attention, but I don't let him distract me. Later on today, Josh's life may depend on how well we keep watch.

It isn't much longer before slight movements of the vehicle tell me that Josh is up. He's always awake before Harry. Usually before me.

Soon the hatch opens and his head appears, dark hair

and terracotta skin damp from the shower. He settles in another seat, leaving the hatch open, of course, since it's just the two of us, and offers me a mug. I accept it and sip eagerly, though it's only boiled water. After sitting up here for hours, the night chill is getting to me, even in this milder region.

Josh stares up toward the crags as he sips his steaming water, his expression bleak. Has he done a rex nest since his dad died? I'm sure he talked about doing some with his Uncle Z. It seems to be a point of pride among hunter-borns that each HabVi does one or two nests each spring.

Despite the danger.

Finally, Josh gives his head a slight shake and turns his chair around, putting his back to the nest. "Any activity?"

I shake my head. "It's quiet. There are various herbi'saurs around. I kept a record, but if you stay alert and don't walk into them, nothing dangerous."

"Good."

HARRY

Hot water for breakfast. Nothing else. Then Josh burns a little pile of dried willow clippings up in the turret and mixes the ash with some Holy Water, reciting several hunter prayers seeking Saint Des's intercession for a safe and holy Lent.

He ends up with a pot of soggy ashes not unlike the ones Father Ben gives each household shortly before Lent—though I think Father Ben makes his out of old palm crosses. Occasionally he's even at the farm on Ash

Wednesday to administer them himself, but a rural priest can't be everywhere.

As the eldest, Josh stands in for Father Ben, the way Dad always did, carefully marking a cross on my forehead—"Remember you are dust, and to dust you shall return"—then on Darryl's. "Remember you are dust, and to dust you shall return."

For once, it doesn't make me want to giggle, everyone getting smeared with ashes. Today, out in the wilds, it feels really . . . real. What Josh is going to do later is dangerous, and there's no getting around that.

"Harry, you're the youngest." Josh offers me the pot.

Oh, do I have to do him? I take the pot and dip my finger—he bends his neck. I wipe the ash onto his forehead, trying to make a neat cross. "Uh . . . remember you are dust, and . . . to dust you shall return . . ." Annoyingly, my voice vibrates slightly, but Josh just smiles a thank you and takes the pot back.

No doubt there's a tradition for disposing of what's left!

JOSHUA

It's mid-afternoon. Almost time to make my move.

My heart's pounding in my chest.

I've gone over and over each scenario with Darryl and Harry, since they've never rex-nested before. They only need to fly the drone and lure the rex away and, above all, keep lookout. I trust 'em to do it. It ain't them I don't trust today.

Sweat trickles down my spine.

All three of us have stayed on watch for most of the day and we ain't seen no carni'saurs. No need to postpone. Part of me's disappointed, but part of me's glad. If I'm finding it this hard, even on this special holy day, how much worse will it be tomorrow?

I make one last check and force myself to stand. "Right." Ugh, my voice sounds like Harry's when he were ashing my forehead. I strengthen it, sounding too loud instead. "I'm gonna go below, get ready. Darryl, come down in a minute and collect the meat for the bait. Put Kiko in the critter cage—no distractions."

I slide down the ladder and move to the table, where my rex-nesting backpack sits—Uncle Z's, it were before—with its proper silent-release buckles. Not a scrap of Velcro, no zips, nothing to clink or clank and draw eight tons of motherly wrath with a mouthful of ten-inch teeth.

Opening it, I check the contents, though I only packed it earlier.

In my head, I hear my own voice, younger, higher pitched:

"Can't I do it? I'm fourteen now. I've done several rex nests already. Don't I need the practice?"

Sterilization fluid. Syringe. Odor neutralizer. Check . . .

And Dad's voice:

"Not this nest, Josh. You're not doing this *nest, not while your Uncle Z or I are around to do it."*

They ain't around to do it . . . no more. I'm the oldest and most experienced. I have to do it. Though I no longer wanna.

Oh, why *did West give me* this *nest?*
Please, Saint Des, give me strength!

DARRYL

When I slide down the ladder with Kiko on my shoulder, Josh is carefully applying scentBlock cream, pushing up his sleeves to do well above his elbows and smearing it down under his shirt at the neck. His hands shake slightly. I thought the only thing that bothered him this much was going in-city.

The cream is mottled brown-green for extra camouflage, which the now-smeared ashes on his forehead only help with, though Josh's darker skin always gives him an advantage over Harry or myself—except in snow.

I shut Kiko into the cage. "Josh?"

"Everything's ready." He grabs the little pack and swings it onto his back.

"Josh, are you okay?"

"I'm fine."

He steps toward the side door—but when he gets there he places his palms against it, leaning over, staring at the floor, breathing hard. Still shaking.

The possibility of being eaten is ever-present for a hunter, but it's never seemed to faze him. *Why* is this different, here, today? Is it just because it's a rex nest, and that's how his dad died?

Or is it . . . Oh, no, surely not!

"Josh, is *this* where your dad died?"

JOSHUA

When I don't reply, Darryl grabs my arm, pulling me around to face her. "Oh, Josh, it *isn't*, is it?"

I nod without speaking. My gaze rests on the floor beside the door—for a moment I'm down there, wrestling with Uncle Z as he tries to stop me from rushing out to help Dad—'cos it's too late.

"Josh! You don't have to do this nest!" Darryl's fierce voice breaks in on the memory. "You don't! *Ever*."

"The nest needs doing, and we got the contract." My voice comes out tight and flat. "So I do."

"No! *How* could West give you this nest?"

"He didn't know!" I snap, hating hearing my own accusation coming from her mouth. "He had two rex nesting contracts, and he simply gave me one. *I* didn't even open the file until later that day. Why would he? There's a lotta rex nests in this state!"

"You don't have to do it, Josh! Look, I'll . . . *I'll* go do it!"

"No. Absolutely no *short-circuiting* way!" I'm wearing a throat mike, and I lower my voice to double-check it's working. "Harry, all clear?"

"Y-yes?" Clearly he's heard what we've been saying.

"Good. I'm going. Darryl, be ready to lure the she-rex away."

"Josh—!"

I feel one hair from sitting down in the corner and sobbing and never moving again; the only thing that might get me out of this vehicle is the thought of her going up to that nest instead of me. *Yeah, that works . . .*

I hit the door's "open" button and leap to the ground.

"Josh!"

Letting it slide closed behind me, I set off up the hillside at more of a blind sprint than a jog.

No, calm down, Josh. You're out-'Vi. Get it together.

I pause behind a large boulder and draw in deep breaths, fighting for control.

"Josh, you okay?" Darryl's voice comes through my earpiece.

"Fine."

"Please come back." Her voice catches slightly. "You shouldn't have to do this."

"Shouldn't? What the heck does that even mean? It's a rex nest that needs doing, and that's all there is to it. We've done everything just the way we should. It'll be *fine*."

I turn and move up the slope again, at a gentle jog this time, watching for danger.

Harry's nervous voice comes from my earpiece. "But I thought your *dad* did everything just the way—*ooph*." He breaks off as though his breath has been driven from him by a sisterly elbow.

Yeah, thanks, Harry. Dad did *do everything just right, but that ain't really the most helpful thing to hear right now.*

Or mebbe it is. Dad did everything just right and he still got et up, which means it were his time. And if it's your time, it's your time. What am I worrying about? I just have to do my part the very best I can and the rest is up to God and Saint Des. *Yeah, stop being an idiot, Josh.*

I keep moving, nice and steady. My hands have finally

stopped shaking. Good. I guess making it out of the 'Vi were the hard part.

"Darryl," I say, as I get higher up the slope, almost out of their sight. "Start luring the rex away. Going silent now. Don't speak to me unless it's critical."

HARRY

Darryl pilots the drone with a chunk of meat dangling from a strong spiderline, while I maintain watch. It takes a huge effort to keep my eyes on my task and not glance at the drone screen to see what's happening. Without the drone, my field of vision is vastly reduced.

Darryl clearly appreciates how much of a struggle it is because—our mics carefully muted—she keeps me up to date.

"Okay, the she-rex has smelled the meat. She's getting up. Yep, she's following the drone. I'm trying to catch the meat between the two rocks Josh picked out. Almost . . . okay, the meat's off the line. She's maneuvering toward it, but not too fast . . ."

JOSHUA

By the time I reach the nest hollow, the she-rex is moving away, her featherless hide rippling as she stomps along. She-rex barely eat for three months while guarding their nests—she ain't gonna turn down a tempting morsel she can snatch quickly.

Okay, she's far enough out of earshot. I creep down into the hollow, placing my steps with great care. If I knock two rocks together, she'll be back faster than you can say "RIP Josh."

Here's the nest, a well-built, hard-packed mound. I inspect the eggs quickly. Four. Okay, this one looks the very best—large, strong, with good color. Rex Junior. Opening my backpack, I swiftly inject sterilization fluid into the other three, spray the nest with odor neutralizer—though this rex probably associates human scent with a tasty snack—and begin creeping back up the slope.

I've been real quick. That's good.

But I'm only halfway when Darryl speaks softly—and tensely—from my earpiece. "Rex on her way back."

Already? I move as fast as I possibly can, step by careful step. Heck, I chose a position for the meat much further away than last time. And she still got it too soon. Clever girl.

Heavy footfalls from the entrance gully . . . My heart's pounding but I keep moving, careful, careful . . .

The lip of the hollow looms ahead. Nearly there. Nearly . . .

"Josh, freeze!"

Misfire! I drop gently onto my belly on the slope and lie motionless, clinging tightly to my calm. It's okay. They know what to do. Just call the drone back, re-bait it, and lure the rex away again. And I lie nice and still here and try not to take a nap.

Nap, yeah right. This is *exactly* what happened to Dad. The rex coming back too soon . . .

Yeah, but that weren't why she *caught* him. She only

caught him 'cos the approaching Utahraptors forced him to make a run for it. So I'm *fine*. I just lie here quietly until the rex leaves again. So long as I don't move, I'm just a boulder to the she-rex.

DARRYL

My heart pounds wildly. With the drone on route back to the turret, Harry and I can't see Josh anymore, and that's almost unbearable. We just have to trust he's okay. "Josh would never move an inch near a rex, Harry," I say, though my voice sounds strangled. "You know that. He'll be fine. Just keep watch."

Pale-faced, Harry obeys.

Ugh, come on, drone, come on!

I've got the drone on the fastest setting, but a glimpse of something on the screen and I bring it quickly to a halt, zooming in one of the cameras.

A wave of coldness washes from my head to my toes.

No!

JOSHUA

Darryl's voice comes very, very softly, 'cos she knows the rex is in the hollow with me—in fact, the rex-mom is relaxing at the bottom of the slope, lying slightly on her side, huge head stretched out as she enjoys a ray of sun.

"Dakotaraptors coming from the north. About four minutes until they cut you off."

I squeeze my eyes closed, my cheek pressed to the rock, fighting, fighting to keep breathing ever so slow and steady and inconspicuous, fighting to keep hold of myself so I don't start to shake visibly.

This is exactly what happened to Dad.

Different species of raptor—brown instead of grey and a foot shorter, a little lighter, much difference that will make! *Saint Des, help!*

"Josh, what do we do?" Darryl's still speaking very softly, her voice shaky. 'Cos I ain't given 'em instructions for this scenario. There ain't nothing they *can* do.

Just audibly, I breathe, "Stay in the 'Vi. It'll be fine."

Liar. But what can I say? I've the same choice Dad had. Lie still and let the raptors cut me off from the 'Vi—almost certain death—or make a run for that lip right away and hope the rex lets me go if I make it over—very probable death.

But number two, beat the raptors back to the 'Vi . . . it's now or never.

DARRYL

I cut our mikes again, staring at the drone screen, where one camera now shows Josh, flat on that slope, while the other shows the rapidly approaching Dakotaraptor pack.

Fine?

"Liar, Josh!" I whisper, my hands clenched so tight they hurt. What to *do*? He's going to die, just the way his dad died!

"Darryl?" stammers Harry.

Josh thinks there's nothing we *can* do, that's clear enough. I mean, if the raptors come close enough, we could shoot at them, hope it sends them off in a different direction. But they look more on a trajectory for the rex nest. Are they hungry enough after the winter to try to steal her eggs? It's a large pack, ten adults and no fewer than five juveniles, their plumage many shades of Dakotaraptor-brown. Yeah, they're going for the nest, aren't they? And they're not going to come within range of our rifles. Curse this terrain! We can barely move the HabVi around on it at all, most directions blocked by huge boulders.

"Darryl?" Harry practically sobs the word. "We've *got to help him*!"

JOSHUA

I've been raised to be real decisive in a crisis, yet now I lie motionless, racked with indecision. *Weigh the odds . . .*

The odds say I make a run for it, like Dad did—but I know too well how it will end.

What will Darryl and Harry do? Oh, please God, let them stay inside! If they try to come help me, to attempt to drive the pack off . . .

Heck, if I get one hint of that, I'm gonna jump up right away, take my chances with the rex. Two rifles ain't enough to fend off a whole pack of Dakotaraptors. They've *gotta* stay safe in the 'Vi!

DARRYL

Saint Des, help!

Lord . . .

Panicking, drowning in helpless desperation, I slide down the ladder and throw myself to my knees in front of the gun cabinet, my forehead pressing against the cold metal. *Lord, please, oh, please! How can I save Josh? How?*

Deep down inside me, a little voice whispers that I can't. I simply *can't.*

I'm quivering on the point of total break-down when another little voice, that isn't quite like my own little voice, says: *But I can.*

I can.

I . . .

My brain thrumming with white-out hope, I leap to my feet and dive for the main console. Tapping quickly, I cut off Harry's communication with Josh, then type in a code Josh shared with me that will stop the doors being opened from the inside after they're next closed, until the override is input.

"Darryl, what do we *do*?"

Ignoring Harry's wail from the turret, I hurtle back to the gun cabinet, place my hand on the scanner, wait, then yank the door open. I genuflect, then place my hand on the scanner again to open the inner explosives-box-tabernacle, waiting impatiently. *Come on, come on . . .*

A year later, the lock clicks. I swing the door open, dip down to the floor and up again, then move aside the shimmering feather-fabric curtain with a trembling hand. There's the pyx, the size of my palm, covered by its lace veil. Drawing the veil off, I carefully pick it up, turning the knob at the back to open the lattice, and move toward the door.

I pause for a moment, drawing a deep breath. But . . .

I can.

HE *can.* The certainty that floods me is . . . absolute. Complete. Indescribable. I take one hand from the pyx and open the door, then climb carefully down to the ground.

"Darryl? What the heck are you—?" The closing door cuts off Harry's panic-stricken words as his head pops down through the turret hatch. *Sorry, Harry.*

Holding the pyx before me, I head steadily up the slope. Less than half a mile, an easy walk on the grass winding between the outcrops. Five to ten minutes to reach Josh?

"Okay, Josh," I speak very softly, "looking at your position right now, the very best thing you can do is stay still and wait, okay? Don't reply, don't make any noise. Just wait. I'll tell you when it's safe to move."

Considering the she-rex is resting comfortably right beside her nest, teeth bare yards from his heels, Josh must be puzzled by the idea that he should soon move. But he stays silent. Waiting? Good.

Because another thing I'm sure of: if Josh knows I'm out here, he'll feed himself to the rex at once if it will get me back inside the 'Vi faster.

HARRY

My mind spins, terror trying to overwhelm me. Josh is trapped in a rex nest and Darryl . . . Darryl is walking calmly up the slope, holding the pyx out in front of her like she's taking part in some kind of . . . solemn procession.

She's going to get eaten! They're *both* going to get eaten and there's nothing I can do!

"Josh, Darryl's out-'Vi; do something!" But how can he help her when he's stuck himself? *"Josh?"*

He doesn't answer. Is he ignoring me? He wouldn't ignore *that*. I check the console. My mike is muted. I try to turn it back on, but I can't. From that little symbol on the screen, the doors are locked, too. How did Darryl do that?

Movement on the screens . . . Oh no, the raptors have scented Darryl! She's not wearing any scentBlock. They're flowing toward her . . .

I yank the lever to raise the windows and position my rifle's tip through the bars . . . but they're too far up the slope. A few glimpses of feathery tails behind distant boulders, nothing more. I glance at the screen again, at the drone camera's view from above, my insides clenching up—

Darryl keeps walking right toward them. Has she lost her mind? They cock their heads, eyeing her, colorful ruffs flaring around their leathery faces. They dart back a few massive, bouncing, yards-long strides—Dakotaraptors are big, man-high, taller than Darryl. Then they cock their heads to inspect her again.

Again, they dart away, killing claws held clear of the ground. Why are they running? Is it her they're looking at—or the pyx?

Whichever, they keep moving away and she simply keeps walking, with reverent steps, through the Dakotaraptors and up toward that rex nest . . .

JOSHUA

"Okay, Josh." Darryl's voice again, still so calm that there must be some hope. Have the raptors moved away? Are they about to lure the rex again? "I'm here. Just get up and walk slowly to me."

What? Fear closes around my throat like a raptor's jaws, my eyes jerking upward, my head turning slightly before I can stop it.

She *is* here. Literally, *here*. Standing right on the rim of the hollow, holding . . . holding the *pyx*? The pale golden circle of Our Lord's Body shows behind the open lattice.

What the—?

My eyes dart down into the hollow as the she-rex moves, rolling, getting her feet under her. But she stays sitting, staring up at Darryl, at Him, her bushy reddish-brown crest feathers rising.

"Lord," Darryl speaks clearly in a gentle, soothing tone appropriate for an anxious mother, "please bless this she-rex and her un-hatched chick. *Come on, Josh.* Please grant them health and long life and plentiful prey . . ."

Oooookay, the rex still ain't attacking. Slowly, carefully, I ease to my feet and begin to move up the slope, resuming the chaplet of Saint Desmond I were partway through.

Jesus, I trust in You . . .

Jesus, I trust in You . . .

The mother rex carries on staring at Darryl. Or mebbe at Him.

"Lord, please keep them away from fences and from all conflict with humans. Please don't let them ever eat anyone or need to be shot."

No one *else*. Softly, softly, I pick my way upwards, step by step.

"And we pray, Lord, for the repose of Isaiah Wilson and beg your blessing on his son, Joshua . . ."

I swallow a lump in my throat. I'm literally walking over the exact spot where those motherly teeth sank into Dad . . .

"Lord, please bless this she-rex with mild winters and gentle summers . . . *Come on, Josh . . .*"

I creep faster, afraid to make sudden moves, but also fearful Darryl's inventiveness will run out and the blessing end before I get up there. Irrational, 'cos it sure ain't *Darryl* that's keeping that rex sitting there . . .

"Lord, may this nest be a safe place for this mother. May no raptors steal her eggs or harm her chick."

And I'm stepping up onto the rim of the hollow beside her, staring down at the she-rex.

"Amen," Darryl finishes.

Despite everything, I have a moment of silent struggle with myself. I don't wanna hate nothing, even this she-rex . . . "Amen," I whisper, adding my blessing to Darryl's—then I step slowly backward when she does.

"Just . . . stay behind me," says Darryl, as she turns around to face downslope.

"What—? *Oh . . ." Great.*

Dakotaraptors. A large pack, spread across the hillside, watching us. Darryl starts toward 'em, calm as anything. I guess she walked through 'em to get up here, right? After what just happened at the rex nest . . . I take hold of the hem of her jacket and follow close behind.

Is this all a strange dream? I feel awake. Uncle Z told me how he went berserk, once, under extreme stress. Ran at a pack of Dakotaraptors, single-handed, just him and his rifle, screaming like a lunatic. Chased 'em off. Has Darryl gone berserk? Like, spiritually? There's probably a special word for it.

Our Lord is obviously smiling on us right now, anyway. A big, beaming, luminous smile, bathing us in this inexplicable protection. It's beautiful. I just wanna enjoy the moment. Try not to be scared . . .

Darryl is watching her footing too carefully to pray for the raptors, so I recite Saint Des's "Blessing Over a Sick Carni'saur" as we walk. Okay, they quite definitely ain't sick—sleek feathers and rippling muscles—but I ain't feeling too inventive. The raptors follow us the whole way, peering curiously, whisking away, peering again, in that way they do when they ain't sure about something.

Soon—incredibly—we're coming into sight of the 'Vi, where a lonely figure stands in the turret, rifle raised.

"Harry," I say softly, "hold your fire."

This is a miracle. Has to be.

So nothing needs to die today.

DARRYL

Josh types in the override code to open the doors while I stand, still holding up the pyx as though inviting the raptors to adore Him. They keep staring, though I'm not sure if they're worshipping or just trying to figure Him out or simply not being allowed to attack us, somehow.

Despite the unearthly sense of confidence that I've floated in since that little not-Darryl voice spoke inside me, the sound of the sliding door hissing back has rarely been so welcome. Josh grips my waist, steadying me and boosting me as I place one heel into the foothold and climb up backwards, keeping Our Lord pointed toward the raptors.

Josh rolls in after me and hits the door's "close" button.

Hiss. Click.

Safe. My legs sag as the reality of what I just did hits. Josh catches me and lowers me to my knees. "Darryl? You okay?"

Nodding, I clutch the pyx to my chest in a rather unorthodox fashion because my arms are shaking so much that I'm afraid I'll drop it. Huh, what will Father Ben say about me taking it out there like that? I hope that was okay.

Then Harry's down the ladder, throwing himself on us and enfolding us in a tight hug, sobbing hysterically. Josh wraps his arms around us too, and Our Lord ends up squashed in the middle of the hug, but it's hard to believe He minds, there's so much love in it.

"I thought you were gonna die," Harry gasps, once we're all smeared with ashes and scentBlocker and sweat and tears and probably some snot. *"I thought you were both gonna die!"*

"I'm sorry, Harry," I whisper. "I didn't have time to

explain."

"Explain what?"

"That it was going to be okay."

"How could you know that?"

I hesitate. Here's where I'm going to sound like a crazy person. I'm limp and shaking now, but I still remember that absolute certainty . . . "I was thinking how I couldn't save Josh and a voice inside me that wasn't me—I think it was Our Lord—said . . . well, communicated, that *He* could. That's why I took the pyx."

"A voice you thought was God said He could save Josh so you *took the pyx and climbed out of the 'Vi?"* Harry's voice rises incredulously as Josh listens silently.

"Uh, yeah?"

"But when God says things like that it usually means, like, *don't worry that Josh is going to get eaten because I'll save him spiritually*—his *soul,* right? Didn't it even *cross your mind* that's what it meant?"

I pause, my mouth hanging open. "No," I say at last. "No, that wasn't how I took it."

"Perfect faith," murmurs Josh. "Like Saint Des. That's why God honored it. Whether you misunderstood or not."

Okay, this conversation is getting *way* embarrassing. Since when do *I* have *perfect faith,* like Saint Des? What I just experienced . . . that was a gift from God, it wasn't *me.* This is total speculation, anyway.

"Look, I need to put the pyx away . . ." I raise it with shaking hands. Josh takes my wrist, steadying it, then leans in and touches his lips to the glass and I've never seen a kiss more sincere.

"Thank You," he whispers.

Yeah, I know how he feels. I kiss the pyx too. *"Thank You."*

Shaking, wild-eyed, Harry leans in as well and kisses it without a trace of embarrassment. "Thank You!"

I stand, wobbly-legged, long enough to return the pyx to its secure home, then sink down on the floor again. Harry remains slumped nearby.

"That . . . that was a miracle, right?" he whispers. Looking at Josh, the resident animal behavioral expert.

Josh smiles, his eyes bright, his expression radiantly dazed. "Sure were."

"Is anyone ever going to believe us?"

"Nope," says Josh. "We can tell Father Ben. But there ain't much point in telling no one else about something like this—unless he wants us too." He glances up at his blue feather. "Trust me on that."

HARRY

We sit in silence for a while, until my stomach gives a mighty gurgle. "I am *so* hungry," I groan.

Josh and Darryl open their mouths—I scowl, cheeks hot, wishing I'd kept quiet. *"No!* I am *not* eating anything after God just *saved* you two like that. Forget it! Not *one bite* until midnight."

Darryl laughs so hard she holds her sides, and so does Josh.

"What?"

"Sorry, just picturing you hovering beside the fridge at one minute to midnight, waiting."

"Yeah," smirks Josh. "'Cos I promise you, *I* shall be asleep in bed."

I have to grin, too. "Oh. Yeah. Guess I will be too. We are allowed breakfast tomorrow, right?"

Josh nods. "Sure. Oatmeal. With the last of the ashes in it."

The ashes. We're going to *eat* them. Of course we are.

Welcome to Lent, hunter-style.

For some reason, I'm becoming increasingly sure I want to be a farmer. Unlike my big sis.

But we're all *alive*. Yeah, after today, nothing a hunter-Lent can throw at me is gonna make me waver. Grumble a little, probably—but not waver.

Thank you, God!

###

To find out how farm-kids Darryl and Harry came to be living a Hunter lifestyle with Joshua, pick up the first quick-read in the unSPARKed series: *Please Don't Feed the Dinosaurs*. Or for a full-length pro-life adventure, pick up the prequel novel: *BREACH!*

ABOUT THE AUTHOR

CORINNA TURNER has been writing since she was fourteen and likes strong protagonists with plenty of integrity. Although she spends as much time as possible writing, she cannot keep up with the flow of ideas, for which she offers thanks—and occasional grumbles!—to the Holy Spirit. She is the author of over twenty-five books, including the Carnegie Medal Nominated I Am Margaret series, and her work has been translated into four languages. She was awarded the St. Katherine Drexel award in 2022.

She is a Lay Dominican with an MA in English from Oxford University and lives in the UK. She is a member of a number of organizations, including the Society of Authors, Catholic Teen Books, Catholic Reads, the Angelic Warfare Confraternity, and the Sodality of the Blessed Sacrament. She used to have a Giant African Land Snail, Peter, with a 6½″ long shell, but now makes do with a cactus and a campervan.

To learn more, visit: www.IAmMargaret.com.

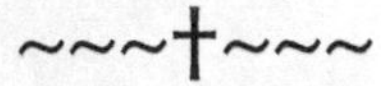

8

Historical

LUCY AND THE FORSAKEN PATH

by Antony Kolenc

The midday sky darkens—nearly as black as Father's mood. We trot in single file along the stony path behind Lord Barksdall and a half-dozen of his men. It feels like we've been riding for all of 1185, even though we departed for home only two days ago, after a fortnight's rest in London.

I caress my horse's mane and hum softly. The poor beast needs comfort from the approaching storm.

"Lucy, have a care!" Father says for the third time this hour.

I think he's forgotten that I'm almost thirteen. Mother was nearly that old when she married him and started our family. But he doesn't seem to trust me to do *anything* these past few months. In March—after he fetched me from Harwood Abbey for this trip—he seemed much more agreeable. But ever since that night in Lincoln Cathedral, his tone toward me has grown sharper while his faith in me has grown duller.

Specks of rain deepen the blue of my traveling frock.

"How many times must I tell you to tighten your reins, Lucy?" he calls back, shaking his head.

"Aye, Father."

I don't like to shorten my reins because it feels too much like I'm forcing my horse against his will. Plus, Midnight—that's my horse's name, his coat blacker than my hair—never heeds me anyway. He's a bit like my stubborn brothers. Truth be told, I miss all three of my brothers, especially Aubrey. I can't wait 'til we gather them from the miller at Leeds next week. It has been far too long since we've been a proper family . . . even longer if you count the years since Mother died.

"We should have taken that narrow path back yonder," one of the men grumbles. "Those clouds are about to burst upon us like Noah's flood."

Lord Barksdall turns in his saddle. "Nay, not *that* forsaken path. Better to take our chance in the storm."

Drizzle sprays our faces in the gathering winds. The cool, tiny flecks soon turn to round, hard drops. The rain pelts our skin and soaks us to the core, even flattening Father's thick hair.

He keeps staring back, and I can almost hear him repeat his latest refrain: "*You almost died, Lucy.*" He always says those words as though 'twas all my fault. Maybe he's right. Maybe I *shouldn't* have gone with Xan into that spooky Lincoln Cathedral in the middle of the night. But what kind of person would I have been to let my friend face that danger alone? Plus, I *didn't* die.

Father pulls his brown mare beside me. "I told you to keep your mount closer to mine."

"What did his Lordship mean just now?" I say to him. "What's so terrible about that little path?"

Father frowns. "Never you mind. Just focus on showing that horse who is in charge, Lucy."

Except I already know which of us is really in charge . . . and so does Midnight.

A rumble approaches. Two golden flashes wrestle on the shadowy clouds. The horses grow so restless that even the strongest riders must use their full skill to stay in control.

Midnight and I fall behind again, but this time Father is busy calming his mare.

"C'mon, Midnight," I say, gently tugging his reins.

Suddenly, a yellow flash forces my eyes shut, like the burning of ten thousand torches.

A deafening crack pierces my skull, as if God's hand has flicked an enormous whip to my ears.

A craggy tree bursts into flame along the road, throwing the men and horses into chaos.

Too late do I pull on the reins. "Whoa, boy!"

My frightened mount bolts away from the fiery tree, while Father cries out my name. Soon, all I can hear is the thudding of hoofs, the splattering of water, and the panting of Midnight.

Save me, Lord!

Lord Barksdall said he'd rather face this storm than take

that little path, but Midnight disagrees. He gallops along the forsaken path, away from the flashes of light and crashes of thunder. Nothing I shout seems to matter to the horse, so filled with dread that all he can do is run.

My grip loosens from the powerful impact of his hoofs upon the road. The saddle grows slippery. If I fall and break my head, Father will say once more that I was too young to take on this journey.

I keep jerking on the reins, shouting as loud as I can. "Slow down, Midnight!"

Another crack splits the air beneath the golden flashes and the shimmering raindrops.

A faint feeling washes over me like a wave.

My weak foot slips from its stirrup, and the strength in my legs fails. I fumble for the slick leather strip.

Then I fall from Midnight's back, and everything turns to blackness and silence.

I lie flat on my back. The puffy clouds hide the sun in the gray afternoon sky.

I know I'm not dead because my head pounds as though Aubrey is hammering a board next to my bed. Before I went to Harwood Abbey last year, my jesting brother would startle me awake most mornings.

The storm has passed, but I cannot fathom how long ago it ended. All I can say is that I'm alive and that neither Father nor Lord Barksdall's men are with me. Also, my horse has run off to who-knows-where.

On the third try, my weary, stinging body finally sits

up. My damp frock is torn in several places and covered with mud, which has coated every bit of my hair, too. My achy head seems filled with fog.

Why do they call this path *forsaken*? It looks like any other road: pits filled with rainwater, stones strewn about the muddy earth, weeds growing in bunches. *There*—Midnight's hoofprints in the mud heading farther down the trail. Perhaps he's grazing on the side of the road over that hill on the horizon.

This path may be forsaken, but no one called it *forbidden*, so I suppose I can search for my horse without breaking any rules. Plus, if I don't find Midnight, Father will probably yell at me again.

I stumble to my feet.

Praise God, I can still walk.

Travel goes slow at first, my muscles throbbing the whole time. At least the rain and clouds have cooled the worst of the heat. A pleasant breeze warms my face and dries my frock enough to pick off the mud.

When I finally clear the hill, Midnight's hoofprints continue down the road. He fled this way for certain.

I'm not the only person walking this path today. On the downslope, a bent figure trudges toward me. He wears a tattered, hooded cloak that runs to the ground—not a monk's robe, but nearly as dark and bulky. He has a cap on his head and a round object on a rope around his waist. Perhaps *he* has seen Midnight.

"Pardon me," I call, when he's close enough to hear. My voice sounds distant in my foggy mind.

He stops, straightens his shoulders, and takes hold of the round object. He rings it three times—a bell. That's supposed to mean something, I think.

"Can you help me, please?"

He doesn't respond except to shake his head rather crossly. Then he crouches to the path and gestures with his right arm for me to pass. His hand is covered with cloth, balled up to hide the tips of his fingers.

I draw closer to him. "I'm looking for my horse."

His arm thrusts again for me to move past. For a moment, the light exposes the secrets of his face, and it suddenly all makes sense: the cloak, the bell, the balled-up cloth, the refusal to speak to me.

That must be why they call this the forsaken path.

His cheeks and forehead bear many open sores: craggy wounds with greenish-brown gooey edges. His nose has partly dissolved into his face—obvious signs of his disease.

A leper.

My eyes recoil from the revolting sight, and my feet suddenly want to run away.

Nay, don't you dare do it, Lucy.

Jesus treated lepers with kindness, and the Church says giving alms to the sick is a Christian duty. Also, there's the matter of Ingrith, that sweet girl from my village. She too was a leper, living at my manor for years before suffering a horrible death from that disease.

Ingrith's family took good care of her, but they never let her speak with anyone from a close distance. They were especially concerned that she stay downwind from the rest of us. They feared the wind might blow her disease in our direction. Some in our village would grumble because she didn't carry a bell to announce when she drew near. Still, Father taught me to always be kind to her.

I walk several steps beyond the leper to place him downwind from me. Maybe now he will speak.

I greet him again without looking at his face. "I'm sorry. I didn't realize you were . . . you were—"

"Cursed?" he says, his voice hoarse and deep.

Some in my village used to tell Ingrith that God had cursed her with leprosy to punish her wicked sins, but Father said not all lepers are sinners. The blessed King Baldwin of Jerusalem caught leprosy when he was an innocent child, incapable of serious sin.

I shake my head. "Not cursed. I—I just didn't know who you were."

He draws his hood a bit closer; perhaps he's noticed how my eyes shy away from his wounds.

"You mean you did not know I was one of the *living dead*. That is what they call us lepers, lass."

I've heard such insults. A bratty boy once called Ingrith a *walking corpse* . . . but I'd seen her laugh. One time, she cried while petting a dog that licked her hand as if she were like the rest of us. Corpses don't cry.

I might not have alms to give this man, but there *is* something I do possess. I offer him my best smile. "I only meant to ask if you'd seen a black horse—Midnight. He threw me from my mount in the storm."

He glances at me and offers a droll smile, raising the

cheek that is unmarred by any sores. "Your ragged clothes and hair look nearly as wretched as those of us who live here at St. Mary's."

'Tis as I suspected, then.

This path is forsaken because it leads to a leper commune. Such places exist all over England—chapels with groups of lepers cared for by healers and priests. Father told me a council of bishops met a few years ago and made a rule that lepers couldn't live with the healthy anymore.

"Right," I say, sniffing at my shoulder. "I probably smell terrible, too."

The leper points to the place under his hood where his nose should be. "How would I know if you did?"

That was a jest, but I shouldn't laugh at it. "Maybe I can come and wash up at St. Mary's, if 'tis not far. Then I need to keep searching for Midnight and Father."

He nods. "Your horse is tied outside our chapel."

"You found him? That's wonderful news!"

"Aye, lass. I was surprised anyone would abandon such a magnificent beast."

"He abandoned *me*, actually." I laugh and force my eyes to rest on him without wincing. "By the way, my name is Lucy."

A *real* smile graces his face this time, raising both his cheeks high. "I am Flint."

"Thank you for helping me, Flint. Let us walk together to St. Mary's."

As long as I stay downwind, Flint talks quite a lot as we make our way along the forsaken path. He speaks to me as an equal, not as a child.

Before he got leprosy, Flint was a great man of London. He tells of times when he traveled to Flanders and Paris; he once saw the Pope at the Vatican in Rome. I wonder if he has anyone to listen to his stories. I suppose lepers are a rather depressing group, if they see themselves as walking corpses.

"How long have you been here at St. Mary's?" I say, as the commune's fence comes into sight ahead.

"'Tis five years since my son, Walter, shut me away here. Actually, that is the reason you found me on this path: I am expecting his annual visit today."

"How nice that your son comes to see you."

Flint's head droops. "Walter comes only with a document for me to sign. You see, he needs his yearly stipend so that he can live in comfort. I suspect that he waits for my death so he can finally inherit it all."

How sad. The only time Flint sees his son is when Walter wants some worldly possession from him.

"I'm sorry."

Flint shakes his head. "I am one of the lucky ones. There is a man here whose family held a funeral for him before sending him away. His sons divided their inheritance before his very eyes."

"Can they do that?" That sounds like a practice that King Henry's judges would find improper.

Flint shrugs. "Who will complain about it—a living

corpse?"

The path leads us to the chapel at St. Mary's, with its two sections of light-colored stones and a triangular roof that points to Heaven. Its walls are decorated with carvings of flowers and with that symbol of victory over death: the cross of Calvary where Jesus was crucified on Good Friday. Four wooden huts stand near to the chapel.

Flint points with his cloth-covered fist. "There is your mount, lass."

Midnight's dark frame stands out against one of the chapel walls, near to several lepers milling about dressed in robes similar to Flint. None approach Midnight, though. Perhaps they are forbidden to touch the property of others for fear of spreading their disease.

My horse seems healthy and refreshed, drinking water from a bucket and nipping a clump of grass. He doesn't seem to care that I'm back, either, as I stroke his mane and tell him how naughty he's been.

Flint points me to a well that is used by the priests—untouched by any leper. There I wash my hair and face and scrape the rest of the mud from my frock. While I clean up, three lepers tell stories, joking with each other near the chapel door. Two women—cloaks on their backs and veils over their faces—take turns throwing a stick to a fuzzy black dog, who retrieves it with a wag and a bark. Another leper woman picks vegetables in a fenced-in garden, while a man with a hood covering his face tends a few sheep in the field.

"Is it always like this here?" I say to Flint, when I return from the well. These lepers do not seem at all like living corpses who spend their days weeping and complaining. "You seem to be managing well."

"A local earl used to give alms to soothe our suffering, but nowadays we mostly fend for ourselves. We live in these huts like monks and nuns—men separated from women. We promise obedience to the rules to remain in this place. We abstain from meat, except on Tuesdays and Thursdays, if we can catch a coney or spare a sheep. Nor do we speak at table. Those who cannot abide these rules are expelled from here."

"Or they are given a beating," one of the other men says with a wink—a man with only one eye.

The rules here do sound similar to the ones used by the monks and nuns at Harwood Abbey.

Yet is there not sweet simplicity in such a life?

For months I've desired stillness and silence, especially with all the coarse talk of Lord Barksdall's men, and with Father correcting me at every turn.

"We pray *all* the time," the one-eyed man adds. "Seven times a day."

Flint nods. "Not all are happy here, of course." He points to three men sitting with their backs against the chapel wall. They are not laughing, but have a lost look in the black eyes within their sore, sunken faces.

"If it would be all right, I would like to go pray in your chapel," I say. "I long for—"

Just then, hoofbeats echo from the forsaken path. Two of Lord Barksdall's men gallop toward us on warhorses and draw to a halt: Sire Humphrey and his servant, Landric.

Father and Sire Humphrey were not friendly with each other back at my manor, and they have barely spoken all these months we've been together on this journey. My brother Maurice once told me that Humphrey and Father were both in love with Mother when they were young, and that Humphrey never forgave Father for marrying Mother. Even though Mother died, their dislike for each other did not.

"Lucy!" Humphrey's eyes widen with either anger or fear, I'm not sure which. When he looks upon Flint, though, his stare turns to rage. "Lucy, step back from this cursed filth!"

Humphrey draws his sword from its scabbard and points the edge of his blade in the leper's direction. Flint already is crouched on the dirt, hiding his face in the sleeve of his robe.

I do not move from Flint's side. "All is well here, sire."

With a huff, Humphrey urges his horse toward me, forcing me to take several steps back. Landric's mare follows close behind. They've put much more distance 'twixt us and Flint now.

Humphrey dismounts and towers over me. "We have been looking for you for hours. Lord Barksdall has ordered us to search for you in every direction. Your father is nearly frantic, you willful girl!"

I tell Sire Humphrey about Midnight and the storm and how I was thrown to the path. His expression softens a bit until I mention that Flint found Midnight and tied him to a post.

At that, he spins toward the leper. "You touched her horse with your cursed hands, you fool?"

Flint doesn't budge from his spot. Maybe he fears Humphrey's sword, or perhaps he stays down so that he doesn't risk infecting us with disease. The other lepers have moved far away from these newcomers.

"Please leave him be!" I say. "He's done nothing wrong. He was helping me."

Humphrey spits on the ground next to Flint. "Look at this creature, Landric, spreading its filth to all those around." He gestures to the other lepers. "And who knows how many others these have infected?"

Landric dismounts and stands beside him. "Shall we take care of this problem ourselves, sire?"

Surely these men of health and honor would not strike down a poor unarmed leper who has done nothing but try to help a girl and her horse! Still, Humphrey seems to be considering the idea.

"How many others are here, Landric? Are there any priests around?"

Landric gives a nod and stalks off to circle the chapel, apparently seeking answers for his master.

"You cannot possibly be thinking of such a wicked act," I say.

Humphrey stares down at the leper, who still has not moved. "*He* is the wicked one."

I stand 'twixt him and Flint. "But some say that lepers

are closer to God than we healthy ones . . . suffering their penance of purgatory here on this earth. They may go straight to Heaven when they die."

Father had used similar words to defend Ingrith in our village years ago. But if Father were here watching us now, he would see only a little girl chittering away at a grown-up.

Humphrey dismisses my plea with a wave of his hand. He is a hard man, yet nothing in his nature these past months has shown him to be the kind of person capable of slaying innocents. The few times we have spoken, he has usually been kind in his speech to me, even looking upon me with a gentle gaze.

His reaction to these lepers goes beyond any typical fear. Something deeper must be fueling his rage.

Why does he hate them so much, Lord?

"Sire, can I speak with you a moment in private, 'ere Landric returns?"

Humphrey grunts at me, but he steps away from Flint to a more secluded area for us to talk.

I follow him. "I know that I am only a girl, and you owe me no explanation on any matter. But please—is there not some other cause in you for this violent reaction? These lepers pose us no threat; they have broken no rule in their treatment of me or my horse."

His face hardens into rock, but then he gazes at me a long moment and his mouth turns down in sorrow. "Lucy, you look so much like your mother, you know. She too had a way of somehow piercing my armor."

He told me once before how I reminded him of Mother, though he never mentioned his feelings for her.

Now he lapses into a long silence.

"What happened to you, sire? Tell me, please."

He leans against a fencepost. "My sister's husband . . . when he returned from the Holy Land after his service there—" He sighs. "Little did the man know he suffered from such a disease. The signs had only just begun to plague him: numbness in his fingers and toes, loss of his balance."

He pauses, and it seems he might give up on the story.

"I see this is difficult for you, sire, but please go on."

His eyes hold only sadness in them now. "My little niece . . . so sweet was she to her father and so fond to sit close and hold him tight. By the time they knew of the man's disease, he had already cursed the dear girl with it, the fool. If you had seen the pain in her tiny face during her years of torment . . . if you had seen how the sores consumed her body and her soul . . ." He shakes his head.

"That all must have happened 'ere I was born."

He raises a gloved fist. "If this filthy leper were to cause you harm, Lucy, I . . . I do not know how I—"

An empty, far-off look enters his eyes. My face must remind him too much of Mother, whom he has already lost twice—once to Father and the other time to the grave.

"Let us go, sire. We need not disturb these poor lepers any longer. Come . . . let us ride away together."

That's when Landric rounds the corner, his footsteps heavy and purposeful. "There are only twelve of them, sire, and no priest or healer about—nothing at all to protect them. What are your orders?"

I breathe my silent plea to the Lord until Humphrey finally lifts his head from its stupor.

"Put down your sword and take up your mount, Landric. We must ride from this place."

Only after the horses of Humphrey and Landric have taken to the path does Flint finally rise to his feet. Though I sit high upon Midnight's back, the leper keeps his distance from me even now, making the Sign of the Cross with his cloth-covered hand. "God go with you and your kind heart, lass."

"And with you," I say. "I will pray God's healing for you . . . both soul and body."

Flint shakes his head. "From ashes this body came, and to ashes it shall return; that is the way with all of us. Your kindnesses today were enough . . . better alms than any I have received even from my own kin."

Though my heart breaks for him, I smile once more. It no longer seems difficult to gaze upon his sores.

Thank you for that, Lord.

I ride off with Humphrey. Perhaps he will tell Father about what I have done here today, but will Father find my actions good or bad? He will probably say that I should never have walked with a leper at all.

As we finally near the entrance to the forsaken path, a rider gallops toward us: Father. For a moment it seems his face has lit up with joy, but his expression sours by the time he halts at Midnight's side.

"You let that horse get the best of you, Lucy. Why did you not tighten the reins when I told you?"

"Do not be hard on the girl, Jonas," Humphrey says. "You should be proud of this one; she has courage."

Father glares at the man. "I will be the judge of my own daughter. Now go and let his Lordship know we have recovered my wayward child."

Humphrey shakes his head disagreeably, but does not argue. He and Landric spur on their horses.

After they've gone, Father speaks again. "You must tell me all that went wrong with you today, Lucy, so I can give a full account to his Lordship when we return to camp."

I ride with Father side-by-side along the forsaken path. I don't know whether he is angry with me, but he has barely spoken a word since I told him all that happened with Midnight and Flint and Humphrey.

As we near the intersection of the path with the main road, a rider approaches on a pony—not one of our company, but a young man in a red tunic and black pants. We halt beside the stranger, whose pony is much shorter than Midnight. 'Tis odd to see a man riding such a small mount: a beast usually reserved for women.

"Have a care, friend," Father says to him. "This path you are traveling leads to a commune of lepers."

"Aye. My father dwells there among them."

I cannot help but smile. "You must be Walter, then—Flint's son."

He nods. "You have met my father?"

"A wonderful man! He is eager to see you. I am Lucy, and this is Jonas, my father."

Father and Walter exchange the customary greetings.

This chance meeting with Flint's son seems covered with God's handprints. Perhaps I'm meant to give even greater alms to Flint this day—a chance for his son to see the great need in his suffering.

"Father, can we ride with Walter to St. Mary's? You would not mind our company, would you, Walter?"

"Not at all," he says, a bit reluctantly, probably wondering why I would make such a request.

Father eyes Walter distrustfully and then turns to me. "We must go, Lucy. Lord Barksdall has already set our camp for the night upon the main road."

"Then he shall not miss us if we are gone a while longer."

Father's brow darkens and he pulls his mare closer. "*Enough,* daughter," he says in a throaty whisper. "I will not risk further contact 'twixt you and those lepers."

He doesn't trust me anymore. He doesn't even ask why I want to ride with Walter. He doesn't care that I seek to comfort a good leper who suffers in this world as though in the fires of purgatory itself.

"You can't protect me from everything, Father. If you're afraid of lepers, then ride on to camp yourself. I'm not a little girl anymore. I can care for myself and go where I please if I—"

Father slices the air and strikes my mouth, the back of

his hand as angry as his glare. The pain on my lips burns more than the scrapes on my back from when I fell. A drop of blood sours the tip of my tongue.

"I said *enough*! If you take so much care, then why have you almost died *twice* upon this trip?"

I cannot stop the tears, they burst forth so quickly from the depths of my wounded soul. Only then do Father's eyes soften. He turns his red face away, his gaze as empty as the one Humphrey showed me earlier.

What must Flint's son think of me—a sobbing, bratty girl who needs her father's discipline? But Walter says nothing, his head hung low. Nor does he move to leave.

I somehow smother the sorrow within me before it overflows from my eyes again. Then I wipe the wetness from my cheeks with the rough sleeve of my frock and lick a blot of blood from my swollen lip.

By the time Father looks upon me again, his anger seems to have melted into regret, just as Humphrey's wrath at Flint seemed to fade only upon feeling great sorrow in *his* heart.

"Perhaps a small delay is possible, Lucy, if we take extra care at St. Mary's." The tone in Father's voice is gentler than I've heard in weeks—almost apologetic. "Walter, we can accompany you, if you'd like."

Flint's son nods politely. "Very well, then."

While we ride, Father and Walter share news of the world. I stay silent, but my muteness has less to do with Father's discipline and more to do with Flint's son. How can a stranger like me—a weepy child in his eyes—ask a grown man to love his father better and to visit Flint more often than he does?

Give me wisdom, Lord, to help open his eyes and to not offend with my words.

All the while that Walter speaks with Father, he studies me from the edge of his vision, his expression growing more curious as we go. He does resemble Flint, if I imagine the leper without sores on his face.

Eventually, Walter shortens his reins. "Let us stop a moment to rest."

Father and I dismount without incident but, as Walter swings from his saddle, he stumbles when his foot touches the ground. I almost point and tell Father that girls aren't the only ones who can make mistakes on a horse, but I don't want to humiliate Walter, whose face already has turned a shade of pink.

"Pardon my misstep," he says.

Not long after this, Father excuses himself from our presence under the pretext of stretching his legs. He heads into the brush and will probably be gone a little while.

Walter opens his pack and removes a flask of ale, from which he takes a long draught. He does not offer me a sip, though that would be customary. Maybe he is still embarrassed by his misstep.

"You're probably wondering why I wanted us to ride with you," I say.

"The thought crossed my mind."

"I want to speak about your father. He is a good man

who carries his cross with patience and faith."

"You are kind to say so," Walter says. "How did you get to know him?"

I explain to him about the storm and about Midnight.

"You are lucky to have survived such a fall," he says. "I tumbled from my horse last year and nearly broke my neck." He gestures to his pony. "This smaller mount has proven to be a bit safer for me."

While we speak, his left hand massages the fingers of his right.

"Did you hurt your hand when you fell from your horse last year?" I say.

"Nay." He stares at his hand a moment and then sips his ale. "What is it that you want from me, Lucy?"

I clear my throat. "Your father—did you come here today with another document for him to sign?"

Walter's eyebrows raise high with surprise. "He has told you about my stipend?" He folds his arms. "And why is my personal business of concern to a girl I have just met?" His voice is sharp.

"My apologies. I do not mean to pry, but . . . 'tis just—Your father yearns for the fellowship of a son. Could you not visit him more often? Would that not be a kindness you could show him in his suffering?"

Walter turns his face from me and begins to massage his hand again. I may have angered him.

"If you must know," he says, "today will be my last visit with the man."

"But what of your stipend?"

"I will come into my inheritance today." He points to his pack, where he must have put the documents.

"You mean for your father to sign away his entire estate to you?" That seems little better than the leper whose family held a funeral for him. I must make him see that truth.

He nods. "'Tis my birthright. Anyway, his estate is useless to him. The lepers at St. Mary's must share all their property in common. It does him no good to have a fortune he can never spend."

No doubt, Walter plans on spending that fortune himself.

"So you would leave him to die here without family?" I say, but with too coarse a voice.

At that, Walter thrusts the ale flask into his pack and stumbles to his feet to load his pony.

"You have no idea what 'twas like being raised by such a man. In his days of health, nothing I did was ever good enough for my father. You see him today as a kind, sickly leper, but he was not always so. Indeed, *your* father reminds me quite a bit of my own back then."

If Flint was like Father, then Walter must have spent his frustrating youth being treated as a little child.

Walter studies my eyes again. "Perhaps you *do* understand. I saw how harshly you looked upon your father when he struck you. Do not be so quick to judge me, Lucy. One day you may feel as I do now."

"Never," I say.

If Father got sick, I wouldn't abandon him to die in a

leper commune. I would visit him often . . . unless, perhaps, my visits brought sad memories; then I might stay away a bit longer. But surely I wouldn't take his property . . . unless there was some great need in my life, or in my brothers' lives. But, I would never—

Wait, Lord . . . is Walter correct about me?

The throbbing in my lip gives an answer I don't like in the least. For months I've resented the way Father has constantly worried over me. If this were to continue another year . . . two years . . .

I push that thought away and focus on Walter again.

"Whatever happened is in the past," I say. "You must see that your father needs you *now*. Can you not at least consider coming to visit more often to bring him comfort in his sickness?"

Walter reaches up to his pony's reins. The sleeve of his shirt slides down toward his shoulder, revealing a dark circle on the back of his upper arm.

Could it be true? Does Walter even know?

"You didn't offer me a sip of your ale," I say, as he climbs into his saddle.

He makes no reply.

"And your balance is getting worse—falling from your horse, stumbling here today."

He carefully slides his feet into his stirrups.

"Your hand is numb and tingly—that's why you are always massaging it. And just now I spied a dark sore upon the back of your arm."

Walter's face reddens and his head droops low.

"You are a leper, too! That's why you would not share your flask with me. And now I realize you have kept yourself downwind this entire time. How long can you hide your disease from those around you?"

He does not deny my guess. A moment of silence turns into many awkward moments without words.

"What will you do with your father's fortune once you get it?"

He straightens in his saddle. "I will enjoy whatever life I have left. I will deny myself nothing—no pleasure, no food, no comfort. I have earned the right to my father's estate with my very life."

Walter seems ready to continue his journey alone, but maybe there's a better way for him to consider than the plan he has confided in me. At Harwood Abbey, Sister Regina told me that the pleasures of this world cannot bring true satisfaction. Such peace of heart can only come through prayer and loving others.

Walter might be on the verge of denying himself true meaning in what remains of his life.

"Will you consider one thing?" I say, stepping closer as he tightens the pony's reins.

He stares down at me with dumb eyes. "What?"

"The estate that you seek from your father—if you were to donate it to St. Mary's it could provide the lepers years of sustenance. You could join your father in the commune. You could pray and find peace of soul, just as I found when I was at Harwood Abbey."

Walter's expression shows that he is truly hearing my

words.

"You can make peace with your father and with yourself," I say. "You can make peace with God. Would that not be a better life than the one you are planning?"

He spurs on his pony to a slow walk. "Farewell, Lucy. I wish you happiness in your future."

"Will you at least consider my words?" I call after him.

He continues riding but—before he is beyond reach—turns in his saddle. "I will think on what you say."

Perhaps that is the best I can do for Flint today, with such a brief time to speak with his son.

Help him, Lord. Help Walter see the truth.

With the end of my prayer, Father reappears on the side of the path. The throbbing of my lip and the grudge I now see within my own heart confirms Walter's warning to me.

Maybe this was how Walter felt when he was thirteen years old. Perhaps over time, the resentment and sorrow of a child can grow into the indifference of an adult. If I don't abandon this path that I walk upon, I might end up exactly like Flint's son—not even caring whether my father suffers death from a horrible disease—ready to claim my inheritance and let him die alone.

"Where has Walter gone?" Father says.

I cannot lie to him. "It turns out that he was a leper. He has gone on to St. Mary's without us."

"A *leper?* Did he touch you, Lucy? How close did he come to you?"

Father's eyes burn with the same intensity as when he struck me, but then the fire fades into that empty gaze again—the one Humphrey bore when recalling the loss of Mother.

That's when it finally makes sense. I am everything that Father still possesses of Mother . . . his only daughter. How must he have felt when he nearly lost me forever at Lincoln, and again today? All this time, instead of seeing the painful loss in Father's heart, I have only heard the anxious words upon his lips.

Thank you, Lord.

Today I wanted more than anything to open the eyes of Walter, and even of Humphrey. Now I see that they have been the ones to cure *my* blindness—to remove the log from my own eye, as Jesus would say.

I go to Father and embrace him as I haven't done since I was a child.

"Do not be overly anxious for my life, Father. We have to trust in God's will for us, do we not?"

He hesitates, but then pulls me closer. "You are a good daughter . . . the best girl a father could hope for. But when I think of this world taking you from me, it fills me with such—"

Warm tears wet my shoulder in the silence, until he can speak again.

"Can you forgive an old fool for his lack of faith, Lucy?"

I smile. "If you can forgive a willful, reckless daughter."

We hold each other a long while without saying anything else. Finally, we wipe away our tears.

When Father gazes at me again, the pride and love in his eyes has overcome any fear or anxiety.

My heart bursts with joy, for now I know there is still hope for Flint and Walter.

"Come, my dear," he says. "Let us fetch your brothers from Leeds and make our family whole again."

###

If you enjoyed this story, be sure to check out The Harwood Mysteries by Loyola Press. Lucy is a main character in that series, where she and her friend, Xan, solve spooky mysteries at Harwood Abbey and beyond. There are four books in the series thus far: *Shadow in the Dark, The Haunted Cathedral, The Fire of Eden,* and *The Merchant's Curse.* The short story in this anthology takes place shortly after the events in book two, *The Haunted Cathedral.*

ABOUT THE AUTHOR

ANTONY BARONE KOLENC is the author of The Harwood Mysteries, a multi-award-winning historical-fiction series for youth published by Loyola Press. He is a long-time member of the Catholic Writers Guild, and his novels all have the Catholic Writers Guild's Seal of Approval. He retired as a Lieutenant Colonel from the U.S. Air Force Judge Advocate General's Corps after 21 years of military service. A law professor who's had his works published in numerous journals and magazines, Kolenc now speaks at legal, writing, and home-education events. He and his wife, Alisa, are the parents of five children and have been blessed with three wonderful grandchildren. To learn more about The Harwood Mysteries and its author, visit www.AntonyKolenc.com.

9

Contemporary

BREAD ALONE

by T. M. Gaouette

Hunger gnawed at my insides like a rat on a bone. In my fourteen years of existence, I couldn't remember ever being this hungry. It had been almost a year now. You'd think I'd be used to it.

Mom joked that I was a growing boy, eating her out of house and home. She said it with a wide smile, but I still felt bad whenever I grabbed a bite.

I pushed my feet into my sneakers, tied the laces, and stood up, my toe pressing through the sole to the old carpet. I combed my fingers through my disheveled brown hair, avoiding a mirror that would reflect my thinning face.

A growl that would put a lion to shame escaped from my stomach, accompanying my walk through the hall into the frigid kitchen. I missed the warmth of our old home. The warmth of the hall rugs. The warmth of the cream walls lined with family pictures that were now boxed away in the back of a closet. The sun didn't shine through these windows. Not for me anyway.

Yanking the fridge door open, I stared at its pitiful insides. A lonely piece of cheese, barely a quart of milk, and half a tomato stared back at me.

I glanced over my shoulder at the counter and the few slices left in the bread bag. Enough for a tasty cheese and tomato sandwich . . . for one. My stomach growled again, urging me on. I straightened with a sigh, allowing the fridge to close. Mom would be hungry and she had to go to work. Her day job, after a long night shift cleaning offices. A big change from her former stay-at-home-mom gig, which she and I both missed desperately. She needed the food more than I did.

I grabbed the cereal bag, shaking half of the remains into a bowl, then covered it with enough milk to make it enjoyable. It went down so well and disappeared too quick. Mom would have made me finish off the bag. I'd have to leave before she woke up. One last, hopeful look in the cupboard. Three cans of lima beans. Who buys lima beans? Evidently someone thought it a good idea, then changed their mind. Now they sat in our cupboard.

With a sigh, I closed the cupboard door. It wouldn't be long before I could get a job too. Help out.

I stepped out into the cold morning, adjusted my backpack strap over my shoulder and attempted to zip up my jacket. Stupid jacket. You get what you pay for. Heading toward school, dodging slush puddles on the sidewalk, I held my breath as I passed a coffee shop. Last thing I needed were those sweet breakfast smells mocking my hunger. I could hold off till lunch. I always did. Course it'd be a cold sandwich. Mom was late paying for hot lunches again. I didn't have the heart to tell her. Besides, a sandwich was a banquet.

"Yo, Ethan, wait up."

The voice was like a slap on the back. I didn't wait up. I increased my speed, knowing it would be useless. He'd make sure to catch up to me.

Devin's footfalls pounded closer from behind me, then a hand grabbed at my backpack, pulling me to a stop. He swung around me to cut me off, his grin more of a jeer.

"You heard me, right?"

I didn't say anything. His hand clutched the front of my jacket now, preventing me from walking off. His beady eyes pierced mine, his forehead creased with frustration. He looked me up and down. "Man, you deaf?"

I eyed his clean Levis, leather jacket, and brand new sneakers. He always wore new stuff. "I'm late, Dev."

"You're not late. You're right on time." He released my jacket and his agitated expression melted into a grin.

I commenced my march toward school and he matched my stride, swinging an arm over my shoulder like we were best friends. I sucked in a breath and released it slowly. I knew what was coming.

"Listen, I spoke with Micky. Just two more hits and you're in."

He made it sound so easy. "I can't talk about it right now." I quickened my pace. My stomach grumbled. Not in front of him, *please*.

Devin laughed. "You hungry?" He stopped.

I didn't answer but continued forward, passing a crowd of people exiting a church. They spilled onto the sidewalk, breaking up in all directions. A small group lingered in conversation, blocking my path. I meandered around them just as Devin grabbed at me again and shoved a twenty in my face. "Breakfast's on me."

As I stared at it, my stomach protested harder, begging me to accept it, but my eyes found the faces of some of the parishioners around us. Signs of penance marked in ashes on their foreheads. That time already? My breath caught in my throat as I heard my father's voice in my head. *We use ashes as an outward expression of penance, repentance, and a fresh start.* I pushed the words from my mind, just as my eyes drifted to a face looking right back at me. A boy, maybe a few years older than me, stood amid the chatty group. His light blond shaggy hairstyle swept across his forehead in a surfer-dude way, making it hard to see his ashes. His stare caught me off guard and I twisted away.

Another laugh from Devin, who I assumed saw the ashes too, and I knew he construed them a different way.

I continued my journey, speeding to a jog as I crossed the street.

On my heels, Devin called after me. "You want this or not?"

"No thanks," I said, not looking back. But my rejection caused my stomach to growl its annoyance. "Quit it," I muttered.

"I'll wait for you after school," he said, finally giving up his pursuit.

"Don't bother." I threw the words over my shoulder. I knew I was pushing my luck with him. But I didn't care.

"Yeah, you got this all figured out, don't ya?"

I ignored the comment, widening the distance between us.

Still, his voice rang out, loud and clear for the world to hear. "If you're so smart, how come you can't feed yourself?"

Anger welled in the pit of my stomach. I spun to face him, walking backward a few steps as I yelled back, "There's more to life than food."

"Ha!" he yelled back. "Tell that to the growling bear in your stomach."

What a loser. Although, honestly? How much was I willing to widen the gap between us? How far was I really willing to go?

Repentance. A fresh start.

Devin had a way of manipulating me. I saw that now. But back in the day when we were young, I was blind to it all. Maybe he wasn't a bad kid back then. Maybe he changed over time. He seemed all innocence, hanging out with his small group of friends, welcoming me into the crowd. I don't know what changed him, if he changed at all. Maybe he was always corrupt inside. What do I know? Still, he was able to pull me in.

I'd made it easy for him, if I had to be honest. At least this last year. Opening myself up to doubt and depression.

He'd recognized that too and pounced. But it wasn't till recently that things got seriously out of hand. When I noticed the real change.

I remember the moment, clear as day. Him, leaning against a wall between Jim's Pizza and Bubbles Laundromat, ankles crossed, spying on me from afar, like he sometimes did. A devious smile twisting his lips. He pushed off the wall and headed my way. My insides knotted. He had a proposition. He'd heard about my dad and was sorry, and he wanted to help.

That was a couple months ago, maybe three. I forget. Did it matter? I recalled that moment so many times since. It could have gone so many ways, but the path I'd chosen was the worst. Why hadn't I just said no? Why hadn't I remembered my father's words? *There will be times when you're tested. Stay strong.* But it was hard to stay strong without my dad. Everything had changed and his strength had been taken away from me in more ways than one.

The smell of incense wrapped around me like a warm blanket, bringing me back to a time I wanted to forget, but still missed. Who'd have thought I'd be in church? Although not by choice, but rather by chase. Or maybe hide. I was avoiding a confrontation with Devin again. After our interaction on Wednesday, he'd been lurking around. I felt his presence like a stinking fog, eyes on me from afar, waiting. I didn't want to deal with it. I didn't want to give in.

I gazed up at the image of Jesus, bent low from the

weight of His cross. A woman reached out to Him. His mother, Mary. Her features drenched in agony. Whispered prayers drifted to me from my left, and I glanced at the small group gathered by the wall, praying the Stations of the Cross. I moved up closer to them, so I didn't stand out, but remained one Station behind.

The next scene showed Jesus crouching lower with His burden and a man taking hold of the cross, helping Him.

"Simon of Cyrene," someone whispered beside me, making me jump out of my skin.

I hadn't noticed his approach. I recognized the blond hair, flopped over his face, and I wondered if his folks couldn't afford a barber either. Except, his white shirt and khaki pants were clean and crisp. And what was that scent? A warm and musky fragrance that I could not describe broke through the incense, instilling a familiarity that I struggled to place. And while I knew we'd never met, he didn't feel like a stranger to me.

He grinned perfect white teeth and his eyes shone a weird blue. "Imagine going through that," he said.

I returned my gaze to Jesus. I couldn't imagine going through that. Instead, I walked to the next Station. This scene showed Jesus, the cross weighing Him down, even with the help of Simon. A woman extended a cloth toward Him, attempting to wipe His face.

"Veronica," the boy said softly, staring solemnly at the scene. "She's wiping the blood from Our Lord's face. You know it left an imprint of His Face on the veil."

Of course I knew. I opened my mouth to speak, but a

gurgle from my stomach responded before my words could. My cheeks burned.

He just smiled, adding, "You'll come down and share in a Lenten meal with us, I hope?" Then he wandered toward the praying group ahead of us.

A Lenten meal?

I stood in the vestibule of the church, choosing my path. The exit out into the cold and an empty fridge or the stairway to my right and a hot Lenten meal. I knew which way I wanted to go. The faint aroma wafted from the hall downstairs, enticing me. Should I? Would it be weird?

The boy appeared at my side. "Are you coming?" He headed down the stairs, turning back to see if I was following.

I wanted more, but one bowl curbed my hunger. I glanced around the room from my secluded table in the corner. The priest had invited me to sit with him and some others. I thanked him, saying I was fine, and found a table alone. I didn't want to talk or explain myself. All seemed like nice people—I even recognized some of them—but I didn't feel like I belonged with them. Not now. Not anymore. Maybe Father sensed that in me. Maybe he understood. He hadn't insisted. He'd just nodded and smiled. The servers had happily filled my bowl with soup and handed me a warm roll.

"Would you like some more?" the blond boy asked, by my side again. He sure knew how to sneak up on a guy.

The smell of musky spice wafted past me. Ugh, why did that scent seem so familiar?

"No," I said, standing quickly. "I have to go."

"I'm Angelo, by the way," he said.

"Ethan." I wedged my arms into the sleeves of my jacket. Like a fool, I attempted my zipper. What was I expecting, a miracle? Then as quickly as I'd thought it, the zipper worked. For the first time in . . . I couldn't even remember how long. I grinned at Angelo, but he just offered me an amused smirk. He must have thought I was some crazy homeless person.

I trudged the darkening streets thinking about Jesus, a bread roll dipped in soup, and a possible new friend. While the meal hadn't completely satisfied my hunger, it would sustain me for a while.

But the evening had left me with something else. A familiar feeling. Comfortable. Like when my father had been around. I crossed the street, pausing to let a car pass, and resumed my trudge and thoughts.

"You try'na avoid me, Ethan?"

The voice broke out of the dusk and made me start. I slowed and looked behind me in both directions. A silhouette stepped out of the shadows.

I groaned and mumbled, "Why would I do that?" I couldn't shake this guy! I quickened my pace.

Devin marched up beside me and slung his arm over my shoulder, his face so close to mine his sour breath turned my stomach. "You close, man. Don't mess it up now."

"Yeah, well, I changed my mind."

It took a second for him to cut me off and shove me against a wall. Benny's Burger Bar. Perfect. He didn't bother to hide his expression of shock.

I grunted when my back hit the bricks.

"What? You're as good as in."

"I decided I don't want to do that. I really wasn't into it in the first place." It was true. I did it in a moment of desperation. I was in a low mood, what with my dad and all. The sadness and worry in my mother's eyes. The fear that ate at me.

He pulled me off the wall and hung an arm around my shoulder again, with more force than usual. He guided me down the street. "It's like you just don't know a good thing when you see it."

Oh, I'm beginning to see it. I'm beginning to see it all.

He turned down a side street. "I'm trying to help you."

I jabbed him with my elbow and shoved him off me with my hands. But he rebounded fast to my side and directed me toward the window of a store, practically pushing my face against the cold glass.

"Look . . ." he said, nodding into the store.

I eyed the sparkling and glistening offerings on display and in jewelry cases. I knew the store. I passed it often.

He released me. "This is your next hit," he said bouncing his eyebrows. "A sweet, innocent-looking kid like you . . ." He looked me up and down. "They'd never suspect a thing."

I wasn't sure how to take that. "Not interested," I said.

Devin glared at me. Then he glanced around, as if about to share a secret. I didn't want to know what it was, but he pulled a wallet from his back pocket. "You know as well as I do, this is a good gig." He opened his wallet and revealed a wad of hundreds that choked me.

That could buy a lot of burgers.

I blinked and glanced away to prevent my eyes from widening, desperate to appear nonchalant. If Devin knew my need . . . if he really knew it, to its core, he'd have had me with a little more prompting. But he said nothing, just glared into my eyes with a look of disgust, as if I'd lost my mind.

I sneered. A weak attempt at a response, I admit. But the words that had gathered in my throat pushed against the back of my clenched teeth, eager to be released were, *Yes, okay, let's do it. Let's do it now.* All they needed was a thief. I could do it. I'd done it before. I was hungry. My mother was hungry. My father was gone. I needed this. We had bills. Rent was late, funeral expenses left unpaid. Medical bills from a long stretch of cancer. I could see my mom now, sitting at the table, head in hands with a messy pile of bills in front of her . . . didn't they justify this? "They're trying to squeeze blood out of a stone," she'd said, releasing a soft laugh when she saw me watching from the shadows, but the tears in her eyes revealed her pain.

"Seriously, man?" Devin's voice jogged me from my thoughts. "What are you doing? I have rank. Know what

I'm saying? I can recruit you now. Just say the word. I can help you. You can have all this too. You can get out of this hole. You don't have to stand there looking like you're homeless. Come on. You're practically skin and bones."

He was half right. I snorted. It's all I could muster. Even after my Lenten meal, the hunger was back and it ate at me.

"Don't do that." He shook his head obstinately. "Don't diss me like that. If you knew what I could do for you, you'd be on your knees."

I tipped my head. "My dad used to say that there's only One I should kneel before."

Now he snorted, turning away from me. "Your dad's dead, dude. Who cares?"

My hands clenched into fists. I could have pounded him. I wanted to pound him. He knew I could pound him. I'd done it before. When we were in elementary school together. When we *were* best friends. Instead, I pushed him out of my way and walked off.

"You're making a mistake, Ethan. Not kidding. This was your way out. You just blew it."

I blew it. I blew it. Sometimes I wished I could just blow it all up.

Shhh. A voice whispered in my head. *Don't talk like that.*

I was going crazy. I was poor, hungry, and now insanity was setting in. *Oh, God. God, it's been so long. Ever since Dad died. What was it—almost a year ago?*

The following week dragged, but finally it was Friday. I

had soup and a bread roll on the brain. But it wasn't just that. I really wanted to pray the Stations again. It brought the warmth back. I missed the warmth.

Angelo stood next to me as we prayed the Stations in synch, lagging one Station behind the main group like last time. He didn't seem to mind.

"We adore Thee, O Lord Jesus Christ, and bless Thee. Because by Thy holy Cross Thou hast redeemed the world."

Each Station reminded me of the extent to which our Lord was willing to go for us. The depth of His mercy. For me. For my sins. And how did I repay Him?

Repentance. A fresh start.

How did the world flip over so fast? How had I so easily forgotten? It's all I could think about until time came to eat, leaving me with an ache that paralyzed me.

As I stood in line waiting to be served, my eyes stung and my chest constricted, freezing me to the spot.

"Are you okay?" Angelo stood beside me.

"No," I whispered, looking at my sneakers. "No, I'm not okay." Warm tears dropped onto my cheeks.

I turned away and headed to a nearby table, where I slumped onto a chair. How long could I go on this way? I'd held onto this agony for so long with a vice-like grip, it actually hurt to try and let go. But I couldn't hold on forever.

As Angelo sat opposite me, waiting in silence, a server appeared at my side and placed a bowl of tomato soup in front of me. A bread roll beside it.

"Thank you," I whispered, not looking up. The delicious steam curled up toward me, its heat touching my skin, its aroma falling flat on my senses.

"It won't be enough," I said, as a tear plunged into the red abyss. I wiped my face with the heels of my hands. "I'll still be hungry."

I looked up at Angelo, who nodded, as if he knew what I meant. I doubted he did.

"I'm always hungry," I said. "And I'm always cold. And . . . it's like something broke inside me."

He remained quiet, holding my stare as if his life depended on it. Or maybe mine did. He probably felt sorry for me, and that's definitely not what I wanted. I don't know what I wanted. I don't know why I'd said what I'd said. It was so revealing and weak. I shook my head, resting my elbows on the table on either side of my meal, and grabbing my hair with fists.

"Of course it won't be enough," Angelo said, finally, leaning in toward me as he spoke. "Your hunger is deeper than that."

I crunched my brows. How did he know that? Of course he knew. Everyone at this parish probably knew. They knew my dad. They knew what happened to him.

I had to stop. I needed to crush this pity-party. It was too . . . honest. "It's nice being back here," I said, looking past his shoulder at the group sitting together eating their Lenten meal. "I used to come here. With my mom and dad. Until . . ." I couldn't say it.

"I know," he said. "I'm sorry."

I narrowed my eyes. "I don't remember you being here."

"That's okay," he said. And then he held my stare as if he was planning on saying more, but he didn't. He just stared. There was something so familiar about him, but I was absolutely sure I'd never met him. There was no doubt about that.

Finally, I blinked, breaking away, and looked down at my soup.

"My mom won't come back. Too many memories, I guess." I shrugged. "Or maybe she doesn't want to be pitied. Doesn't want people to feel sorry for her. I'd have her come here with me, but she has a hard time accepting charity."

"This isn't charity," Angelo said. He looked around. "This is just friends praying and sharing a meal together."

I looked around too, mulling his words and seeing the group at the long table laughing and chatting enthusiastically. I knew he was right. I saw it that way too.

"What about your mom? Does she mind you hanging out with me this whole time?" I stared at the group again, singling out the woman I guessed was his mom.

Angelo smiled, not looking back. "I'm talking to my friend."

Leaving the warmth of the church, I held the covered bowl of leftover soup for my mom. A movement on my left caught my attention, and I blew out a heavy breath.

Devin stood leaning against the railings lining the path

from the church entrance to the street. "I thought you were done with this place," he said, pushing himself off the railings and moving into my path.

My chest tightened. "What's it to you?"

"They can't help you. You know that, right?"

I passed him. "Why you always in my business, Dev?"

"Just trying to help."

I shook my head.

"What? You think your God can fix it all? You think He can save you from this life? This pitiful existence? Oh, that's right, all you have to do is pray, right? How's that worked out for you?" And then he laughed. "Oh, man, you are stupid."

I chose to ignore him, walking again and hopefully leaving him behind.

"You think I'm wrong?" His footfalls scurried behind me. "Alright then. Get on your knees and pray now, beg Him to fix it all, and let's see what happens. Let's see if He'll save you. Better still . . ." He ran around me, cutting me off in his usual fashion. He seemed almost desperate in his demeanor. "Kneel in the middle of that busy road and pray. Pray hard like your life depends on it, 'cause it does, and see if He stops all the traffic and makes all your dreams come true."

Start fresh.

"You're an idiot." I scoffed, pushing passed him. "It's like you've never learned anything." I stomped off but turned back to look at him.

He stood in the same spot. Evidently, not interested in

following me now.

I stopped with a few yards of distance between us and glared at him. "We both went to this same church! Learned the same things! We both know that's not how it works." It was hard to believe, really, how Devin had changed so drastically. "Why do you keep talking like you're bigger than it all? You know what will happen. You know how it will end. I made my choice. Time to give up the act, Dev, and make yours."

Devin held my glare only for a moment. A moment in which he could have turned it all around. A moment in which he could have snapped out of his madness. But he snickered at me instead. "I made it," he said, gesturing his hands out from his sides with his palms up, as if presenting a better self. Then he spun on his heel. "You're on your own," he called back, throwing a hand up and waving me away.

Was I though?

As I watched him walk off, wondering if this would really be the last time he harassed me, something caught my eye at the church entrance. Angelo stood there, watching. Had he heard? If he had, he showed no reaction. He watched Devin walk away, and then he shifted his glance to me and smiled, holding my gaze for a moment before he waved. Then he turned back, disappearing into the church.

The next afternoon, Saturday, the doorbell rang. Mom opened the door to a group of five women. I recognized them from church.

Pots and bags weighed them down. The woman heading the group, the one I guessed was Angelo's mother, smiled at Mom. "Oh, Maria, we hope you don't mind," she said. "We miss you, and we waited as long as we could, but we just had to see you. Do you mind at all?"

Mom smiled in return and eyed the stuff they carried. "Masey, what is all this?"

"This? This is just an excuse to see you."

"I don't know what to say."

"It's no trouble. We're your church family. May we come in?"

"Of course." Blushing, Mom stepped back and to the side to allow the women in.

"Thank you. Come on, girls."

"The house is a mess," Mom muttered, running her fingers through her tangled hair and straightening her shirt.

"We don't mind. Is that the way to the kitchen?" Masey pointed and set off in its direction.

I flicked my glance from face to face as they passed me, and then over their shoulders and toward the open door, wondering if Angelo was among them. It had been nice to have a friend again. But all I saw was Devin strolling past my house on the other side of the street, hands in his jacket pockets, his eyes on me, a smirk on his lips.

Mom tugged at my shirt and widened her eyes. I shrugged and eased out a comforting smile as I followed the ladies to the kitchen.

As they set to work emptying their bags, Mom sidled next to me. "What is all this?" she whispered, eyeing the women.

The women offered Mom kind words of reassurance that everything was going to be okay as they carried on with their tasks, filling our cabinets and fridge with groceries that could make even lima beans taste good. Masey started warming the food in pots.

"It's okay, Mom," I said, squeezing her arm. I knew how she felt about charity. I knew she didn't want me to worry or to think that she couldn't take care of me. "We know what it feels like to be on this end. But one day, we'll be the ones helping, right?"

She nodded hesitantly, then looked at me with suspicious eyes and asked in a low voice, "You do this?"

I shook my head. "No, but I'll bet Angelo did."

"Angelo?" She drew her eyebrows together.

"He's a friend from church. You should meet him."

The playful smile crunched into a frown. "Oh, Church?"

I bobbed my head slowly.

She bit her lip.

"I really want us to go back to church, Mom," I said. "Can we?"

She sighed heavily. "I don't know, Ethan."

"Please, Mom."

She peered over my shoulder, anxiously eyeing the women at work. "Can we talk about this later?"

I followed her glance, seeing a mom placing cereal, rice cakes, and pop tarts into a cupboard. So many choices, but

I had to focus. We could talk about it later, but it all ate at me now and I just needed to get it all out. "Mom, I miss Dad too."

Her eyes shot back to me, and her mouth opened as if she was about to respond. But no words came.

"I just feel like . . . we need to go back. He'd want us to."

"Oh, Ethan." Tears filled her eyes.

"It wasn't His fault, Mom."

"Whose?"

Who *was* I talking about? But I knew. "God's . . . Dad's . . . neither of them did this."

"I know that." She looked to the floor. "I'm sorry. There's just still so much anger . . ."

I struggled to swallow the rock in my throat. "Dad would want us to go back. We need to go back."

"What's the point? I mean, look at this." She turned, gesturing at the small kitchen around us and the pitifulness of it all. So different from the house we shared with Dad, when we could afford a house.

"Yeah," I said, nodding. "Look at this." And I gestured to the women around us laughing and preparing food. The sun shone through the window, beaming its warmth into the space. I looked back at Mom. "Even Jesus needed someone to help carry His cross."

Mom's sad expression warmed into a smile.

A woman approached, brows lifted in question. "Was wondering if you minded us setting up in the living room?"

"Setting up?" Mom's eyes narrowed.

"For brunch," the woman said. "We'd love to share this meal with you, if that's okay."

Mom bit her lip, and I knew she was holding in more tears. "I'd love that," she managed to mutter. "Please, let me help you." And she left my side to assist.

"Angelo isn't here?" I asked Angelo's mom, as she stirred meatballs and sauce in a pot.

She offered a warm smile. "Angelo?"

"Your son. We're friends."

The woman's forehead creased. "I'm sorry, honey, you must have me mixed up with someone else. I don't have a son."

Hmm. Misjudged that one. "Well, you probably know who I mean. I met him at Stations. Blond shaggy hair, always wears a white dress shirt and khakis."

The woman looked off into space and bit her lip as if trying to recall. Strange. If Angelo wasn't her son, she should at least recognize his description. She must have seen him. He literally hung out with them the whole time. Standing by them, praying alongside . . .

As I thought about it, my chest tightened. I'd never actually seen Angelo interacting with the others. He wandered around them but never talked to them, and he seemed to appear as if by—

A warm and musky scent overcame the aroma of meatballs, circling around me. I turned, searching the small space. I didn't see him. But I was sure—as sure as I was standing there myself, as sure as I now was about who Angelo was—that he was by my side, where he'd always been every day of my existence, and would continue to be until my last day on Earth. My real best friend. One who would never lead me astray, but instead light, guard, rule, and guide my every move. Reminding me of my father's words. *Repentance. A fresh start*. Which reminded me of my Father's mercy and a hope-filled future. It wouldn't be easy and I'd have to make amends.

Maybe after brunch, Mom would agree to go to confession with me so that tomorrow we could return to Mass and receive Jesus. Joy welled in me at the thought. And for the first time in a long, long time, I was sure that I truly wasn't alone, and that I didn't ever have to be hungry again.

###

In the Gospel of Luke, we are told that for forty days Jesus remained in the desert, fasting and praying. When He grew extremely hungry, the devil tried to tempt Jesus in His vulnerable state, but He prevailed. He remained strong and steadfast and loyal to His Father. "Bread Alone" is a reflection of Jesus' experience in the desert. Ethan is also tempted during his time of personal suffering. He had his moment in the desert during Lent, when he felt all was lost and he was so close to giving in. But like Jesus, he held on and with the help of his angel, he prevailed. We have those moments too. And we can

prevail if we hold strong to Our Lord, reminding ourselves of his love and great mercy.

T.M. Gaouette's novels and stories often reflect the struggles and temptations that teens face. For more stories with exciting twists and colorful characters, reflecting God's mercy, check out her Faith & Kung Fu Series.

ABOUT THE AUTHOR

T.M GAOUETTE is the award-winning author of the Faith & Kung Fu series for young adults. This series won a second place Catholic Media Book Award in 2022 for Best New Religious Book series. The last book in the series, *Loving Gabriel,* also won second for Best Books for Youth (17-21). Gaouette is also the author of *The Destiny of Sunshine Ranch, Shadow Stalker,* and *For Eden's Sake*. The latter received an endorsement from Evangelist Alveda C. King in addition to winning a first place Catholic Press Association award in 2020 for Books for Young Adults. She also contributed to the last three Catholic Teen Books anthologies, *Secrets: Visible & Invisible* with her short story "Sister Francesca," *Gifts: Visible & Invisible* with "Just Jesus," and *Treasures: Visible & Invisible* with "In Mouth of Friend and Stranger." Her novels have received the Catholic Writers Guild Seal of Approval.

Born in Africa, raised in London, England, Gaouette now lives on a small farm in New England with her husband, where she homeschools their four children, raises goats, and writes fiction for teens and young adults. A former contributor for Project Inspired, Gaouette's desire is to instill the love of God into the hearts of her readers. You can find out more at www.TMGaouette.com.

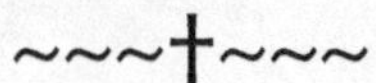

10

Historical

PREPARE THE WAY

by Theresa Linden

Somewhere between the Jordan River and Jericho, Asher spotted shadows moving along the craggy hills on either side of him and his goat, Juniper. Bandits! His hand slid to the sizeable bag of coins that hung from his leather belt.

Juniper pulled a wagon half-loaded with goods: salt, honey, spices, pottery, and fabric that his mother and sisters had woven. Asher had sold quite a bit at the marketplace in a little village just west of the Jordan River. With a heavier coin bag than what he'd brought home his last few market days on his own, *Abba*, his father, would be pleased . . . provided Asher and the goods that didn't sell made it home safely. Along with the money. Once the weather warmed a bit more—maybe in a few weeks—the river would go down and he'd be able to sell at the marketplace in Bethabara beyond the Jordan.

A skeleton lay ahead on the path, maybe of a gazelle or a goat. Asher's gaze shifted to the craggy hills on his right. Then to his left. No sign of the bandits he'd detected a moment ago. Where had they gone?

"*Hashash,* Juniper. We need to get home." Asher grabbed the lead attached to Juniper's harness and trotted a few paces ahead of her. The good little goat always followed him, even without Asher holding the lead, but he wanted her to hurry.

While tugging Juniper's lead and alternating between walking and jogging, Asher tried to relax. Bandits wouldn't bother with him, a lone fourteen-year-old boy and his goat, would they? They sometimes hid in caves or craggy spots in hills or mountains along busy highways, not in little passes with low hills like this one. And they mostly went after companies of Romans, which Asher appreciated—not just because he should be able to feel safe now but because the Romans caused trouble for Jews. He couldn't wait for the coming of the Messiah some talked about. The Messiah would set things right.

Asher spun his staff over his wrist one way and then the other. Maybe one day he'd use his staff in the service of the Messiah . . . if he ever really learned how to fight. He'd learn tonight if he got home in time for the Zealot meeting. His first Zealot meeting.

The Zealots mostly talked and schemed, but they did a bit of training too. His friend Uri, two years older than he, had invited him to the meetings months ago, but Asher had never been able to attend. He would tonight.

The staff swung a bit too close to the goat, whooshing by her ear. Juniper bleated and tugged against the lead.

"I won't hit you. I've been practicing." He smiled at the tan-and-white goat. She seemed to smile back. White streaks started at the top of her head—where horns would've been she if wasn't a polled goat—and ran above her lazy eyes and down to her smug little grin and the tuft of fur hanging under her chin.

Pebbles skittered down the hillside on his left. A cloud of dust kicked up as a figure raced toward him, weaving around shrubs and boulders on the hill. Two figures. And another one on his right.

Asher's heart thudded in his chest, and his stomach clenched. Juniper bleated and leaped to the side. His father's voice spoke in his head. *Never travel through the craggy hills north of the wilderness. It may seem the quick and easy way, but it can lead to great trouble. Take the safer route through villages.*

"I'll protect you, Juniper." Wishing he had more confidence, Asher dropped the lead and gripped his staff with both hands. He couldn't run, couldn't abandon his father's goods or the money he'd made. He turned toward the nearest robber, throwing glances in every direction to see how many came against him.

Three men with turbans and covered faces rushed him. Three against one!

Heart racing out of control, Asher lifted his staff overhead, ready to defend himself. Then he swung at the nearest man. Juniper's bleats filled the air as the goat jerked against the harness, trying to escape.

The man grabbed the staff mid-swing, his strong tan fingers curling around it, his dark eyes glaring over the cloth hiding his face. Then he kneed Asher in the gut.

The pain released Asher's grip on the staff and sent him to his knees.

One bandit barked out hasty commands in Aramaic to the other two. "Take this pack. Carry that. And here—"

"Why don't we just take wagon and all?" another said.

Between gasping for breath and doubling over from the pain, Asher glimpsed his staff not too far away on the ground, all but ignored by the bandits as they busied themselves with the goods on the cart. If he could just snatch it up and swing it with two hands, cracking one bandit and then the other with a surprise attack . . . But how would he take down the third man?

Before wrapping his mind around a solid plan, zeal to protect his father's goods consumed him. Asher lunged forward and snatched his staff from the ground. Ignoring the pain and gaining momentum, he spun toward the bandits ready to strike.

Not halfway through his spin, something cracked hard against his temple. The world tilted, and the ground shot up to meet his head. Dirt and grit found their way into his mouth before the pain even registered.

Raindrops sprinkled the side of Asher's face as he lay sprawled face-down, palms open and one cheek to the dusty road. His head throbbed as if he'd been kicked by a mule, and his gut ached. The bandits' voices—along with the bleating of his goat—had trailed off, but defeat held him down.

A righteous man falls down seven times and gets up, Abba

often said when encouraging Asher and his sisters, quoting Proverbs. But another proverb spoke louder in Asher's mind. *Pride goeth before a fall.*

With a heavy sigh, he forced his eyes open, rolled over, and sat up, one arm holding his abdomen. How far had the bandits gotten with his cart?

Gray rainclouds hung above him, speeding through the sky. The rain never lasted long this time of year, almost the month of Nissan, the first month of spring. The bandits had surely kept moving, not letting a little rain stop them.

An empty path stretched out in either direction, winding around the low, craggy hills. No goat. No cart. No bandits in sight. They'd even taken his staff and—Asher's hand shot to his belt, to where he kept the money bag, and his heart sank. No money either. One of the robbers had roughed him up after he'd fallen to the ground, he vaguely remembered, and must've been searching for his money then.

Asher yanked a kerchief from his leather belt and secured it around his head with a cord to keep the rain out of his eyes. Nausea rolled inside him as he got to his feet. What would he tell Abba? Abba had been counting on him. And he'd warned Asher about this shortcut, but Asher had taken it anyway. What could he say in his defense?

Asher looked each way down the path, reorienting himself. How long had he been out?

The sun sank toward the hilltops to the west. He would not have light for much longer, and he still had close to an hour to go. He'd better hurry home. He could think on the way about how to explain this disaster.

Asher walked stooped for a few steps, the pain in his head and abdomen begging him to take it easy. Then he forced himself to straighten up and set his gaze on low shrubs in the distance. His steady pace and the fresh, damp air distracted him a bit from his discomfort.

He should've listened to Abba and taken the safer route, but he just couldn't see himself making the long schlep through towns when the path through the craggy hills offered such a direct route.

Abba wouldn't like that reason. And he wouldn't care that Asher had wanted to hurry home so he could hear the Zealots tonight—which he definitely wouldn't get to do now.

While Abba never went out of his way to hear them speak, he had seemed favorable to the Zealots. What Jew wouldn't be? They defended the Torah and Jewish customs. And they, like every good Jew, hated the piece-of-dirt Romans, their occupation of Israel, the oppressive taxes, and the rule of Judea by an outsider—King Herod.

The Zealots put action behind their beliefs and tried doing something about it. Of course, Abba did not agree with their techniques. True, sometimes the Zealots stirred things up a bit, inciting people to join them in rebellion, but the restlessness of the people had been growing anyway. The Zealots also refused to pay tribute to the Romans, and, okay, they sometimes used violence.

Abba lived in the past. He longed for a return to the

glorious days of King David, but he preferred a more peaceful approach. *"Bloodshed follows bloodshed,"* he would say, quoting Hosea, the prophet. And he spoke often of the coming of the prophet . . . the Messiah . . . who would show them the right way.

On that, they all agreed. The Messiah would soon come and deliver Israel from all oppression. The signs were everywhere. Some said he would come from David's line, from the tribe of Judah, and he would rule as king and conquer all their enemies. Others thought maybe from the tribe of Levi.

Rumor had it that a heavenly army appeared thirty years ago, announcing the birth of the Messiah at Bethlehem. Was it true? King Herod had believed so, and in his fear of losing power, had massacred all the male children around Bethlehem. An unforgiveable crime. Yes, the Messiah was here, living among them somewhere, and one day he would reveal himself.

Wishing he still had his staff, Asher swung his fists in the air, his right, his left, his right. The motion sent sharp pains through his abdomen, so he stopped and rubbed his belly. He'd find another staff. He would be ready to fight when the Messiah appeared.

Thinking of home and Abba, Asher dropped his hands to his sides and sighed. With all this on the near horizon, he had no reason to bring up which route he'd taken home. He'd been robbed by bandits. That could happen anywhere. Admitting that he'd taken the shortcut would change nothing, except to make Asher lose Abba's trust.

Before long, the low hills gave way to flat land and the main roads. Jericho stretched out in the distance. Palm trees grew along a stream that weaved back to the Jordan River, and a scattering of other trees and shrubs broke up the pale desert landscape of the low valley. A scattering of single- and two-story, white-washed homes with flat roofs blended into the neutral shades.

He couldn't see his family's home yet, especially now that the sky had grown a deeper shade of blue, but they lived on the outskirts of Jericho. Asher's father and uncle would have arrived home from Jerusalem by now, if their business trip had gone well.

Asher's stomach churned. How was he going to explain this? He'd lost the goods, the money, the cart, and even his goat to bandits. His hands curled into fists, and an ache started in his heart. Why did they have to take Juniper?

Having no time for grief, he pushed the emotion back. He couldn't tell Abba about the shortcut. He wanted Abba to trust him. He would not take the route again, no matter what. He would be trustworthy from now on.

Abba would need to trust him now more than ever since they'd lost so much today. Maybe Asher could work even harder, hit more marketplaces, and charge more for goods until the amount was recovered. They'd need to replace the wagon . . . and the goat too. A tear came to his eye, but a deep breath stopped it from falling. *O Lord, keep Juniper safe. Bring her back to me one day.*

Home came into view, a short jog away now. The setting sun illuminated one side of the limestone wall surrounding their two-story house, several rooms built around an open courtyard. Figures stood on the rooftop, enjoying the evening—or on the lookout for him? They might have been worried. He was late. In a few minutes he would have to explain why.

On the tenth day of Nissan, Asher followed his father through the bustling marketplace to help select a lamb for Passover. In previous years, Abba had seen to the task alone. But Abba had been keeping Asher close at hand since the day he'd come home beaten up and robbed. His parents had only seemed to care about him and his bruises that night, but Asher suspected Abba's confidence in him had dropped a few notches.

Chatter and excitement filled the dusty streets today. A savory aroma of grilled fish carried on a cool breeze. Then the wind shifted, and a foul odor replaced it. Asher wrinkled his nose.

They'd left his mother and oldest sister, Dina, selling goods at their regular booth on a less crowded street. Asher wouldn't have minded helping with that or being near Dina, who sang his favorite songs while she worked. His other two sisters busied themselves at home with spring cleaning—a task Asher was glad to avoid. His family made a thorough spring cleaning an annual event, as many families did, preparing for the fourteenth day of Nissan, when the patriarch would lead the family through the house by candlelight and remove all leavened bread. They would eat only matzah, unleavened bread, during the seven days of Passover as a reminder that the Israelites hadn't time to bake bread before their hasty departure from Egypt.

Bleating filled the air as they neared a pen of goats and lambs. A smile came to Asher's face as a little black lamb stuck its head between the horizontal beams of the temporary pen. He liked lambs and goats well enough, but it always made him a little sad picking one out, knowing it would be slaughtered in a few days' time.

Asher's thoughts flitted to his goat Juniper, and he glanced around as if he might see her following behind someone or standing in the shadows. She was a good goat. The robbers would likely find her useful—if they didn't eat her.

Rather than spot Juniper, he caught sight of his friends Uri and Nathan with a few others that Asher couldn't recognize at the distance. Standing to the side of a fishmonger, smoke from a grill drifting over them, they talked excitedly among themselves and threw glances as if waiting on someone.

Jealousy teased him. Maybe they were going to train with the Zealots. Or maybe something else was going on. Something big. Asher had been unable even to hear the Zealots speak and had to rely on second-hand information.

"Asher, come." Abba motioned him over to the pen.

The seller stood in the middle of the pen, boasting about the quality of one lamb and then another. He grabbed one by the snout and turned its face from side to side, then he lifted it up to give Abba a closer look.

Asher stood beside Abba and peered down at the lamb, a solid white male. Only a perfect, unblemished lamb would do for the Passover celebration. His father had taught him that years ago. Abba began instructing him in the Law from the moment he'd first learned to talk.

The verse he'd first learned came to mind. *Hear, O Israel: the Lord our God is one Lord.*

"Why did the Lord have regard for Abel and his offering, but for Cain and his offering he had no regard?" Abba gazed at Asher, the confident look in his eyes saying he knew Asher could answer the question.

"Abel offered the firstlings of his flock, the very best of what he had," Asher answered, his eyes on the white lamb—with a tiny spot of black on one leg. "Cain gave an offering of the fruit of the ground, but not the first fruits of his harvest."

Abba nodded, the wrinkles deepening around his eyes as he smiled.

"Not this one." Asher pointed to the one the seller held. Then he looked over the other lambs in the pen, avoiding the goats that reminded him of Juniper. The little black lamb with his head sticking out of the pen looked healthy with bright eyes and a clean mouth—and no spot of white or any other color. "This one." He reached over the pen and patted its head.

The seller lifted it for Abba's inspection. Then Abba traded him coins for the lamb and placed the little creature on Asher's shoulders.

Asher held its legs against his chest as he balanced it,

the warm, soft body pressing against his neck. He had to force down the desire to name the thing. That would only make the fourteenth of the month that much harder.

"Let us take it home—" Abba's head turned a bit, as if he spotted something or someone in the distance. Worry creased his brow. He squeezed Asher's arm. "You take the lamb home. Secure it and then return to help your mother."

"Yes, Abba." Asher followed Abba's gaze to a man a stone's throw away in a brown skull cap and cloak next to a Roman soldier with iron-plated armor over a short red tunic. Both looking Abba's way.

"Go," Abba commanded Asher. Then he weaved through the crowd and approached the men.

Puzzled, Asher stood a moment longer and watched.

The man in the skull cap tapped his fingers as if tallying something up, while the soldier stood gazing down at Abba with an arrogant tilt of his chin. Abba shook his head and gestured while he spoke, his every move humble and sincere. Maybe he hadn't been able to pay his taxes because of their setbacks. Maybe he needed more time. Or worse . . . could he have taken out a loan? Did he blame Asher for their loss? He didn't know that Asher had taken the shortcut, that he truly was to blame.

"Asher!" Nathan cut into the space right in front of Asher, blocking his view of Abba. "You look pale. Are you all right?"

Asher glanced over Nathan's shoulder, but the crowds blocked the view of the tax collector and soldier and

Asher's father.

Uri came up too, a sturdy walking stick in his hand and a proud grin on his face. He liked being associated with Zealots.

Pushing feelings of guilt aside, Asher stroked the legs of the black lamb and shifted its weight. He smiled at his friends. "Saw you over by the fishmonger. Learning a new trade?"

"Ha, no," Uri said. "Too slimy of a job for me." He'd been learning his father's trade, stonecutter.

They walked with the crowd in the direction Asher should've been taking anyway, since his father had told him to take the lamb home.

"We're on our way to the Jordan River. Thought you'd want to know," Nathan said.

"The Jordan River?" Asher considered warning them not to take the shortcut through the craggy hills, but they were probably going with a group of Zealots. They'd be safe enough.

"We're going to hear a prophet out there, a Nazarite who lives in the wilderness," Uri said. "He's been preaching for the past few weeks."

"Wish I could go." Asher sighed. "Next time you see me, tell me what he said."

"From what I've heard," Nathan said, "he speaks of preparing the way . . . for the Messiah."

After sundown on the fourteenth of Nissan, Asher sat with his family and extended family in a spacious room in his grandparents' home in Jerusalem. Saba and Savta had both passed away, so the property actually belonged to Abba, as the eldest of his brothers, but he preferred to rent it out to pilgrims rather than to move to Jerusalem just yet. He would know when the time was right, he always said.

They rested on thick cushions around a low table, preparing to eat Shlomo—the one-year-old black, unblemished male lamb that Asher should not have named. He should also not have let it sleep with him on his mat on the roof. He should not have fed it from his hand. And he should not have insisted on carrying it for so much of their two-day journey to Jerusalem.

Asher's younger sisters and he sat glumly staring at their plates. Following tradition, care had been taken to break no bones as the lamb was prepared and the meat cut for serving. But why did they have to roast it on two spits in the form of a cross?

Abba said the prayers over the first cup of wine. "Blessed are you, O Lord our God, king of the universe, who has created the fruit of the vine . . ." And they all ate bitter herbs dipped in vinegar, passing the dish from one to the other, beginning at the head of the table.

Jabyn, the youngest of Asher's cousins, asked the questions this year. "Why is this night different from all other nights?"

Following tradition, Abba recounted the history of Israel from Abraham to Moses and then the giving of the Law. Abba placed much emphasis on the Exodus, when Moses had freed the Jews from four hundred years of slavery to the Egyptians.

"They wouldn't have needed freeing if they hadn't turned from Yahweh to begin with," one of Asher's uncles said.

Abba explained the significance of the food, and then everyone sang the Hallel Psalms. More handwashing followed. Then servers brought out the Paschal Lamb with vegetables and unleavened bread wafers, which Abba blessed.

"Blessed are you, O Lord our God, King of the universe, who brings forth bread from the earth . . ."

More wine, more prayers, and the final Hallel Psalms. But what stuck in Asher's mind was the verse: "Blessed is he who comes in the name of the Lord." His skin prickled as he sang along. He sensed the time had come.

Between cups of wine, a conversation arose concerning the sacrificing of lambs. "The Passover lamb is the peace offering," his father explained with an aura of wisdom, "but the scapegoat on Yom Kippur, the Day of Atonement, is the sin offering. Together they make a single offering for sin."

"Scapegoat?" Asher's youngest sister, Moriah, put her little hand to her mouth and giggled.

Abba shifted his eyes to her, an amused sparkle in them. "Yes, *hamuda,* scapegoat."

Asher smiled at the term. Moriah certainly was *the cute one*.

Abba continued, "As the high priest places his hands on the head of the scapegoat, he lays the sins of the people on it. It becomes the atoning sacrifice, which is then sent to the wilderness."

"The sins don't matter then?" she asked with a tilt of her head.

More smiles and light chuckles from around the table. Then Abba answered, "The people must still think about their own sins and repent and recognize their utter dependence on Yahweh for redemption. Only with repentance can the sacrificial animal stand as a substitute."

Asher had chuckled too, though he still didn't entirely understand. One rabbi had taught Asher and his friends that the anointed one would bring greater understanding.

"He who covers his sins will not prosper." Ima, their mother, looked in Moriah's direction, offering a compassionate little smile. "But whoever confesses and forsakes them will have mercy."

Asher knew the verse from Proverbs. And for some reason his cheeks burned. He didn't want to think about confessing sins. He wanted to recover the excitement he'd felt when singing about the one who would come in the name of the Lord. "Has anyone heard about the prophet preaching out at the Jordan River?" His face burned hotter now as everyone turned toward him.

"I have heard of him. He is a Nazarite. His name is John," Uncle Lantz said. "What have you heard of him?"

"He speaks of preparing for the Messiah, just as the Zealots do." Asher looked to Abba to see what he thought.

"Not as the Zealots do," Abba said.

"No," Uncle Lantz said. "Not as the Zealots. Perhaps

more like Jonah."

"Or Elijah," Ima said, smiling at Asher. "I hear he lives in the wilderness and wears a garment made of camel's hair." She set down her glass of wine, her gaze resting on it for a moment. "He eats only honey and wild locusts, with no care for worldly comforts."

"And he calls people to repentance," Abba added.

Asher shook his head, wishing someone understood the urgency. "We don't need repentance now. We need freedom from our oppressors."

Abba gave him a long look. "We always need repentance."

On his way home from running errands, Asher sliced the air with the staff his uncle had given him a few days ago, on his family's last day in Jerusalem.

"Made from a cypress tree," Uncle Lantz had said. "It's good wood, strong and durable, used for the building of the Temple, you know."

Asher hadn't known, but he liked the weight and feel of it. Uncle Lantz—a woodworker—had carved it himself, sanded it smooth, and treated it with some kind of oil. It made a nice whooshing sound when whipped through the air. And for whatever reason, it reminded Asher of his goat Juniper. Maybe because he'd lost Juniper and his original staff on the same day.

A few others strolled in the distance, along the gently rolling roads and paths in the outskirts of Jericho, walking to and from homes. Various fruit and palm trees grew here and there, breaking up the bald landscape.

Asher's home soon came into view. The midday sun shone brightly on their two-story home and the pale stone wall around it, throwing a narrow shadow toward the front of the property. A thin gray line of smoke snaked from the courtyard to the blue sky above.

Asher's stomach growled. Ima and the girls probably had something cooking.

As the front of the house and the solitary opening in the gate came into view, Asher stopped in his tracks and squinted to get a better look.

Two horses stood out front, one of them in the narrow strip of shade cast by the wall. Only the wealthy and sometimes soldiers rode horses. A man mounted one of them. Someone already sat on the other. Wait, no, two people sat mounted on the other, a young woman and . . . The horse stepped from the shade, revealing the bigger person seated behind the woman. Red tunic, shiny breastplate—a Roman soldier!

Panic surged through him. Asher bolted for home, willing himself to cross the remaining distance in seconds. But the horses took off just as he did, headed away from him.

Sucking in sharp breaths and pumping his legs, Asher raced on. The world seemed to jiggle and fall apart around him as questions raced through his mind. Was Abba home? Was the family safe? Why would a Roman soldier come to their house?

Asher raced through the gate and bounded into the

courtyard, stopping with a thump a short ways in. Pottery lay smashed on the dirt floor in a puddle next to the well. A black pot hung over a little fire near the open kitchen, smoke shifting to the middle of the courtyard with a breeze.

Beyond the smoke, Abba leaned against the back wall of the courtyard, as though defeated and nearing collapse, next to the wooden door to Asher's uncle and aunt's room. His ashen face spoke of misery unlike Asher had ever seen.

Ima stood beside Abba, angled toward him but hiding her face with one hand. Her other hand stroked little Moriah's back. Moriah clung to her, bawling, whining, "Why, Ima? Why, Abba? Don't let it happen."

Asher's second youngest sister sat on her haunches a short distance from them, head bowed, hair falling forward, arms hiding her face. He could not see his oldest sister, Dina, anywhere.

"Where is Dina?" Asher demanded, his voice scraping out his constricted throat. "What happened here?" He peered through the dark doorways on his left and right. Not seeing his sister, he pounded the end of his staff on the hard dirt floor. "Dina!" he shouted, "Dina!"

"It is only for a time." Dod, his uncle, stepped out from the shadows on the right of the courtyard. He squeezed Asher's shoulder, compassion in his eyes.

"What is just for a time?" Asher needed to hear it. No one had explained anything yet. He'd come home to destruction, to his oldest sister gone, and everyone distraught.

"Your sister—"

"They took her," Moriah shrieked, collapsing to her knees.

Abba leaned over her, lifted her into his arms, and rubbed her back. Then he looked at Asher.

Abba spoke and Dod spoke . . . while Ima and the girls wailed . . . and little Moriah kept saying, "They took her, they took her."

Asher struggled to sort out what they were saying, his ears wanting to close against the truth, the smoke choking him, and his stomach threatening to empty itself. As understanding dawned, he backed away, taking one step and then another. The Roman soldier had taken his oldest sister as a slave to repay Abba's debt.

"We have to get her back," he shouted, looking from Abba to Dod.

"We will." Dod grabbed his shoulder again. "We will get her back."

"No." Asher turned to him. "We get her back now!" He slammed the end of his staff against the ground.

Dod smiled, a forced smile, one meant to pacify, but his eyes couldn't hide his anger at what the Roman had done. Or was it fear that this would not end well? "I assure you it won't be for long. Remain calm. We will get her back." He paused, then said, "All of Israel are responsible for each other," repeating a common Jewish saying.

In the next moment, Asher was running. While a part of him meant to go after Dina, he did not head in the direction the riders had taken. A part of him also meant to find the Zealots, to join them and not return home until the chosen people were free of foreign power. But he did not head toward the heart of Jericho, to the places where they often met. He raced toward the wilderness.

Sometime later, unable to keep up the pace, body tingling with sweat and near the point of exhaustion, he found himself on the path that wound through the craggy hills. Ignoring his father's past warnings, he continued, swinging his staff, envisioning Roman soldiers in the arc of his swing.

He would find a way to get his sister back. He would work extra hard at the marketplace to raise the money. What else could he do? Maybe he could find her. Would she be sold as a slave, the money going to the tax collector? Or was she to be the tax collector's slave until he considered the debt paid? Or was she to serve the Roman soldier he'd brought along?

At the thought of the Roman soldier sitting behind Dina on the horse, he gripped the staff with two hands and swung hard.

Every Jew believed the Messiah would soon come. When he arrived, would it change all this? Would he lead an army against their enemies and bring the Israelites to victory? Would he free the captives and usher in an era of peace?

"How long, O Lord, how long?" Asher shouted. *How long will our enemy exalt over us?* "Show me, O Lord, what I can do to prepare for the coming Messiah."

His mind grew numb as he continued walking, running,

walking again. As he neared the end of the path, he was not alone. Figures appeared ahead. A family with a wagon and a mule—and children—had just started down the path through the craggy hills.

Protective instincts kicking in, Asher scanned the hills on either side. The hills, lower here as the path neared the Jordan River, offered few places for hiding. He saw no sign of bandits, no threat at all . . . until he turned again toward the family.

A cloud of dust on each side alerted him to bandits. The one behind the family was most obvious, a man with a cloth drawn over his nose and one arm flailing as he rushed down the hill.

"You!" Driven by a surge of anger, Asher bolted toward him. He gripped his staff with both hands, ready for the robber's attempt to take it from him, as had happened last time. "It's all your fault!" he shrieked. "If you hadn't robbed me, my father could have paid his debt. My sister would not have been taken!" While still some distance from the man, but racing closer, he swung his staff and growled with anger.

The man skidded to a halt and backed away, lifting one arm defensively, the other keeping him balanced. "I-I don't even know you. I'm just trying to retrieve my goat."

A goat bleated behind Asher.

Confused but sensing no danger from the man, Asher lowered his staff. He looked to the family, but then something nudged his leg.

A tan goat with familiar white streaks running down

the sides of its face pressed against him.

"Juniper?" Asher's voice cracked with emotion.

The goat bleated and nudged him again and nibbled the end of his mantle.

Joy and thankfulness overwhelmed Asher. He dropped his staff, fell to his knees, and threw his arms around Juniper's neck. "I can't believe I found you. Or should I say, you found me?"

"What, this is your goat? I-I thought it wild and claimed it as my own," the man said.

"This is Juniper." Asher straightened, doing his best to regain composure. "I was robbed some time ago. They took everything, including my goat. I can't believe I've found her again."

Juniper tilted her head, gazing up at him through her strange little eyes.

"Okay, I understand. The goat is yours." The man lifted his hands and backed away.

"I am sorry." Asher wanted to explain. "I thought you were a robber, you know, since I was robbed here some time ago."

The man took off, so Asher turned toward the family, each member staring intently at him. "Do not take this path. Take the route through town." Asher pointed, directing them to go back the way they'd come. "Bandits hide in these hills and will rob you of all you have, especially your animals." He glanced at their gray mule loaded with packs.

The man and woman exchanged looks of uncertainty.

"It may seem the quick and easy way, but it can lead to great trouble," Asher said, repeating the words his father often said to him. He saw his father's weathered face in his mind, his caring eyes and the wisdom of his countenance. Abba had been right.

"Thank you," the father of the family said. "And we are sorry about your sister, the one you said had been taken. We are sorry." Then he turned the mule and wagon around, and he and his family went back the way they came.

Asher stood there a moment longer, Juniper beside him, the family moving away, and the man he'd mistaken for a robber long gone. He'd chosen the quick and easy way when coming home from the marketplace just west of the Jordan River. And he'd found great trouble. Abba had warned him. If he were to be honest with himself, his own spirit had warned him that day too. Then once he'd lost everything, he hid the truth—again taking the easier path—but that had only compounded his feelings of guilt.

Taking steps forward now, the Jordan River his destination, Asher continued examining his conscience. He'd put off thinking about it since it had happened, but he'd chosen the quick and easy way over obeying his father. He'd wanted to attend the Zealots' meeting and had put that first. Then he'd lied about it. Well, he hadn't actually lied. Abba had assumed he'd taken the route through the villages, as he'd been told, and Asher had not admitted his disobedience. He'd allowed Abba to believe something good about him instead.

And now—Asher's heart clenched—Dina was gone. His sister had to pay the price for his disobedience.

Guilt weighing heavy on him now, Asher plodded down the path. Juniper trundled along beside him, as content as she'd ever been. The sweet little goat had probably escaped the bandits and been looking for him ever since.

If only he could lay his sin on a scapegoat as a sin offering on the Day of Atonement and send the poor thing into the desert.

Asher watched Juniper for a moment, her jaunty gait, smug grin, and floppy ears. He smiled, deeply happy to have the goat back. He wouldn't want to place his sins on her. He needed to take care of them himself, with the help of the Lord. He needed to repent . . . to give them to the Lord and to recognize his need for help.

Repent and turn from all your transgressions, he'd read in Ezekiel, *lest iniquity be your ruin. Cast away from you all the transgressions that you have committed and make yourselves a new heart and a new spirit!*

A bud of hope blooming, even as sorrow for his mistakes weighed heavily, Asher hastened his steps. He knew now where he was going, what he intended to do, what his spirit had wanted even before he'd recognized it.

As the path met up with the longer route through villages, he found others heading in the same direction, convincing him that he was on the right track. When not sure which way to go, he followed them. They seemed to know. Soon, a trail of people formed, everyone heading for the Jordan River.

Before the river became visible, the prophet's voice rang out. "Repent, for the kingdom of heaven is at hand. Repent and bear fruit in keeping with repentance."

A moment later, the river came into view, narrow and twisting in some places, wide in others. Those walking with Asher didn't hesitate as they approached. They simply stepped into the cool waters and continued trudging toward the prophet. But Asher stood off to the side, among tall reeds, watching . . . and waiting. What was he doing here? Was he really going to—

"Confess your sins and be baptized, every one of you." Lean, tanned, and wild in appearance, the prophet stood in the middle of the river, dressed in a garment of camel's hair with a leather belt around his waist, his hair unkempt and beard long. "Repent," he cried, scanning faces, his gaze pausing—on Asher? "Repent and be baptized for the forgiveness of sin."

Asher shifted under the prophet's gaze, wanting to hide among the reeds, but the prophet's words stabbed Asher's heart. Truly, this was what he needed to do, to repent of his own sins. "Though your sins are like scarlet," the Lord said in Isaiah, "they shall be white as snow."

A gentle breeze accompanied Asher to the water's edge as the heat of repentance burned his soul. He gripped the neckline of his tunic, and deep inside himself he rent his heart, splitting it apart and tearing it to pieces, acknowledging his brokenness, his need for forgiveness and restoration.

He stepped into the river, cool water sloshing over his sandals as he found his footing. Step by step he joined the others in line. Step by step he came alone before the Lord. Before long he stood face to face with the prophet, whose amber eyes seemed to read his soul, evoking a confession from him.

"Repent," the prophet said, almost whispered this time, so gentle was the invitation.

Gladly, Asher poured out his sins. He was sorry. Sorry that he had disobeyed, sorry that he had kept the truth from Abba, sorry that his sister had to pay the price, sorry for many other things that came into his mind as he stood gazing into those golden eyes. He didn't need a scapegoat; he needed to repent, to confess his sins to the Lord and then to his father. He would work hard to repair the damage.

Having confessed everything that had come to mind, Asher shut his mouth.

A glint of joy passed the Baptist's face, then he plunged Asher down into the cool water. That joy transferred to Asher as the water enveloped him. Then the Baptist lifted him up. Water cascaded from his face and down his body, sparkling in the sunlight, giving him freedom and peace.

Six months later, Asher sat on the bank of the Jordan River with his staff resting across his legs. He watched and listened to John the Baptist, as people now called the prophet from the wilderness. A great crowd gathered this month, on both sides of the river, much larger than the first time Asher had come. Some simply watched, as he did today. Others stepped into the water.

A short distance away, Juniper foraged through reeds swaying in the wind along the bank. Every now and then she glanced back at Asher, as if checking that he hadn't wandered off.

"Make ready the way of the Lord," the Baptist cried, and the next in line waded to him through chest-high water, head bowed and ready to confess his sins. A long line of penitents stretched along the bank and into the river.

The breeze rustled the *tzitzit* on a corner of Asher's cloak, the tassel worn as a reminder of Yahweh. Everything John said stirred Asher's soul, especially his words about the coming of the Messiah and the repentance needed for each person to individually prepare for him. The more Asher listened, the more it made sense.

The chosen people were to be faithful to the Commandments given to Moses. The Torah made it clear that unfaithfulness brought punishment, which then brought repentance and a desire to return to holiness. *You shall be holy, for I am holy* (Leviticus 11:45).

Yeah, he still wanted to join the Zealots, wanted to learn to fight, but somehow this felt more important. Winning the battle inside. If only sin did not come so easily . . . Perhaps the Messiah would show them the way to remain faithful.

As the next penitent emerged from the water, Asher closed his eyes. After his baptism, he'd gone home and confessed to Abba, promising to make things right.

Eyes glistening with tears, Abba had lifted Asher off his knees and pulled him into a hug. He had known all along that Asher had taken the shortcut. He forgave Asher even before Asher had repented.

Asher had returned to the Jordan River monthly, making a sort of pilgrimage out of the experience, moving himself to self-examination and repentance again and again, though he only came forward for baptism the first time. His family had even come with him once—all except for Dina. While Abba understood what motivated the Zealots, he approved of the Baptist's message.

Dina remained in servitude somewhere, as far as Asher and their family knew. He and the rest of the family worked hard to earn what they could, but the tax collector expected more from them each time, it seemed, and the price set on his sister was high. Asher intended to find her as soon as he could. He'd already followed the tax collector home. Dina was not there. He had not been successful following the Roman, but he vowed he would be eventually.

Abba suspected she'd been taken to the outskirts of Jerusalem, and he spoke of moving the family to his property there. He daily consoled Ima that they would find her.

"Behold!" the Baptist cried in a clear, loud voice, his tone awestruck and humbled and exultant.

The wind stopped and silence fell. Everyone turned to where John the Baptist pointed.

A man about thirty years old strolled from the direction of the wilderness. With the hair and beard in the style of any other Jewish man, he did not seem extraordinary. Still, Asher found himself transfixed. The man's expression, gentle as the breeze that stirred Asher's soul but also powerful as a storm, and something else . . . the look in his eyes . . . authority, purpose, and love . . .

John spoke again. "Behold, the Lamb of God, who takes away the sin of the world."

###

"Prepare the Way" is a prequel to Theresa Linden's upcoming historical-dystopian novel tentatively called *Three Days to Forever.* Linden spent time researching landscape, time period lifestyles, and Jewish customs so that readers can step into the past and walk with Asher, the main character, in first-century Israel—where our Lord and Savior walked.

ABOUT THE AUTHOR

THERESA LINDEN is the author of award-winning Catholic fiction, including the West Brothers contemporary series and the Chasing Liberty dystopian trilogy. One of her great joys is to bring elements of faith to life through a story. She has more than a dozen published books, three of which won awards from the Catholic Press Association. Her short stories appear in several anthologies, including *Secrets: Visible & Invisible*, *Gifts: Visible & Invisible*, and *Treasures: Visible & Invisible*. Her articles and interviews can be found on various radio shows and in magazines, including EWTN's *The Good Fight*, *The National Catholic Register*, *Catholic Digest*, *Today's Catholic Teacher*, and *Catholic Mom*. Her books are featured online on Catholic Teen Books, Catholic Reads, FORMED, and Virtue Works Media.

A wife, homeschooling mom, and Secular Franciscan, she resides in northeast Ohio with her husband and children. You can learn more about her at www.TheresaLinden.com.

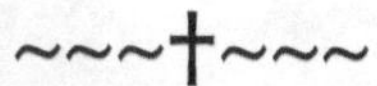

BOOKS FOR TEENS & YOUNG ADULTS by THESE AUTHORS

CAROLYN ASTFALK
Rightfully Ours

T.M. GAOUETTE
Destiny of Sunshine Ranch
Freeing Tanner Rose
Saving Faith
Guarding Aaron
Loving Gabriel
For Eden's Sake
Shadow Stalker

ELLEN GABLE
Julia's Gifts
Charlotte's Honor
Ella's Promise

MARIE C. KEISER
Heaven's Hunter

ANTONY B. KOLENC
Shadow in the Dark
The Haunted Cathedral
Fire of Eden
The Merchant's Curse

AMANDA LAUER
A World Such as Heaven Intended
A Life Such as Heaven Intended
A Love Such as Heaven Intended

THERESA LINDEN
Roland West, Loner
Life-Changing Love
Battle For His Soul
Standing Strong
Roland West, Outcast
Fire Starters
Chasing Liberty
Testing Liberty
Fight For Liberty
Anyone But Him

CYNTHIA T. TONEY
8 Notes To A Nobody
10 Steps To Girlfriend Status
6 Dates To Disaster
3 Things To Forget
The Other Side Of Freedom

CORINNA TURNER
I Am Margaret
The Three Most Wanted
Liberation
Bane's Eyes
Margo's Diary
Brothers
The Siege of Reginald Hill
Someday
Drive! *(Unsparked 1.0)*
A Truly Raptor-ous Welcome *(Unsparked 2)*
BREACH! *(Unsparked Prequel)*
Elfling
Mandy Lamb and the Full Moon

LESLEA WAHL
The Perfect Blindside
eXtreme Blindside
Into the Spotlight
Unlikely Witnesses
Where You Lead

MORE CTB ANTHOLOGIES
Secrets: Visible & Invisible
Gifts: Visible & Invisible
Treasures: Visible & Invisible

Visit
CatholicTeenBooks.com for even more authors & titles.
And subscribe to our newsletter for new titles *hot off the press!*

www.ingramcontent.com/pod-product-compliance
Lightning Source LLC
Chambersburg PA
CBHW021140310726
48971CB00002B/422

* 9 7 9 8 9 8 5 3 4 8 5 1 4 *